W9-AVW-533

The Love Song of
A. Jerome Minkoff
— *and* —
Other Stories

❊

Books by Joseph Epstein

The Love Song of A. Jerome Minkoff

Fred Astaire

In a Cardboard Belt!

Alexis de Tocqueville

Friendship

Fabulous Small Jews

Envy

Snobbery

Narcissus Leaves the Pool

Life Sentences

With My Trousers Rolled

Pertinent Players

The Goldin Boys

A Line Out for a Walk

Partial Payments

Once More Around the Block

Plausible Prejudices

The Middle of My Tether

Familiar Territory

Ambition

Divorced in America

The Love Song of
A. Jerome Minkoff
—— *and* ——
Other Stories

❖

Joseph Epstein

Houghton Mifflin Harcourt
BOSTON • NEW YORK
2010

For information about permission to reproduce selections from this book,
write to Permissions, Houghton Mifflin Harcourt Publishing Company,
215 Park Avenue South, New York, New York 10003.

www.hmhbooks.com

Library of Congress Cataloging-in-Publication Data
Epstein, Joseph, date.
The love song of A. Jerome Minkoff, and other stories / Joseph Epstein.
    p. cm.
ISBN 978-0-618-72195-5
1. Jews — United States — Fiction. 2. Short stories, Jewish. I. Title.
PS3555.P6527L68 2010
813'.54 — dc22   2009034898

Printed in the United States of America
DOC 10 9 8 7 6 5 4 3 2 1

These stories were previously published elsewhere: "Casualty" in *Sewanee Review,*
"My Brother Eli" *in Hudson Review,* "Kuperman Awaits Ecstasy" and "Danny
Montoya" in *Standpoint;* the rest of the stories appeared in *Commentary.*

For Ivan Dee,
good friend

Contents

The Love Song of
A. Jerome Minkoff
— *and* —
Other Stories

✳

The Love Song of
A. Jerome Minkoff

D R. A. JEROME MINKOFF, family practitioner, three
years a widower and coming up on his sixty-fourth
birthday, met Larissa Friedman, two years into her
widowhood and fifty-two, at a charity dinner at the Ambassador
East Hotel in Chicago for ALS, dreaded, goddamn Lou Gehrig's
disease, from which both their spouses had died. Each had do
nated $25,000 to the annual national ALS fundraiser, where they
were seated next to each other at the same table near the dais.
Mrs. Friedman gave the few things he said full-court-press attention. She smiled. She agreed emphatically. More than once she
touched his forearm, gave it a gentle squeeze.

Since Marlene's death three years ago, Minkoff had been considered, if not by himself then by friends, many patients, and all
female acquaintances, a highly eligible bachelor. He had gone out
with a few women, but nothing resembling a relationship came
of it. He grew wary. Divorcées recited ghastly sagas of grievance
that were lengthy and painful. Others were far too willing to share
their many problems. Minkoff, who had never in his life uttered a
word of complaint to anyone but his wife, preferred to devote his

problem-solving prowess, which he thought not inconsiderable, to the patients in his large family practice.

Minkoff found himself acting rather coldly to Larissa Friedman, not responding to her attentions, directing his own conversation to others at the table. Back in his apartment on State Parkway, getting into his pajamas, he had a touch of bad conscience. Why had he assumed the worst? After all, like him, she had gone through the hell of seeing someone she loved put through the tortures of ALS. She was alone in the world. She was generous in her giving. She had done nothing to warrant such chilliness.

Larissa Friedman lived in Los Angeles, and Minkoff recalled her saying that she was staying at the Drake. Late though it was, he called her there and asked if he might drive her to O'Hare tomorrow, a Wednesday and a day off for him.

Minkoff picked Mrs. Friedman up at nine-thirty A.M. in front of the hotel. Her plane departed in three hours, but she had mentioned that she liked to get to the airport early. The traffic on the Kennedy was unusually light, and they arrived a touch after ten. She suggested a cup of coffee, and so Minkoff pulled up in front of the O'Hare Hilton, turning his Honda over to a young Mexican guy at valet parking. In the hotel coffee shop, they exchanged talk about the cruelty visited upon their late spouses by disease and about their own lives, as she put it, "as bachelors." She was small, dark, with black eyes, and wore makeup with evident artistry. She had a French haircut, or so he thought of it, with one side falling across her well-sculpted forehead. More than once Minkoff felt her knee touch his. Concerned about the time of her flight's departure, he checked his watch.

"Not to worry," she said, smiling. She called United Airlines from her cell phone and rescheduled her flight. She leaned toward Minkoff, giving off a strong whiff of expensive perfume, and whispered into his ear.

✳ ✳ ✳

Minkoff looked at his eyes in the rearview mirror. He had spent four extraordinary hours in a room upstairs in the airport Hilton with Mrs. Friedman—make that Larissa. After checking his male patients for testicular cancer, Minkoff always inquired, "Everything all right down there?" Who knew how many prescriptions in recent years Minkoff had written for Viagra, Cialis, Levitra, and the rest? He hadn't himself entirely neglected things down there, but Larissa Friedman had refreshed his memory of how revivifying they could be. She was a woman of experience. Although himself an easy A student in anatomy and the veteran of nearly forty years of medical practice, she was in possession of a few things about the physiology of the human body that until now had not occurred to Dr. A. Jerome Minkoff.

She told Minkoff that she planned to be back in Chicago early next month and hoped they might be able to spend some time together then. Yes, sure, of course; he would look forward to it. They kissed, and she patted him, twice, on his bottom as he walked out into the cool hallway of the O'Hare Hilton.

Things progressed quickly. Larissa called to say that she was returning to Chicago two weeks earlier than expected and would have the use of an apartment in the 900 N. Michigan Avenue building that was owned and used as a pied-à-terre by a neighbor of hers in Brentwood. Their week together left Minkoff exhausted. Every night Larissa made reservations at one of those restaurants Minkoff used to read about with less than casual interest in *Chicago* magazine but had never taken Marlene to: Tru, Trio, and Charlie Trotter's, where well-connected people ate—a great privilege, apparently, this—in the kitchen. Larissa had acquired tickets to the symphony, to a Goodman Theatre production of *Death of a Salesman,* to Steppenwolf, where they saw Lady Macbeth deliver her monologue in the nude. Afterward, she and Minkoff retired to the pied-à-terre and did not sleep much.

They were invited to dinner at the apartment, on East Lake

Shore Drive, of Larissa's old high school friend Rita Greenberg, whose own date for the evening was her personal trainer, two decades younger. A locally famous interior decorator of whom Minkoff had never heard was there with his partner. The conversation covered mainly new restaurants and movies and vacation spots. Minkoff hadn't much to contribute and, despite Larissa's efforts to bring him into the conversation whenever possible, felt out of it.

Perhaps it was just fatigue. Minkoff worked long hours. He began making his rounds at Rush–St. Luke's at seven A.M. He saw twenty patients a day. His schedule was no heavier this week than any other, except that instead of shuffling off to bed at nine-thirty every night, he was out with Larissa Friedman, whose energy, in bed or out on Michigan Avenue, appeared to be inexhaustible.

Minkoff was also distracted by a pathologist's report he received earlier in the day. It confirmed that one of his oldest patients, Maury Gordon, had pancreatic cancer. Maury — he had insisted that Minkoff, whom he always called Doc, call him that — was a wealthy man of eighty-five. He was large — six foot one, close to 220 pounds — and in his dress and manner gave off fumes of high prosperity. He had owned seven or eight movie theaters around Chicago, which he sold at just the right time, before the multiplexes took over. He had invested well and, as he put it to Minkoff one day at the conclusion of his annual physical, was "out of the financial wars before I was fifty."

Maury Gordon had a taste for ample generalizations. "If you have eighteen or so million in the bank it's awfully easy to relax and be an entirely moral man," he once said, "though I realize lots of money doesn't have this effect on certain *chazerim,* who, let's face it, wouldn't be content with eighteen billion."

When he turned sixty-five, Maury Gordon began getting physicals twice a year. He also came in once a month for a B_{12} shot.

Over the course of four decades, their relationship gradually deepened. Shortly after Marlene's death, Maury asked Minkoff if he thought he would remarry. A bit put off by the question, Minkoff said that he didn't feel it was a pressing question just then.

"Oh, well, married, single," Maury Gordon said, "neither is a solution."

"A solution?" Minkoff asked. "What's the problem?"

"Human existence, that's the problem," Maury replied. "Maybe you've noticed." Maury then told him that he had had a wife who had died in her late twenties, of colon cancer of a kind now easily treatable. They had had no children, and he had never remarried.

"No children, no sense of futurity," Maury said. "There's just you, alone. You die—*poof!*—show's over."

Minkoff was himself without children, but not for want of trying. His wife and he had gone through the ordeal of a fertility clinic. He could remember rushing home when he had calls from Marlene that she was ovulating. The whole exercise made him feel like nothing so much as a field-goal kicker, called in to perform at odd, usually inconvenient times. Marlene, with her sweet sense of humor, would phone the office and say, "Send in George Blanda." She was referring to the man who had been the Chicago Bears kicker when they were kids. But it all came to nothing. They talked about adoption, but finally decided that an adopted child was too much of a crapshoot, and so childless they remained.

Shortly after Marlene died, Minkoff had a note from Maury Gordon.

Dear Doc,
I am sorry to learn about the death of your wife. The toughest deals are those in which you lose both a wife and a best

friend, which, from the few things you've told me, suggests this must have been the case with you and the late Mrs. Minkoff. Welcome to the sad fraternity of widowers. If you ever feel like talking things over, let me know, and I'll be glad to take you to lunch.

Sincerely,
Maurice Gordon

Minkoff did not socialize with his patients, and he certainly didn't let down his hair with them, or with anyone else. He didn't take Maury up on his invitation to lunch. But he was touched by the note and found himself sharing bits of information about his social life with the older man. Only a few days before the cancer diagnosis, Minkoff revealed his surprising relationship with Larissa Friedman.

"What did her late husband do?" Maury asked.

"He was commissioned by Nike to make their sweat socks."

"A sweat sock baron. What a country!" Maury said. "Is she rich?"

"I suppose," Minkoff said. "Though how rich I don't really know."

"Worth knowing," said Maury.

Minkoff soon found out. Only a day after she returned to Los Angeles, she called and asked him to come on the following weekend to attend a dinner party a few friends in Los Angeles were giving for her fifty-third birthday. At LAX, after picking up his bag, Minkoff discovered a limo driver holding up a sign with his name on it. He and the driver exchanged few words, but when they were near Larissa Friedman's house in Brentwood, the driver pointed out a house across the street: "This is where O.J. lived when he knocked off his wife and her boyfriend." As they pulled up in front of Larissa's house, Minkoff noted in the driveway a convertible of a dazzling blue in a make he didn't recognize. "Maserati," the driver said.

Larissa's house was capacious. She had a full-time maid, also a houseman to work on her lawn and garden and do other jobs. The dinner that evening was at a restaurant called Spago. Four other couples were there. Everyone called Minkoff by his first name. Two of the women obviously had had plastic surgery; the other two were younger than their husbands by twenty or so years. Larissa was wearing a ring with a formidably large diamond. Lots of talk about the food; large quantities of wine were drunk. Once again Minkoff felt himself the odd man out, but the glitter of the room absorbed much of his attention. He spotted a man with an ambitious hairdo a few tables away who was, he was fairly sure, the singer Steve Lawrence, now bleached by age. Later a tall man with large and too-white teeth came over, and Larissa introduced him to Minkoff — everyone else at the table knew him — as Garry Marshall, a television producer of some fame.

When the check came, Minkoff insisted on paying his and Larissa's share. The men each put credit cards down, and when the waiter returned with the check, his part of the total came to $680. The tip was included.

"I have to tell you, I'm not a $680-a-dinner guy," Minkoff told Larissa when they were back in her living room. "It's not that I can't afford a dinner like that from time to time. It's just that I feel there's something intrinsically wrong about it. People lie and cheat and even kill for money. This being so, I've always felt that the least I can do is respect it. Spending that kind of money for a meal isn't, in my opinion, respecting it."

"Sweetie," she said, placing a hand on Minkoff's cheek, "sit a minute. I want to show you something." A few moments later she returned with a heavy leather folder. She ran through the pages of the folder with him. By the time she was done, he had learned that her net worth was somewhere in the range of $64 million.

"Really, baby," she said, closing the folder, "I don't think we need worry about a $680 dinner."

Later that night, as she lay beside him, Minkoff thought about that $64 million. He had not slept with all that many women in his life, and it occurred to him that hitherto he had never slept with a woman worth more than $2 million. Just before he drifted off, he heard her voice in his head, saying, "I don't think we need worry about a $680 dinner." He would need to think more about that word "we."

Back in Chicago, Minkoff had his monthly session with Maury Gordon. The worst of medical practice for Minkoff was conferring with patients who had been told that there was nothing further anyone could do to sustain their lives. Minkoff had had patients in their nineties asking for third and fourth opinions about their illnesses.

"What did the oncologist tell you?" Minkoff asked Maury in his examining room.

"That it's the ball game," Maury said, "though that wasn't the exact phrase. He gave me four, five months, but said it could also be sooner."

"I'm sorry."

"When you get to be my age," Maury said, "you're just waiting to hear that your time is up. All this crap about sixty being the new forty, seventy being the new fifty, well, I have some friends who've reached ninety, and let me tell you, Doc, ninety looks to me like the new hundred and twelve."

"Everything'll be done to see that you undergo as little pain as possible."

"Good," Maury said, "I'm not fond of pain." There was a

pause, and Maury ended it by saying: "How's life with the sweat sock queen?"

"Moving along a little faster than I'd planned," said Minkoff, admiring the speed of Maury Gordon's transition from his own death to Minkoff's social life, and for once a little relieved to have the conversation shift to his rather than to a patient's problems.

"What's planning got to do with anything? You want to make God smile, tell him your plans. You probably heard that one before."

"She's using 'we' when she talks about us. I'm not sure I'm ready for 'we.'"

"I've heard people say that when widowers remarry, it can be construed as a compliment to their dead wives. They know how good a marriage can be, and so they're ready to sign up for another. At least that's one theory."

"Since you cared a great deal for your wife and didn't remarry, I assume that it's a theory you don't subscribe to personally," Minkoff said.

"Listen, if I met someone dazzling after my wife died, I would have pursued her with the throttle full out. I didn't happen to meet that woman."

"I suppose the question for me," said Minkoff, "is if I have now met that woman."

"Have you ever thought about what she sees in you?" Maury asked.

"Who knows?" Minkoff answered. "Maybe she's looking for a family doctor on the premises." He thought, but didn't mention to Maury Gordon, that maybe she also found in him a man she could manage and easily dominate. Come to think of it, she was already doing a pretty good job on both counts.

Minkoff assumed his life with Larissa Friedman would be lived in southern California, in her house. He imagined himself driving the blue Maserati, top down, the Pacific Ocean on his right, the wind whirring through his thinning hair. He had originally planned to retire at seventy. Would it matter all that much if he knocked off five years earlier?

Minkoff's wife had never taken to California, northern or southern. She thought it thin—that had been her word for it, thin. She would go on about it. "Not that I have anything against good living," she would say, "but a person shouldn't make it the center of his life. Least that's what I think."

Marlene was full of opinions. If you stitched them all together they constituted a point of view about how a person ought to live: for work, for other people, for something outside and larger than yourself. And she lived her point of view, or so Minkoff always felt, which gave her an impressive dignity, a certain standing in his eyes and in those of their friends.

She had taught math to seventh-graders. The salary from her teaching had helped put him through medical school. She would probably have quit teaching if they had had kids, at least while the children were growing up, and they probably would have moved out to Northbrook or Highland Park, where so many of the other Jewish physicians lived. Minkoff felt the disappointment of childlessness that was at the center of his wife's life. Yet she never grumbled about it. She carried on.

Minkoff thought of his wife as one of those people who had always been tested. Her father died when she was fifteen, and, as her mother never really got over his death, Marlene essentially took over the running of the household and the raising of her two younger sisters. Her mother came down with Alzheimer's in her early seventies, and, as the only one of the daughters still living in Chicago, the heavy burden of seeing her mother through the final three years of her life fell entirely upon Marlene. The final, most brutal test was her ALS.

The disease hit when Marlene was fifty-eight. She began to

lose energy, then muscular control, first in her arms, then her legs. Soon she was sleeping with the aid of a mask and an oxygen machine, which eventually she used all the time. Minkoff hired two Filipina caregivers, working in eight-hour shifts, to watch over her when he was at work. She had to be fed soft foods. She sat in a chair in their den, her head drooping, the oxygen machine at her side, listening much of the day to chamber music CDs on the Bose radio–CD player Minkoff had bought for her and placed next to her chair in the den. At night Minkoff carried her to the toilet. The worst of it was when her speech became so slurred that he had to ask her to repeat four or five times what she was trying to tell him.

One Friday, when the younger of the two caregivers, whose name was Honeyjoy, called in sick, Minkoff stayed home with his wife. Mornings Marlene showered. Minkoff wasn't sure how the caregivers arranged Marlene's daily showers, so when he carried her into the bathroom, he took off all his own clothes and went into the shower with her. As he held her up, she seemed feathery light. Leaning against him, Marlene looked up at Minkoff, smiled, dropped her head on his shoulder, and died, right there, in his arms. "Expired" was the word that came to Minkoff's mind. She had expired, was gone, free at last. He stood there naked, the water beating down on him, his dead wife in his arms, befuddled by loss.

"Jesus, a house call, I don't believe it," Maury Gordon said when Minkoff visited him one evening after work at his apartment at 1212 Lake Shore Drive. Maury was now on a light morphine regimen, beginning his final descent, and spent most of the day in bed.

"More like a social call," Minkoff said. "I just wanted to see how you're doing." He could see that the answer was not very well. His normal suntan had deserted Maury, and he must have lost forty or fifty pounds; his pajamas and bathrobe hung on him.

"I've been thinking for some reason about my father," Maury said. "I don't think I've ever told you about my father." And then he did: Like many of his generation, Velvel Gorodetsky came to this country to avoid the lifelong slavery that conscription in the czar's army would have meant for a Jew. He was a man of scholarly interests, but found himself forced to cobble together a living running little dry-goods shops. Maury said his father had wished he could have been a teacher; he admired teachers because they didn't have to worry about an inventory.

"Did he live long enough," Minkoff asked, "to see your financial success?"

"He did. But you know, he would have preferred that I do something better than merely make a lot of money. We're snobs, we Jews. I think my father would have preferred that I had become a professor or a rabbi. He wasn't all that impressed by wealth."

"My own father's ambitions were pretty much satisfied by my becoming a so-called professional man," Minkoff said. "I don't think he thought about the possibility of my ever rising any higher, or that there was any higher to rise. On the other hand, I disappointed him by not bringing him any grandchildren."

"What are Jewish children for," Maury said, "if not to disappoint their parents? Not for nothing was *King Lear* the favorite Shakespeare play in the Yiddish theater. I had two sisters, both of whom had kids, so my father was a grandfather, though I'm not sure it gave him all that much pleasure. My father used to refer to me as his Kaddish — you know, the one who would say Kaddish for him when he died. I never did, and I'm sorry for it now."

"If that's your only regret," Minkoff said, "that's not bad."

"There's others. I wish I had risked more. I see now that I was a safe player. I made my money early, invested it wisely, and got out of the game. I lived comfortably; I didn't get hurt. Big deal. Maybe that wasn't such a hot idea."

"I wonder," Minkoff said, "if we can will ourselves to be something other than what we really are."

"Life offers more mysteries than there's time to solve," Maury said. "I fancy myself a thinking man, but I haven't solved a single one."

Minkoff walked the seven or so long blocks back to his own apartment, feeling as lonely as he had ever remembered feeling.

Later that same week Larissa called to say that she was coming to Chicago, and asked if it would be all right if she stayed in his apartment.

"Of course," Minkoff said. "Shall I pick you up at O'Hare? What airline are you flying?"

"No need. I've arranged for a limo," she said. "Actually, my friend Harriet Ginsberg and I have chartered a plane. With having practically to get undressed for security checks and all that, flying commercial is getting to be a big bore."

Larissa arrived a little after five o'clock with two large Louis Vuitton suitcases for a three-day stay. She told him that they had tickets for the Lyric Opera that evening — Placido Domingo in *La Traviata* — and they needed to be there by eight. There wouldn't be time for dinner until afterward. Minkoff opened a bottle of Riesling, put out some cheese and crackers. Over a glass of wine, they talked about his moving to California.

"I'm a little edgy about it," Minkoff said. "For one thing, I've never not worked. I'm not sure that I'm built for leisure."

"I'll bet something in the way of part-time work could be arranged at UCLA," Larissa said. "My husband endowed a chair at the medical school."

"I don't do research," he said. "I just meet with my patients.

I diagnose, I give advice, I send people in serious trouble off to specialists. That's all I know how to do."

"Don't worry, baby," she said. "We'll have a wonderful time, a full rich life."

Minkoff wasn't sure how things had gotten to this point. He hadn't proposed, but once that "we" had established itself in Larissa's conversation, it was as though she had already arranged for the movers. She had taken to calling him every night. In their nightly conversations, the word "when" began to replace "we," as in "when you move to Los Angeles" and "when we are together . . ." Minkoff also learned, almost by the way, that Larissa's husband who had died from ALS was actually her second husband; she'd had a first marriage, made when she was only nineteen, that had lasted just two years. No children from either marriage. She was a good closer, Larissa, give her that, Minkoff thought.

He slept through much of the last two acts of *La Traviata*. She had tickets for them tomorrow evening to see John Malkovich in *Of Mice and Men* at the Royal George Theatre on Halsted. Life with Larissa would mean many tickets: to operas, plays, movies; lots of modish restaurants and dinner parties and visits to art galleries; trips to Tuscany, Paris, Tunisia. A full, rich life, just as she said. All the happiness that money could buy.

Minkoff arose early the next morning to get ready for his hospital rounds. He made coffee and, trying not to wake Larissa, got into the shower. He was shampooing when Larissa entered. "Hello, darling," she said, with a sleepy smile. "Seems a shame to waste the water, so I thought we might as well shower together." She put her arms around Minkoff's neck.

He remembered the last time he had been naked in the shower with a woman. In this same shower, Larissa's highly maintained body, the work of so many hours in spas and at health clubs with personal trainers, should have filled him with a sense of all the promise that life still held out, even at his age. Instead he felt only a deadening sense of emptiness and betrayal.

"It's not going to work," Minkoff heard himself say.

"That's all right, darling," she said, "we've got all of tonight."

"No," he said, the water splattering them. "I mean my moving out to Los Angeles, our getting married."

"Why? What's wrong, baby?" she asked, looking up at him, water dripping into her eyes from her fine French haircut.

"What's wrong is, I am I, and you are you."

"What's that supposed to mean?"

"What it means is, I'm not California. I'm not Brentwood. I'm not Maserati. I'm not Spago dinners. And the truth is, I have no interest in being any of those things."

"Try," she said.

"I have tried. I've wasted your time. I apologize."

Larissa left the shower. Was she crying? Minkoff couldn't tell. She had wrapped herself in a red towel and, as she departed the bathroom, slammed the door.

Minkoff realized he still had shampoo in his hair, and had had the entire time he was telling Larissa that things weren't going to work out. A nice clownish touch, he thought. "Send in the clowns," he heard himself mutter. "Don't bother, they're here." He didn't know any of the other words of the song, but he began softly humming what he remembered of the melody. In no hurry to leave the shower, he carefully soaped up, finished his shampoo, shaved, and readied himself to haul those two large Louis Vuitton suitcases onto the street and into a cab, so that he could get back to work.

Casualty

AFTER GETTING MY B.A., M.A., AND PH.D. at Yale, and being kept on to teach in the English department there for six years, I was, as they said in those days, "let go," which means knocked off the tenure track, which really meant I had to look elsewhere for a job. I felt, I won't say lucky, but at any rate pleased to have got back on the track, with a promise of a tenure decision within two years, at the University of Illinois at Urbana-Champaign.

The English department there had a solid reputation, though such things inevitably look much better from a distance. A Teutonic Czech — a Jew and a homosexual — was still on the premises, who, with a genuine power for dramatizing ideas, served up in his lectures a fine heavy Germanic intellectual martini, five parts Nietzsche to one part Goethe. He claimed a friendship with Isaiah Berlin, and used to say the name Isaiah with the same reverential excitement that other men reserved for talking about divine sex. A man who had won a Pulitzer Prize for a three-volume biography of Henry Adams and was finishing up a two-volume work on Bernard Berenson was on the edge of retirement. Jewish himself, he seemed not to notice the fact that he had spent his scholarly career working on the lives of an anti-Semite and a self-hating Jew.

A man said to be the greatest living Melville scholar was in the department; failing to write the great book on Melville everyone expected, he dissipated his powers in the grinding complications of a scholarly edition of Melville in many volumes that used up his life, though he always seemed much jollier than one would have thought his failure permitted. Then there was a specialist in the teaching of English composition, a teacher of teachers, who went about always looking angry, except when drunk, at which point he turned even redder in the face than usual and went in for praising everyone well beyond the limits of credulity. The department also had a Blakean whose almost comical mixture of long-out-of-fashion clothes (spectator shoes, polyester suits, too-wide floral neckties) betrayed his claim to being an aesthete; in the attempt to hide his baldness, he had a hairdo of such complexity of construction that I could never be in his presence without thinking to myself, Ah, the long unhappy life of Francis Combover. (American literature is my own specialty.) This man later wrote a book about great romantic couples in literature and opera, which didn't stop him from introducing me to his own defeated wife no fewer, I'm sure, than thirty times: "Mel, have you met Hazel?"

The remainder of the English department was made up of the standard snobs, dry-as-dusts, and small-time academic operators whose dream was in one or another way to get back to the Ivy League schools whence they had been hatched. My own generation among the faculty, not yet in its forties, was already beginning to take on the look that only faces long pickled in disappointment acquire. They would easily be run over by the new historicists, deconstructionists, queer theorists, and other goofies waiting in the wings of history, as the young *marxisant* professors, now wearing black turtlenecks and unlaced Air Jordans, might put it. Of the two women among my generation of teachers, one took her own life in her fifties with a razor blade in a warm bath; the other allowed alcohol to do the job for her at sixty. Three others were homosexuals very far from on the loose; and most of the remainder sought their identity in an ill-formulated leftism that they thought might permit them to keep their youth by retaining what they actually believed was their idealism.

And then there was Leon Meisner . . . but more about Leon presently.

The most famous man in the department, a biographer of Yeats and of Shaw, had recently left to take up a professorship in Oxford at half his old salary; snobbery in those days still trumped money in academic life. His name was Maurice Picard (accent on the last syllable), originally Pinsky (accent on both syllables). With him gone, the department's Anglo-Irish connection was cut off. When he was around, Stephen Spender and Frank O'Connor used to pop up for a semester each year, Spender to chase boys and complain about the low quality of American students for his ill-prepared classes, and O'Connor, I'm told, to give full dollar value, working very hard at teaching what he always announced on the first day of class to be the quite unteachable subject of how to write the short story.

But of course all this was unknown to me when I accepted the offer from Illinois. And even if it had been known, I probably would have accepted anyway. Married and having a two-year-old daughter, I needed a job. Having gone to the serious pains of acquiring a doctorate and having put in six years of teaching at Yale, I wasn't ready to toss it away and begin work in a new line, even though the infestation of campus politics of the 1960s began to make me feel as if I had pledged a dying fraternity. Besides, though I hated to concede the point to GBS, at this stage in my life I was far from sure there was much else I could do but teach.

Not long after arriving in Champaign, I discovered the one man on the English faculty for whom I felt any real affinity, Andrew Berry, whose office was the next one down the corridor from my own. A man already in his late fifties, owing to an absence of published accomplishment Andrew looked to finish his career at the rank of associate professor. Andrew Berry was drowning in irony — an irony so deep that it made even the attempt at serious scholarship seem, somehow, a crude joke. Not that he ever stirred himself to make such an attempt. Instead he published very occasional parodies in such elegantly obscure magazines as *Botteghe Oscure,* the *Carlton Miscellany,* and the university's own *Accent.* I would gradually learn that Andrew's inability to do the first-rate scholarship that one might have expected from him was owing to the deadly combination of a crippling perfectionism and a want of confidence. Andrew wrote amusing letters to friends, drew cartoons too private to publish, looked up the etymology of French words, and, late in life, taught himself the rudiments of Chinese. I came to like him way too much ever to feel sorry for him or to regret his misspent life.

Ted O'Rourke, the department's Irish expert who had overlapped Maurice Picard, was in Dublin the autumn quarter I had arrived on campus. I hadn't known about him, and would have thought that Maurice Picard took care of all things Irish. When I asked Andrew Berry what Ted O'Rourke was like, he said, "A sweetie," adding, "completely *unadorable.* But you'll soon enough see for yourself."

The day I did, I found a large bald pink face leaning in and leering at me, reeking of beer — Buck Mulligan come to life, no lather on his cheeks and a beer instead of a shaving bowl in his hand. It was a Sunday afternoon at the retirement party for Karl Nolte, the department's Thoreau man. "What," he said, his face no more than three inches from mine, "do we need another Israelite around here for, please to tell?"

Flabbergasted, I asked who he was.

"O'Rourke," he said, "Ted O'Rourke. And while I'm at it, I read your recent article on Fitzgerald and O'Hara. Thin gruel, really pukey stuff, boyo. You ought to have been deeply ashamed to have signed your name to it."

What do you do with that? An unopened bottle of wine was on the buffet table before me, and it occurred to me to pick it up and smash it atop O'Rourke's perfectly bald pink head. He was four inches taller and probably seventy pounds heavier than I. I would, I assumed, have only one shot at him. Front or back of the head? I wondered. And then I thought, What am I, crazy? I walked away, saying nothing, leaving him mumbling as he opened another beer.

To say I made a mental note to avoid Ted O'Rourke would be putting it very gently indeed. But it wasn't, of course, always possible. I was teaching on a Tuesday-Thursday schedule, he on a Monday-Wednesday-Friday one. Occasionally, though, we would pass in the department office. He sometimes wore sunglasses; behind him at the Xerox machine one day, I noted that his hands shook.

Why people continued to invite O'Rourke to their parties I cannot imagine. He invariably got drunk; often he would arrive already drunk. Insults would follow. Andrew Berry told me that once, an empty Scotch bottle in his hand, he actually threatened O'Rourke that if he didn't shut the hell up, he would let him have it, a threat that, even in his drunkenness, Ted O'Rourke heeded. Andrew, I neglected to mention, was six foot three and a former Marine.

Not at all shocking to report, O'Rourke was divorced. His marriage broke up a few years before I had arrived in Champaign. Two daughters of the marriage, from reports I had heard, seemed to be getting on quite well as the world measures these things: they had gone to good schools, and one of the daughters eventually became a civil rights lawyer, the other a pediatrician. What toll their having O'Rourke for a father took I could not say, but it couldn't have been light. I assumed that they owed their success to the sensibly departed Mrs. O'Rourke.

Belligerent, not notably handsome, drunk much of the time, O'Rourke nonetheless appeared to have had no difficulty acquiring women friends. In his person he defied the old joke that defines an Irish homosexual as an Irishman who prefers women over booze. In the terms set by the joke Ted O'Rourke was an Irish bisexual. What women saw in him I don't pretend to know. "Lots of women out there," Andrew Berry remarked when I raised the question with him, "apparently are stimulated by worthlessness and the hope of reform."

Perhaps there was a charm to O'Rourke not visible to the naked male eye; certainly I didn't see it. I once went into Seville Florists, in downtown Champaign, to order flowers for my wife on our tenth anniversary, and when I told the owner I taught at the university, which entitled me to a 10 percent discount, he asked me in what department, and when I said English, he inquired if I knew Professor O'Rourke.

"I do," I said. "Why do you ask?"

"Some years he practically kept us in business single-handedly. Used to send two dozen white roses to lots of different women, always with cards of apology attached. Very elegant sentiments, too. Must be quite a guy, the professor."

"A laugh a minute," I said.

The only time I now saw O'Rourke was in our small department lounge, through which he would pass to pick up his mail or collect phone messages. He never came to departmental meetings. One wintry day he was wearing sunglasses, behind which I glimpsed the purplish skin of a badly blackened eye. A bar fight, I assumed. I noticed that, holding his mail, his hands shook more than ever. I saw him one afternoon at the YMCA, where I used to go in winter to jog; he was working out in the weight room, grunting and heaving, his large hairless chest with its undefined muscles straining at the massive weights he was hoisting.

"Liked your essay on Stevens in the *Hudson Review,* old sport," O'Rourke said to me one morning, touching me lightly on the shoulder from behind as I stood at the Xerox machine. I recalled that he also taught modern poetry.

"Thank you," I said, slightly amazed, and waited for an anti-Semitic crack to follow the compliment. No one in our department ever said anything about things I had written, and I was surprised when O'Rourke, of all people, did so.

A week or so later, driving home alone from a concert at the music school — my wife was down with the flu — I passed the Lincoln Hotel in Urbana at whose entrance I saw Ted O'Rourke, his mouth gaping open, head back, being held up under his arms by two young women.

I pulled my car under the hotel portico, parked, and got out.

"Excuse me," I said to the taller of the two women, "everything all right here?"

"Not for the old professor, it isn't," she said. "He's zonked out of his gourd. But before he passed out he wrote down his address and asked us to get him a cab."

"I work with him," I said. "Let's get him into my car. I'll take him home."

I slid out from behind the wheel, took over from the other young woman, and tried to negotiate O'Rourke into the front seat of my Honda. He was pure dead weight, his head bobbing up and back, emitting low groans. Once we got him in the car — no easy job — I took the address and thanked the girls. Driving away, I wondered if I should also have taken their addresses, so O'Rourke could send them the usual white roses after emerging from his hangover.

He lived only eight or so blocks away, one block west of Wright Street. As I pulled up in front of his house, he came awake.

"Many thanks, old sport," he said. "I owe you one."

"You can make it inside OK?" I asked.

"Major O'Rourke in charge from here. Not to worry." He saluted, exited the car with remarkable ease, and put two fingers to his lips, blowing me a kiss, before closing the door. As I pulled away, looking in the rearview mirror, I saw him vomiting violently at the curb.

The "major" bit was in fact not a joke. Andrew Berry told me that O'Rourke had been a B-17 bomber pilot, European theater, in World War II, a man with many missions to his credit and with the medals to prove it; among them, according to Andrew, a Distinguished Flying Cross.

"What's the 'old sport' bit?" I asked.

"That's Ted's *Great Gatsby* act. He grew up very rich on Long Island. His father was a builder of some kind. To hear Ted tell it, there were lots of servants, including a chauffeur. 'You never want to have a chauffeur,' he once told me. 'When he's gone you'll miss him sorely.' In any case, the whole thing went kaboom when the stock market crashed."

When I next saw O'Rourke in the English department lounge, no mention was made of my having driven him home. Did he remember it? Was he embarrassed to be caught so completely snockered in public? In the lounge O'Rourke was strictly business, picking up his mail, handing papers to the department secretary for typing.

I'm no connoisseur of drunks, but I assumed Ted O'Rourke drank himself into a stupor most nights. Whenever I would see him during the day, his skin had an odd pinkness. His hands took on a permanent tremor, which sometimes lapsed into serious shaking, which he did his best to disguise by slipping them into his pockets.

Yet O'Rourke had the reputation of being a good teacher: nothing dramatic, but solid was the word on him, sound, delivered the goods. I looked up a book he had written on Georgian Ireland, and his prose was straight, clear, no tricks about it, calling no undue attention to itself. He taught mostly undergraduates. Along with modern poetry, his subjects were all things Irish — Yeats, Wilde, GBS, Joyce. He used to teach late-afternoon classes, doubtless so that he would have time to recover from the previous evening's sousing. Then after class, often with a graduate student in tow, he would repair to the bar at the Lincoln Hotel and begin relubricating himself.

One night, assigned to meet a candidate for the department's medievalist chair, a Chaucer man, at the Lincoln, I arrived twenty minutes early and slipped into the bar for a Scotch and water, where I discovered O'Rourke, a graduate student on either side of him, holding forth.

"Old sport," he cried out. "Step up to the bar for a drop, won't you? Let me buy you your first."

I could do nicely without this, I thought. But I was trapped.

"How are you, Ted?"

"Couldn't be better, old sport, couldn't be better. Do join us." I tried to gauge his condition: two to two and a half sheets to the wind, out of a possible three, I decided. I also decided that, at the first anti-Semitic crack, I would, without hesitation, kick him very hard in a tender spot.

"I was just telling the boyos here," he said, putting a heavy arm around each of the graduate students, "that killing a man isn't as difficult as it sounds."

"Really?" I asked.

"Were you a soldier yourself, may I ask?" he said, cocking a dubious eyebrow.

"A Cold War soldier," I said. "Fought in the battles of Missouri, Arkansas, and Texas. Awarded the marksmanship medal and good conduct ribbon."

"I don't knock it, old sport," he said, reaching back to the bar to sip at his drink. "My wife — of sainted memory, though she still walks the earth — my wife used to say that she could always tell if a man had been in the service or not, and she thought those who had been were the better for it." He took a serious swallow of his dark drink. "But where was I?"

"Saying that killing a man isn't as tough as it sounds," one of the graduate students, a chubby kid named Larry Ross, said.

"Ah, yes," O'Rourke said. "I speak from limited experience. I only had to do it once, dontcha know."

"A German or a Jap?" the other graduate student asked.

"Actually," O'Rourke said, "an American. Wherein, you see, lies the complication." He took another large swallow from his drink. He had us all captive.

"Our crew was on its thirty-seventh mission, this one a fire-bombing over Hamburg. We were flying low, ack-ack fire popping off all round us. We'd been here before, but the return of German fire was particularly heavy this time out. Nothing for it, you know, but to play on through and hope that none of it found its target."

The other graduate student, a bearded kid with intensely blue eyes named Leslie Knudson, who looked to be fairly gone on drink himself, pulled at his beer and impatiently asked, "So what happened, Ted?"

"Getting to it, boyo, getting to it," O'Rourke returned. "Trying best I could to avoid the German ack-ack, I suddenly feel an arm around my throat and the thick nozzle of a service revolver pressing against my left temple. Looking to my right, I see that my copilot, a good old boy from Birmingham, Alabama, named Lou Wilson, is unconscious, his head slumped down on his chest, blood running from his ear." He stopped for another swallow and ordered one more of the same from the bartender.

"The chap with his arm around my throat and gun at my head is our navigator; Ron Chapman is his name. And he's shouting in my ear, 'Turn this fucking plane around or I'll kill you, you stupid bastard. Turn it around *now.*' Pure panic in his voice. But there's no way I could do so even if I wanted to, which I didn't, for it would have entailed breaking formation, which would bring a havoc of its own. Meanwhile, he's screaming, 'Turn it, you cocksucker, turn it.' This thirty-seventh mission was apparently one mission too many for him, poor chap. With his arm around my throat I could scarcely move, but I knew there was no way I could accommodate him. Maybe he knew it, too, for suddenly he begins to smash the barrel of the gun against the side of my head. Somehow or other I managed to squirm free of him, and the two of us go down on the floor of the cockpit, the plane flying itself. To get to the climax, I tried to wrench the revolver out of his grip, and in doing so, it went off, from the pressure of my hand on top of his, smashing the bones in the middle of his face."

O'Rourke's usually pink face was now red; tears were in his eyes. He picked up his fresh drink with two trembling hands.

"What'd you do then?" the chubby graduate student asked. It occurred to me that these two students, whose biggest problem was figuring out the symbolism in a poem by W. H. Auden, were probably older now than Ted O'Rourke was when flying his B-17.

"What I was trained to do," O'Rourke said. "I regained my seat and completed the mission, with my dead navigator face-down, soaking in his own blood on the floor behind me."

I didn't know what to make of this story, except I felt it was true. I also didn't know what to say in response to it, though I'm not sure any response was required. I was pleased to spot the arrival in the bar of our Chaucer man, and excused myself.

"Not to worry, old sport," said O'Rourke, now hunched over the bar. "See you around the campus." He put the accent on the second syllable of the word, pronouncing it *puce.*

✳ ✳ ✳

That winter, at the MLA meeting in Chicago, I met Maurice Picard, at the hotel, where he gave, to a full house, a brilliant talk on James Joyce. Although his name sounded French and his prose style was pure Oxbridge, in person Picard was unmistakably, delightfully Jewish, old shoe, completely without pretension as only an academic with genuine accomplishments behind him can be, and with the love of a joke and a good laugh.

Sitting in the coffee shop of the Palmer House, he asked me about various members of the department at the University of Illinois.

"And how fares Ted O'Rourke?" he got around to asking.

"Drunk much of the time, near as I can make out," I said, "though I try to steer clear of him. He doesn't seem overly fond of those of us of the Hebrew persuasion."

"Ted's got a little Jewish problem," he said, "no doubt about that. It chiefly comes upon him when he's on the sauce. Sober, he was always very respectful of me. When gone on booze, he took to calling me, with a great show of Irishness, 'Professor Picardski, also known as Moe,' the full epithet. 'Ah,' he would say, 'and what have we here — the good Professor Picardski, also known as Moe, I do believe.'"

"What did you do about it?"

"I returned the compliment by calling him 'Citizen,' meaning, as he couldn't mistake, the great bully in *Ulysses*. He would then usually smile ruefully and move on."

"What's behind it, do you think? I mean the guy's a damn Irishman. It's not as if he were Henry Adams, believing himself present at the creation and entitled to blue-blooded anti-Semitism."

"I'm afraid that Ted is not very keen on the advent of Jews in English and Irish studies. And there've been a lot of us, as I don't have to tell you. He's convinced himself that we're trespassing on sacred ground. Which I suppose in some ways we are."

"He'd prefer we stick to the Talmud?"

"Something like that. And he'd surely prefer that we produced a lot fewer Leon Meisners. How, by the way, is he doing?"

I told Picard that Leon Meisner had two years before taken a job, for an astonishingly high salary, at the University of California at Irvine.

"An operator, Leon, to the highest power. When I was in Champaign, he was usually off in Bellagio, at I Tatti, or some other such place, working a cushy visiting professorship, on leave with a Guggenheim, a Rockefeller, an NEH grant — he seemed to have everything but Marshall Plan money. No less than twice a year, he'd sashay over to the dean's office with an offer from another school in his pocket, which he used to jack up his own salary. Now toss in his New York accent, his scraggly beard, his paunchiness, and we've got perfect typecasting for someone doing Shylock in modern dress in a university setting. An anti-Semite's dream, Leon, and of course a Jew's nightmare."

The next time I saw O'Rourke, three days later, he was out cold, at nine-thirty P.M., lying on the living room floor of Ned and Jean Wynford, at their annual New Year's Eve faculty party. This was the first of the Wynfords' New Year's Eve parties my wife and I had gone to, and I hadn't realized that there was a yearly pool, five bucks an entry, in which one picked the time, within the half hour, that Ted O'Rourke would pass out.

He lay there now, in his largeness, face-down, peanut shells on the back of his double-breasted blue blazer, his white duck trousers badly rumpled, one leg rising high, displaying his pink, hairless, and bulging calf. Everyone walked around him as if he were some potted plant awkwardly left in the middle of the floor. Elsewhere in the room people exchanged their turgid academic ironies, glasses of wine and sherry in hand. Without wanting in any way to help him — and besides, how could I have done? — I felt sorry for the miserable son of a bitch.

At the end of every school year O'Rourke used to give an afternoon party of his own, in his large backyard, for students and faculty friends. I was surprised when, one day in the lounge, he told me about it and suggested that my wife and I drop by.

I went alone. It was sunny, in the low seventies. Two tables had been set up: on one of them fruit, cheese, and crackers were on offer; on the other sat two large buckets of ice with beer cans in them, six or seven bottles of jug wine, and plastic wineglasses. In the center of the yard — a fine touch, this — sat a young woman playing a harp.

"Over here, old sport," O'Rourke called out when he saw me.

I walked over to him, wineglass in hand. He was wearing a seersucker suit whose inner collar, I noticed, had turned yellowish. His white shirt had a number of tiny holes in it. His black knit tie was slightly askew. He had a straw boater, worn at what used to be called a rakish angle, though with its blue-and-white ribbon slightly frayed. He had a bottle of champagne in each hand.

"Toss away that plonk," he said, referring to the wine in my glass, "and gargle on a bit of the bubbly here."

When I did as told, he poured champagne into my plastic glass, his trembly hand causing a fair amount of spillage, some of it on my wrist. Clearly he was drunk. A young girl, no doubt an undergraduate in one of his courses, asked if she could get a soft drink.

"Soft drink?" he said, confounded, as if he had never before heard the two words conjoined in this way. "There's a supermarket three blocks from here that might have what you're seeking, my dear."

"So tell me, old sport, how are you finding the world of thought and deep scholarship on this beautiful afternoon?"

"It's a living," I said, thinking I was passing off a light, mildly ironic remark.

"Spoken like a true Israelite," he said, "albeit a white one."

"What the hell is that supposed to mean? What's your problem with the Jews, Ted?"

"My problem, you see, is that you boys all seem to be in business for yourselves. Which may well have its place, but not, don't you know, in universities, where the spirit of the operation is meant to be rather different than that of a dry-goods store."

"Go fuck yourself, old sport," I said, and turned away from him. Had I the champagne bottles in my hands, I like to think I would have banged one over his boater.

Walking off, I heard him call out, "No need to take it all so personally, boyo."

I needed to use the bathroom, and so on my way out went into the house, where I was surprised to find rooms full of elegant Queen Anne furniture, all of it polished and in perfect repair. I thought of O'Rourke coming home roaring drunk, the bull in this lovely china shop. But everything seemed in splendid order. On a grand piano sat two photographs, in silver frames, of two young girls, very Irish, very pretty — doubtless O'Rourke's daughters. A family lived in this house once. A strange, raging, Jew-hating drunk lived here now, I thought.

The next Tuesday, I was in the English department office to pick up my mail when O'Rourke walked in, wearing sunglasses and a short-brimmed golf cap with a blue-and-red ribbon around it. I braced myself for a confrontation.

"How goes it, old sport?" he said blithely. "Missed you at my party this past Saturday. Pity. I'm told a good time was had by all."

Did he, I wondered, have no memory of my being in his backyard just three days before, nor any of our little dustup?

"It's quite possible the alcohol has taken hold of old Ted's brain at last," Andrew Berry said when I reported this rather impressive lapse of memory to him. "It's been soaking it in for a long while now. It may well be that he no longer has any memory of his behavior when drunk. I don't know if that's a good thing or a bad."

"And what's with his anti-Semitism?" I asked.

"So far as I know, it only emerges when Ted's drunk. I've never seen it when he's sober. Part of his twenties gentleman's fantasy, I imagine. When on the booze, he seems to have forgot that Jew-baiting is no longer an approved sport."

The years, as they say in fairy tales, passed. The old guard among the faculty began to die off. Andrew Berry, the only one I genuinely missed, pegged out at seventy-three, his wife having found him one morning with the television on in their living room, slumped in his chair, his Chinese primer on the floor beside him. I watched the beards of the young Turks in the department grow gray, then white, even as their wardrobes grew more youthful: they are carrying backpacks now.

I was spending the academic quarter at the Huntington Library the year Ted O'Rourke retired. I'm told that, at his retirement party, he planned to deliver a ringing harangue about the death of the study of literature, but he was so drunk that he wound up incoherently attacking, for some obscure reason, the novelist Ralph Ellison.

After his retirement O'Rourke never returned to the English department office. I would see him from time to time around Champaign. He was wise enough not to own a car; had he done so, driving it drunk would surely have finished him off long ago. Sometimes I would spot him with his small gym bag in hand, heading to or returning from the YMCA. Summer months I might spot him with one of his lady friends at the farmers' market in town.

After buying a pair of running shoes one day, and showing my University of Illinois faculty card as identification for my check, the salesman asked if I taught there or was an administrator. When I said that I taught, in the English department, he asked if I knew Professor O'Rourke. I said that I knew him well, and he told me that Ted O'Rourke had saved his life.

"I'm an alcoholic," he said, "and I had drunk myself to the point where I'd lost my family, my job, and finally my apartment. I knew Ted as 'a fellow voyager on the wet way,' as he used to call it. I had no place left to go but the streets, and he took me in, let me live in a room in his house, fed me, set up the conditions that permitted me to dry out, and then lent me the money needed to get my life started again. Without his help I'd be dead now."

"Why do you suppose he never stopped drinking himself?"

"I once asked him that. His answer was that the world looked a lot better to him after five or six drinks."

Occasionally, from my own car, I would discover O'Rourke waiting for a bus or walking out of a restaurant. Once, when I pulled up at a traffic light on Wright Street, there he was, in white trousers and dark polo shirt, wearing another golf hat. He'd acquired a potbelly, but it looked to be a pot made of iron. He spotted me behind the wheel, so I lowered the window on the passenger's side and asked him if he'd like a lift.

"How go things, Ted?" I asked when he'd settled himself in the passenger seat.

"Not so bad, old sport," he said. "No real reason for complaint. I see where Howard Lindstrom died." He was referring to our Blake man.

"In Florida," I said. "I always thought him clownish, vastly overrated as a scholar."

"You're not far wrong," he said. "But given what they've got teaching nowadays, even our old pedants begin to look good. How goes your own teaching?"

"I'm still serving up pretty much the same stuff."

"We teachers tend to live off our capital, I suppose."

"Mine's about to run out. I retire in two years, and think I can just about make it to the finish line."

We were in downtown Champaign, and he asked that I drop him off at the public library. "Good to see you, old sport," he said. "Keep the colors flying." From outside the car he bent to say goodbye with a smile and a salute.

That winter I had a Christmas card from him, sent from Arizona. In a note accompanying the card, he mentioned that he was staying with his brother. "The place is hot as blazes," he wrote, "and much fitter for cactuses than human beings. I'm also having trouble with my hips and may require damnable surgery when I return to dear old Champaign-Urbana."

Was this an invitation for friendship? Had he in his befuddled brain forgotten that I was Jewish? I didn't know. I was sure, though, that I didn't wish to grow any closer to Ted O'Rourke. When next I saw him, again from my car, he was on a cane and looked very much the old bull gone weak in the knees. With his drinking habits, that he was alive at all bespoke an astoundingly strong heart. I had a Christmas card from him from Arizona the following year, with another brief note appended. Then two years of silence.

One night the phone in our bedroom rang at 2:18 A.M. (Digital clocks allow for such precision.)

"Old sport," the voice on the other end asked with real urgency, "have you any weapons around the place from your army days? A carbine, perhaps, or maybe a revolver?"

"Ted," I said. "It's very late. Where are you?"

"At home, old sport. But they're here. They're in the attic. I don't know how many of them. I hear them rummaging around."

"Who's there? Who're you talking about, Ted?"

"The Nips, man. The bloody Japs. Who'd you think?" And he hung up.

Three weeks later I had another phone call from him, this one in the late afternoon.

"You're the only one left in the damn English department who's served in the army, and I'm going to have to count on your services. Will you be ready if called? Might I depend on you, boyo?"

"For what, exactly, Ted?"

"For what do you think? The bloody invasion, man."

"What invasion?"

"The Pacific theater. The Japs, man, the purple-pissing Japs." Again he hung up.

The third call came a week later, this time at nine at night.

"They're here," he said. "Get your ass over here, boyo. I need whatever help I can get, and I need it now."

There was something more urgent in his voice than before. "All right, Ted," I said, "I'll be right over."

"Bring any weapons you've got around the . . . ," he said, and hung up.

I knew he was in real trouble — but not from any enemies other than himself. I arrived at his house on Judson Street and was about to walk up the porch steps when I heard him call out from above. "Did you bring the weapons? They're downstairs and coming up." He was perched precariously on the slanted roof of the third floor. It was a cold night, and he was in pajama bottoms, no shirt.

"Jesus, Ted, go back in the house."

"Can't do it, boyo. The bastards are here. They're in my bedroom. Toss me up a carbine."

In O'Rourke's mushy mind World War II was still going on. I had heard stories of war-weary veterans of the European theater who were terrified of having next to go fight in the Pacific, and were immensely grateful to Harry Truman for dropping the bomb on Hiroshima and putting a quick end to things. In his booze-soaked brain O'Rourke must have believed that he had now to battle the Japanese, and it panicked him.

"Ted," I yelled up, "just hold on. I'm coming up."

The front door was locked. I kicked in a living room window and was able to crawl through. The same good English furniture was there; rushing over to the staircase, I noted the two photographs in their same place atop the piano.

"I'm coming, Ted," I yelled. "I'm coming." At the second floor the door to a storage room was open, and the cold wind came through its open window. "I'm here, Ted. I'm here." When I put my head outside the window, there was no sign of him. I eased my way out onto the roof. Getting as close to the edge as I dared, I looked over and saw Ted O'Rourke lying prone on the hard turf below.

I raced downstairs, out of the house, and onto the lawn. O'Rourke's neck was twisted in a way that didn't leave much doubt about his not being alive. I bent over his body and put my face next to his, hoping to hear breathing, but couldn't make out any. His body was too massive for me to attempt to drag it into the house. I found a phone in his kitchen and dialed 911.

I sat on the front porch, awaiting the police and fire department ambulance. I tried not to stare or even glance at the body on the ground ten or so yards away from me. Why did I care about this tortured man? I thought to mumble the Kaddish, then considered the irony of it and put it out of mind. Instead I found myself chanting Yeats's "Cast a cold eye / On life, on death. / Horseman, pass by!" over and over, my eyes closed, until I heard the approaching sirens in the shivery night.

Janet Natalsky and
the Life of Art

Driving down Sheridan Road, heading north in the right lane, I noticed from the rear a body, a walk, a carriage that looked familiar. It's Janet, I thought. She was wearing a brownish, leopard-skin-patterned blouse, an ankle-length denim skirt with lace trim along the bottom, sandals. I pulled over to the curb. She bent to pick up something, perhaps a coin. Although I couldn't get a clear view of her face, I saw thick gray hair and rimless glasses. I was on the point of calling out — "Janet?" — but, after the slightest hesitation, drove on.

Janet Natalsky had been a peripheral character at Senn, our very social high school — she lacked the clothes or the easy good looks required for any position closer to the center — but she didn't carry herself like one. She carried herself as if she were a great beauty, which she wasn't: she was tall, with poor skin and thickish features and unruly red hair with a too-low hairline. Better, she carried herself as if she were in possession of a great secret, which, it turns out, she was. As I would discover in later years, Janet's secret was that she, alone in all the world, knew that she was destined to be an artist — specifically, a writer.

I, on the other hand, had no secrets at all. In those sweet adolescent days, I was perfectly happy to luxuriate dab in the center. A minor athlete, a jokey Jakey, a casual master of the art of conformity, I floated through high school completely without care, as if on an inner tube on a clear lake on a balmy summer's day that lasted four full years.

I noticed Janet Natalsky, knew who she was, but hardly more. She wasn't in any of the right clubs, didn't live in West Rogers Park or on Lake Shore Drive, wasn't in my set or in any other that mattered. Besides, she was at Senn for only a year. We took first-year Latin together, but next fall she didn't return, having gone off, at fifteen, to the University of Chicago, which then — I'm speaking of the early 1950s — had a program for very bright high school kids.

It was two decades later, in the seventies, that my friend Norm Brodsky called to ask if I remembered a girl at Senn named Janet Burgess. I didn't. "Someone by that name," he said, "has written a blistering attack on the school in the current issue of *Harper's*. And I think you may be in it. Or at least the flat back of your head and your magnificent ears."

Blistering was the word for it. The essay, a memoir really, was about the stifled and yet bizarre life of a sensitive young girl in the barbaric setting of a middle-class, predominantly Jewish high school. Witty assaults on teachers, students, and clubs were launched in an impressively deft way. A caustic paragraph was devoted to Miss Cobb's first-year Latin class, the author seated, staring, behind a curly-haired boy with stick-out ears within whose head, the author was certain, not a thing could possibly have been going on. That curly hair, those ears, that head with nothing going on in it — as Norm had rightly recognized, they were all mine.

Janet Burgess was of course Janet Natalsky. The biographical note said that she lived in Chicago and was "at work on a novel and a study about daily life in a psychiatric ward." As for me, the empty-headed boy now in his middle thirties, I, *mirabile dictu*, had in the interim become something resembling a literary scholar-critic. After a year at the University of Illinois at Navy Pier— "Harvard on the Rocks," we called it—where I proved my seriousness by getting all A's, my father agreed to pay my way to the University of Wisconsin. There I found I was even better at school than I thought. So I stayed at it, going on to Stanford for a Ph.D. in literature. Now I was a teacher myself, a recently tenured associate professor of English at the University of Illinois at Chicago, located no longer at Navy Pier but on a grim, gray concrete campus just west of the Loop and south of Greektown.

It was in this context that Janet reentered my life later that same year, when she participated in a panel, "Fiction and the New Journalism," sponsored by our English department. I had a late-afternoon class to teach, but managed to slip in for the last quarter hour. And there she was, unmistakably Janet, her red hair thicker than ever, her skin still slightly blotchy, her confidence in her sense of election unchanged.

She sat very upright, leaning slightly forward, elbows on the table, which gave her a look of extreme alertness. The various panelists were in the process of summing up: Michael Anton, a hack journalist and unpublished novelist who had wormed his way into the department as a permanent visiting writer-in-residence; Bette Newboldt, our unappeasable feminist whom, I'm fairly certain, God Himself could not have made happy; and Les Feinstein, the dean of Arts and Sciences, author of a book on Alexander Pope and a collection of his own forgettable verse.

Janet was the last to speak. Her manner immediately interested me, combining common sense with deliberately dated clichés and loopy asides, the whole supported by unbending highbrow views. "We can, it seems to me," her peroration went, "argue this point till the cows come home, the bulls following ardently behind. But finally it seems to me that whether journalism, new or old, can ever attain to the status of high art is a question that calls for, indeed demands, throwing out both the baby and the bathwater. Journalism remains journalism. Art, art. And the two do well never to meet."

After the question-and-answer session, during which she handled herself with equally magisterial hauteur, I walked up to her.

"Excuse me," I said, "but I wonder if you remember me?"

She gave me a quizzical smile. "No," she said, "I don't believe I do. Should I?"

I turned around. "The ears, Janet. Miss Cobb's Latin class."

"Oh, my God," she said, "David Nachman. It's really you."

"The man himself," I said. "Nachman comes before Natalsky, which is why I sat in front of you. If my name had been Noskin, my ears would never have appeared in *Harper's*. Are you free for coffee?"

"Sure," she said, smiling. "We can catch up on the bad old days."

"How did Natalsky become Burgess?" I asked as we sat in my small office, sipping coffee from cardboard cups.

"Ms. Janet Natalsky made the serious mistake of marrying a professor of chemistry at the University of Chicago named Ernest Burgess. Three years later he left me for a graduate student. This sounds common enough, I suppose, except that the student was an East Indian boy. I have to admit that it threw me, at least for a bit. I came away from the marriage with a shiny new Waspy name and what was diagnosed as a nervous breakdown."

"The breakdown accounts for your promised book on the psychiatric ward?"

"Some promise," she said. "It's been to eleven publishers with no takers. But fill me in a little on your own life."

I told her what little there was to tell: my dissertation on the writers of the British Empire, published by Yale, and my new book on the reputation of Rudyard Kipling, which had gotten me tenure; my marriage and my two daughters; my relative contentment with being left pretty much alone to teach my small classes and write my books at my own pace. "I never expected so quiet a life," I concluded.

She asked me about the kids we had gone to school with. I reported that I saw a few of them from time to time, and occasionally ran into others in restaurants or at Bulls or Cubs games or movies in the Old Orchard shopping center.

"I can't tell you how much I hated that school," she said. "I especially loathed the girls with their little upstanding boobs swaddled in cashmere sweaters and their certainty that the world was arranged for them alone. If I'd had to stay at Senn for four years, I think I might have taken my life. Which reminds me — I should be candid. I had more than a nervous breakdown after the honorable Professor Burgess left me for his Indian. I actually overdosed on sleeping pills."

"The breakup left you feeling lost?"

"Nothing of the kind," she said. "I was angry at myself for being so stupid in so many ways. A person like me shouldn't really marry, you know. Marriage is not what I'm about."

I was going to ask her what she was about, but she got there first. "I am an artist," she informed me, "and marriage is always a mistake for an artist, and also for the person the artist marries. I won't make that mistake again."

Before leaving my office Janet told me she was living in a studio apartment on Dorchester in her old University of Chicago neighborhood. She spent a lot of time at writers' colonies, published the occasional article, wrote book reviews for the Chicago *Trib* and the *Sun-Times,* took in small honorariums for things like this afternoon's panel.

I couldn't quite get a fix on whether she was disdainful of what I did. Even as a young man, I don't think I kidded myself about it: I wrote books about people who wrote books, and taught students things that only a small number of them cared about. Still, I felt myself privileged. To be allowed to indulge my passion for the writers I loved, at the price of having to teach six hours a week — as I used to say to my father, who spent the better part of his life selling costume jewelry on the road, it sure beat working.

I drove Janet into the Loop, where she was going to catch a bus back to Hyde Park. We exchanged phone numbers, promised to get together for lunch. Neither of us did anything about it. But one day, a few months later, I found in my faculty mailbox a copy of a magazine called *Ploughshares*. It contained another memoir by Janet Burgess, "My Sister Was an Only Child," sent to me by the editors with the compliments of the author.

I'd never read anything quite like Janet's memoir. It was about her proletarian Jewish family, and it was devastating in its vividness and candor. Her father was a fix-it man, doing odd jobs for people; a brutish man, he never spoke, she claimed, other than in monosyllables or in the briefest of sentences. Her mother, who weighed nearly three hundred pounds, did the minimum of cooking and housekeeping, instead indulging her taste for pedicures and the contents of boxes of Whitman's Samplers. A younger sister, with rheumatic fever, used up what little attention was available in the family's dark one-bedroom apartment on Ainslie Street. Janet didn't mention herself until the very end of the memoir, where she spoke of listening to a radio program called *Mr. Keen, Tracer of Lost Persons*. She ended by saying that, with her books and her dreams of art, she always imagined herself as one of those lost persons, except that she wished never to be found.

Her parents were both still alive, I remembered Janet telling me in my office; I wondered what their response might be to this portrait. When I phoned to thank her for having a copy sent to me, we made a date for lunch on the following Wednesday. I picked her up at her apartment. She was running behind, and when I rang from downstairs she suggested that I come up for a minute. The door to her third-floor apartment was open; inside, the room was a shambles of stacked paperback books, magazines on the floor, dishes in the sink, an unmade single bed.

"Oh, hi, David," she said, emerging from the bathroom as if surprised to see me there. She was wearing a thick green sweater with a high turtleneck, a gray, slightly rumpled skirt, and saddle shoes. "Need to use the bathroom before we go?"

"Maybe I should," I said. The chaos was even greater there than in the living room: open jars and uncapped tubes and damp towels everywhere. I washed my hands, dried them on a rumpled towel over the tub, and as I grasped the door handle, found my right hand wrapped in a pair of Janet's underpants. Jesus, I'm in Janet Natalsky's pants, I thought.

We ate at Salonika, a place on 57th Street. Janet ordered roast chicken, I a gyro sandwich. A lot of bulky Chicago cops were at other tables.

"Your memoir was a knockout," I said. "Really strong stuff."

"Thanks," she said. "It's part of an early-life autobiography I'm planning. The *Harper's* piece was another part of it."

"Have your parents or your sister seen any of this?"

"Not that I know of. My sister's married to a dentist and lives in West Rogers Park. My parents are still on Ainslie. None of them is exactly your typical *Ploughshares* reader."

"But what if it were to fall into their hands? What would happen?"

"I guess they'd learn what wretched parents they were. Besides, you know, David, I'm a writer, and I have only my life to write about. If it hurts them, it'll hurt them. It really can't be helped."

After lunch I walked her back to her building. At the entrance, she told me she was planning to move next month to Santa Fe; she didn't yet have an address, but she hoped we'd stay in touch. I wondered if she'd offer me a cheek to kiss as we parted, but instead she put out her hand. "If you need me for anything," I said, rather foolishly — what could she need me for? — "you can always reach me at the university."

It was a warm afternoon, and I decided to walk over to O'Gara's used-book store in hopes of finding a few H. G. Wells items I'd been looking for. On the surface, Hyde Park appeared to be just another Chicago neighborhood, maybe a little more varied in its architecture — fewer bungalows, almost no two-flats — but the spirit of the place was conferred by the abundance of graduate students and the many hangers-on who, long after departing the university, remained in this enclave in a state of suspended studenthood. To the north and south were tough, slummy neighborhoods, but here in Hyde Park all was books and foreign newspapers and older European professors, Hitler's gift to America, walking around in berets and goatees. Hyde Park seemed a good place for high-IQ misfits, blessed with dazzling minds or imaginations but unequipped to take life straight on; a good place for Janet, I thought.

Three years must have gone by before I heard from her again, and then not directly but through the Guggenheim Foundation. She had put my name down as a reference. Her fellowship proposal was for a study of novelists who took Chicago as their subject, among them Frank Norris, Theodore Dreiser, Upton Sinclair, James T. Farrell, Richard Wright, Nelson Algren, and Saul Bellow. As a practicing writer rather than an academic, she claimed that she was in a superior position to understand what it was about the city that attracted these men, not all of whom had been born there.

When the annual list of Guggenheim winners was published,

Janet's name was on it. But whether she returned to Chicago to work on the project I have no idea, for I never had a word from her. Then, some four years after her Guggenheim ran out, she phoned me from San Francisco.

"Oh, David, hi, Janet Burgess." Again I noted her odd tic of beginning every conversation as if she were surprised to see or hear from me, even when the idea had been hers in the first place. After some pleasantries she said she had a favor to ask.

"Sure," I said. "What can I do for you?"

"Oh," she said, "I've applied for a Newberry fellowship to work on my Chicago novelists project, and I wonder if I can ask you for another recommendation."

"Of course," I said. "I'd be happy to supply it. How's it going, by the way? Making much progress?"

"I don't want to make too much progress," she said. "This little item happens to be my cash cow just now, and I expect to stay with it until all udders are utterly dry. Udders, utterly, what a language we've been given to work with."

"Cash cow?"

"Yes," she said, "I've already had three different fellowships with it. The way I've written my proposal seems to ring the bell with foundation people. And the money gives me time to attend to my own writing. I'm not really a critic, as you know."

I let pass what I heard as a touch of contempt directed at the club to which I happened to belong. "But how's your work going in general?"

"Not too badly," she said. "My memoir is making the rounds of publishers. And I'm also living fairly well on kill fees from magazines that decide not to use articles they've commissioned from me. I've had some quite decent ones, from the *Atlantic*, the *New York Times Magazine*, and an especially fat one from *The New Yorker*. No business like lit business, you know."

We agreed to meet for lunch or dinner the next time she was in Chicago, the chances of which, she said, would of course be much increased if she got her Newberry fellowship. She did in fact win it, though she never called to tell me so. Evidently, she did not feel under the normal constraints of politeness — she was, after all, an artist, with better things to do. But perhaps, I was belatedly starting to think, Janet was also something of an operator.

By then I had been made a full professor and had joined the publication committee of our university press. This enterprise was a good deal less than first class. It published lots of stuff about Chicago and Illinois politics and had recently initiated a program to bring regional writers back into print. The newest activity was putting out the work of contemporary poets; the director of this project, Regis Gambon, was the school's head of creative writing.

I had had little to do with Regis Gambon. Behind his back, other people in the department called him "old soft G," after the way he insisted his name be pronounced. I Ie was said to be from Alabama. Now in his early fifties, Gambon was a wide man who looked extremely well fed without being quite fat. His dark hair was ambitiously coifed — I believe he had a permanent — with curls forming bangs that fell over his forehead. A thick mustache covered his upper lip in what the boys at Senn High School would have called a womb broom. The overall effect — soft G, curly bangs, womb broom — was preposterous.

Gambon did not let the fact that he was married with four young children get in the way of a well-earned reputation for sleeping with undergraduates. As for his own poetry, a glance at his most recent book, on display in our department faculty lounge, revealed strong stands against Ronald Reagan, war, and materialism. One poem ended, "Each of us must as best he can /

Stem the senseless hatred of man for man." I remember reading this and thinking that if Gambon were to try sleeping with one of my daughters, both of whom were now in high school, I'd be delighted to show him a fine specimen of the senseless hatred of man for man.

I mention Regis Gambon only because, at our faculty Christmas party, he showed up with Janet Natalsky on his arm. I spotted them at the other end of the room, looking like more than just friends. The spectacle saddened me; I felt that Janet was — how to say it? — sleeping below herself. What did she need from a clown like Gambon?

"Oh, hi, David," she said when I came up to her. "You must know Regis Gambon."

"We don't know each other as well as colleagues should," Gambon said, putting out a paw for me to shake. It seemed unusually padded, more like a well-broken-in catcher's mitt than a human hand.

"Regis is arranging a stint for me in the creative writing program, David. Wouldn't it be lovely if we were to be on the same faculty? David and I went to the same high school," she said, turning to Gambon.

"It must have been a high-powered intellectual institution," he said.

"Quite the reverse," I said, "as Janet will be the first to tell you."

He wandered off, and I asked Janet how she had come to know him. They were on the same circuit, she said. They had first met at Bread Loaf, and then a few years ago they both ended up at the MacDowell artists' colony.

"He has a reputation," I said, getting as much irony into my voice as was seemly, "as a hands-on teacher."

"I'd say he's a hands-on guy in every way," she said with a

knowing smile. Did she also know he was a creep? Did I know her well enough to say so? I decided not to.

"Do you really want the job here?"

"As always, I can use the money."

"Is there anything I can do to help?"

"I don't think so," she said. "Leave it to Regis." She paused for a beat. "Sounds like *Leave It to Beaver*, doesn't it? Anyhow, I always say that where there's a way there's a will. What do you always say?"

"I always say getting what you want isn't the same as wanting what you get. Or did Lewis Carroll always say that? I think he may have."

I asked the department secretary, a genteel southern woman named Estelle Frye, for the paperwork on Gambon's nomination of Janet Burgess. It included some awestruck recommendations from writers I had never heard of. Gambon's own statement was also there, along with six samples of Janet's writing: the *Harper's* and *Ploughshares* memoirs, short stories from *Prairie Schooner, Antioch Review,* and *Georgia Review*, and a longish poem about the death of her father from *Threepenny Review*.

None of the stories, I thought, came alive in the way the memoirs did. Sentence by sentence, the writing was no less amazing — astounding, really, in its virtuosity; but the characters didn't breathe, the situations were implausible, everything seemed willed and dead on the page. Janet, I concluded, had only one story to tell, and in telling it she was at her best when beating up on someone else. Hers was a purely destructive talent. But genuine: on the right subject, she possessed the magic of art.

Sure enough, Janet got the job, which ran for two semesters. We taught on different days. As a visiting writer she wasn't required to attend department meetings and, sensibly, did not. We never once saw each other during the entire school year. I put a note in her mailbox suggesting lunch; she replied, "Love to"; but when I suggested she name a day, I never heard back, and lost all contact with her.

Then, a few years later, I saw her name above an impressive short piece on the death of James T. Farrell. It had appeared in the *Threepenny Review*, a copy of which was lying on the table in the faculty lounge. The author's bio said that Janet was living in Taos and had just published a novel, *The Avatar's Revenge*, with an academic press. A few years later still, she had a coruscating article in the *Chronicle of Higher Education* about the perils, for a writer, of teaching creative writing; the biographical note had her living in College Park, Maryland, and made mention of a forthcoming book of essays, to be published by Greywolf Press.

Several more years went by. My own children had grown up, gone off to college, married. My biography of Joseph Conrad had met with a good critical reception, and I found myself in a chair at Northwestern, having turned down offers from Berkeley and Yale. I was working on a collection of Kipling's letters for Oxford. Now, in my middle fifties, I had pretty much done what I set out to do and was reaping the small but pleasant rewards of a successful academic career. Ahead of me I had only years and, with luck, grandchildren.

Just before ten o'clock one night — my wife and I were already in bed, reading, about to turn out the lights — the phone rang.

"Oh, hi, David, it's me, Janet, Janet Burgess. Hope I'm not calling too late."

"No," I said. "How are you?"

"'As well as can be expected' is the way I now answer that question," she said. "The reason I'm calling is that I'm in town for my brother-in-law's funeral, and I wonder if you'd like to meet for lunch, like maybe tomorrow? The funeral's on Thursday and I'm leaving Friday." She added that she was now living in the Northwest. Oregon? Washington? Vague as always, she didn't say.

"Sure," I said. "I don't teach on Wednesdays. Tomorrow will be fine."

She was staying with her sister in West Rogers Park. She didn't have a car — didn't know how to drive — so I picked her up there on Fargo, a block west of California. It was one of those gray Chicago days, temperature in the twenties, lots of black ice on the road. All the local restaurants I'd known as a boy — Randall's, Robert's, Friedman's, Kofield's — were gone, so I drove us into Evanston and stopped at the Golden Olympic on Chicago Avenue.

Once seated, she announced her liking of the statement on the menu; under the name Golden Olympic ran the slogan, quotation marks and all, "A Family Restaurant with Just a Hint of Greece."

"Nothing like being both tone deaf and dead to the menace that lurks in language," she said, smiling.

Sitting across from Janet, I saw, as I hadn't during the ride, that the years had not been easy on her. She was wearing a heavy black cable-stitch sweater, a tweed skirt, and argyle socks that came up over the knee. Her hair, thick as ever, was now all gray, running into white. Her face had more than the usual wrinkles and pouchiness for someone our age, and she looked permanently tired. She wore very little makeup: no attempts at disguise.

"Condolences, by the way, on the death of your brother-in-law," I said after we had ordered our lunches, a turkey club with a Coke for her, for me an egg-white Denver omelet and tea.

"Condolences are very much 'by the way,'" she said. "He meant absolutely nothing to me. He was a very dull man, so dull that I'm not sure how the paramedics knew he was dead, unless they sensed the relief on the faces of his wife and children.

He was a dentist, and a good moneymaker, I'll give him that. My little sister, poor baby, married a professional man. Made my mother very happy."

"And how go things with you?"

"Oh, all right, I suppose. I have two manuscripts — one of three connected novellas, the other of poems — neither of which has found a publisher. The royalties from my last book, I hate to tell you, might pay for this lunch, but there wouldn't be enough left over for a tip."

"As far as I can see, you write exactly what you want. I admire that," I said, trying to find some way to give the conversation an upward tilt.

"Do you?" she said. "I notice that Scribner brought out your biography of Conrad. I'd kill to have such a publishing house for one of my books, getting me out of the small-audience ghetto — make that minuscule audience."

"You do eventually find publishers, though. I'm sure you will again."

"David, I am fifty-five years old. I have published three books. If I were a man in this position, I would have lots of young girls, students no doubt, fluttering around me, dragging me into bed. As a middle-aged woman, I don't see any men, young or old, doing anything like that."

That eliminated any personal questions I might have had along those lines. We had both taken detours, Janet and I, from the prosperous lives we might have lived. But how much safer mine was: a life of more than reasonable security, a pension waiting at the end. She, on the other hand, had been flying without a net from the beginning. She had her ambition and her talent, and the two did not match, though she could not have known this when she began betting everything on the latter. Did she, I wondered, realize that she had lost the bet?

We made it through the remainder of lunch talking about things of no real interest to either of us. Arriving back at her sister's, I walked her up the ice-coated steps. Janet took my arm. For a coat, she was wearing what in those days was called a fun fur, a great mottled shaggy piece of business, perhaps borrowed from her sister. At the top of the stairs she said, "Well, David, thanks for lunch and everything else," and then leaned in and embraced me. Her thick hair, her heavy sweater, the shaggy fur — for a nanosecond I feared I would never emerge. Her sister opened the door. "Bye, David," she said, and without introducing me walked into the house.

Driving home to Evanston I felt an overwhelming sadness. Janet and I were contemporaries, dammit, and we were both getting to an age where there wasn't much in the way of turnaround time. She had set out to be a hero of culture and ended a martyr of art. Did what I'd accomplished add up to anything more, or was I merely lucky not to have been infected by the virus of real talent?

Another ten years passed. I had retired from my teaching job at Northwestern and was working on a biography of Kipling when my fiftieth high school reunion came along. I dithered. Fifty years, good God. The days and weeks and months and years seemed to run at the same old pace; it was only the decades that flew by. I had lost a lot of hair, put on some weight. But my wife told me I ought to go, and so I sent in my check, noting my so-called accomplishments on the fact sheet that came with the invitation. I didn't much look forward to it.

We gathered in a dimly lit Italian restaurant in the Loop, Maggiano's, famous for its large portions. Perhaps three hundred people were in the room. Someone had brought an old record player and lots of 45s: heavy-breathing, overdramatized numbers sung by Italian men and women who wanted to be loved with inspiration, invited you to make yourself comfortable, and worried that the teacher might be standing much too near, my love.

At such events, you can either mill around or stand still and wait for others to come to you. I decided to stand still. From old schoolmates who wandered over, I was somewhat surprised to learn that I was considered one of the successes of our class. Many had made much more money, but I had something resembling a public life. The fact that I wrote books and, more crucially, had taught at Northwestern seemed to count for something. I speculated that it was because, when we were kids, Northwestern had had a strict 13 percent quota on Jews and Catholics.

After a few never quite satisfying conversations we sat down to a heavy southern-Italian meal: the works, from minestrone to spumoni. As dessert and coffee were being served, our class president, a nice guy named, then as now, Buzzy Lerner, spoke in an agreeable way about how lucky we were to have come of age at the time we did.

When he had finished, he invited others to come up as the spirit moved them. Betsy Collins, a once devastatingly cute cheerleader, herself now devastated by the trials of aging, took the microphone to say what a privilege it was to have gone to Senn and how much she appreciated all the teachers, ending, after a few more platitudes, with "I love all you guys." A heavyset guy wearing an obvious toupee announced that he was Irwin Goodman and that to this day he had never forgotten the advice given him by Ed Dow, our football coach: "Never go into a game thinking you're going to lose." Since our football team almost invariably lost, it wasn't clear how this applied to anything, but tonight, clearly, was not an occasion for close reading.

Then a tallish woman with thick white hair and very little makeup, dressed much less expensively than most of the others in the room, took the mike. No one else seemed to recognize her.

Please, Janet, I thought, don't tell them off for being smug and stupid and middle class.

"Oh, hi," she began. "My name's Janet Burgess, originally Janet Natalsky, and I attended Senn for just my freshman year, so I wouldn't be in the least surprised if no one here remembers me. In fact, I'd be amazed to learn how anyone got my address to invite me to this shebang. Anyhow, after my year at Senn I went off to the University of Chicago, which may have been the best or worst thing that ever happened to me. I became a writer, and I've published five books, though I've written quite a few more, and I seriously doubt anyone here has read any of them. But that's all right. No hard feelings.

"The reason I've got this microphone in my hand is that many years ago I published an article in *Harper's* attacking the school and just about everyone in it. In that article I took no prisoners. I wrote that you were all a bunch of hopeless idiots, utter conformists, absolutely clueless about what is important in life.

"By the time I wrote my article I was pretty certain I knew what was important, and I can tell you what it was in one word: art. Art was important. I wanted to become a writer, and a writer is what I am, however unappreciated my work may be. If I've earned ten thousand dollars from my writing over the last forty years, I'd be surprised. I had a brief bad marriage and no children. If it weren't for art, today I might be living comfortably in Highland Park and worrying about whether my granddaughter Peyton is going to get into Brown and praying before I fall asleep that her brother Tyler isn't gay.

"But as I look around this room, as I see how little all of you seem to have changed, how pleased you are with what you are, I don't feel so bad. Art—I gave everything up for art, goddamn fucking art. But that's OK. I did the right thing, the only thing, and if I ever doubted it, I sure don't now."

Only at this point did it occur to me that Janet was drunk.

Nobody in the room seemed to have a clue about what was going on. Buzzy Lerner, standing off to the side, appeared stricken. Who is this woman, and why is she telling us these things? This was supposed to be an evening devoted to golden memories, uncomplicated fun.

I couldn't let her continue. Getting up, I nodded to Buzzy, slipped an arm around her, tried to take the mike.

"Oh, hi, David," she said. "Hey, everybody, it's brave Dr. Nachman, tenured and tonsured as he now is." She patted the bald spot on the back of my head. "I'll bet he's going to tell me to read two chapters of Henry James and get right into bed." She hiccupped and slumped backward into my arms.

Holding firm, I steered her to my chair. Norm Brodsky helped me get her to her apartment in an exhausted-looking building on Greenleaf, off Sheridan Road. I walked her up the stairs, opened the door with her key. Still tipsy, she said, grinning, "I hope you don't expect to be kissed, sir. This is, after all, our first date."

It was nearly two years after this that I saw Janet from my car and drove on without stopping to offer her a ride. She did not need me, I decided; there was nothing I could ever hope to do for her. Who knows? On that sunny afternoon she may have been thinking up a story, something about a boring academic who had thrown away his life composing dull books about men more talented and courageous than he. Someone, I would not be in the least surprised to learn, with large and fleshy ears.

You Could Also Love
a Rich Girl

T HE WEEK AFTER Ronald Block, my associate editor of
two years, left to take a job at *Newsweek,* I put an ad in
the *New York Times* classifieds. "Wanted," it read, "editor for small-circulation political weekly of liberal tendencies.
Duties include writing editorials, soliciting manuscripts, working with contributors' copy, proofreading. Benefits. Modest salary to begin." The magazine's name did not appear, and the return address was a post office box.

I received 158 responses. Perhaps the most surprising came
from a plastic surgeon who claimed to be making upward of a
million dollars a year but had to stoke himself in the morning
with two shots of bourbon in order to begin, as he called it, "the
day's carvery." More than thirty lawyers applied. Nine among
them, in notes accompanying their résumés, remarked that salary was not a problem. Another respondent, a senior partner at
Goldman Sachs, offered to buy the magazine outright without
knowing its name, adding that he would be perfectly content,
even as the owner, to hold down a secondary editorial position.

After sifting through the mound, I set up interviews with seven candidates who I thought showed serious potential. All were under thirty: what with the low pay, it seemed sensible to hire someone just starting out, and I wanted a person not yet fully formed, someone I could mold to the needs of the magazine.

In the end I chose a young man named Sanford Aronson. He was then twenty-seven, from St. Louis. He had gone to Brown, dropped out of Harvard Law after deciding that the law wasn't for him, and then worked briefly for McKinsey, the consulting firm, which gave him a chance at the big bucks. But he realized, or so he said in our interview, that money wasn't his main objective, at least not now. What interested him more was gaining insight into how the world really worked, and he thought an editorial job on a serious magazine might be an excellent place to start. Not that he expected me to hire him so that he could continue his education: he had been reading highbrow journals since he was an undergraduate, and he thought that in time he could make a genuine contribution to this one. And then he offered an impressive critique of the magazine, showing a brilliant grasp of its strengths and weaknesses (touching on the latter with what I would call a tactful candor). I said I would get back to him, but clearly the job was his before he left my office. Only later in the afternoon did I realize that he never asked about the salary.

As for me, I should say right off that I have little interest in how the world really works. It's not that I wouldn't like to know, but the older I get the more complex life seems, and the less I hold out hope for anything like a unified vision of the world, let alone how it works. I began working here, in the same job I was now offering to Sanford Aronson, when I was twenty-four, close to thirty years ago. Although I had a chance to leave in the early 1980s to work for the *New York Times* in its Week in Review section, I didn't go for it. This, I suppose, was the decisive move I never made—I've heard it said that everyone has one such chance—though whether I would ever have climbed very high on the greasy pole at the *Times,* I cannot say.

I married young, and Charlene and I had three daughters. Today, all but the last, Rachael, now in medical school, are out and on their own. Charlene teaches special education in a public school in Kew Gardens, Queens; we live in an attached house in Flushing. What's left for me? Aside from the pleasure of practicing the craft of editing and enjoying the accomplishments of my three girls, I'm content to be astonished by whatever surprises life and human nature toss my way. Which brings me back to Sanford Aronson, or Sandy, as he asked to be called.

Small, fine-boned, with thin brown hair, Sandy gave an impression of extreme tidiness. Even at the end of the day in our dusty offices on 17th Street, east of Fifth Avenue, he looked only recently emerged from a shower. He was also, I soon discovered, a quick study. He turned out to have a deft hand at fixing poorly written manuscripts and was particularly skilled at convincing their authors of the good sense of his (sometimes radical) changes. At editorial conferences he spoke little at first, yet always made points that needed to be taken seriously. I early began to sense that, before long, he would outgrow us and move on to greater things.

Generally I don't socialize with my colleagues—no special reason, except that I much prefer an evening watching a movie on television at home to arguing about movies or, even worse, about reviews of movies, in a room filled with people for whom altogether too much is at stake in the rightness of their opinions. But when we received an invitation to a dinner party marking the engagement of Sanford Joshua Aronson to Jennifer Daphne Kaiserman at her father's apartment on Park Avenue, I felt we ought to go. I knew that Sandy had been living—so far as I knew, living alone — in the West Village, and he had said nothing about having a girlfriend. But then, at work we hardly ever talked about our private lives, and he certainly owed me no explanations. When I told him we planned to attend, he returned an odd, sheepish smile.

Sandy's prospective father-in-law, Bernie Kaiserman, was, I discovered, *the* Bernie Kaiserman. His specialty was buying and selling businesses — enormous businesses — and forming complicated joint ventures, spinoffs, and conglomerates. His first wife, I later learned, had died of liver cancer when Jennifer, an only child, was fourteen. After a too-quick second marriage to a very young woman, whom he bought off after less than a year, he was now married to an Argentinean, Jewish it was said, and from the photographs I had seen of the two of them in *Vanity Fair,* obviously high maintenance.

He lived in a penthouse triplex formerly owned by Helena Rubinstein. In the elevator with us on the way up was another couple who introduced themselves as Sandy's parents, just in from St. Louis. A small man, bald, the father — "Call me Ira," he insisted — owned three dry-cleaning shops. Arlene Aronson, who was wearing a mink jacket, didn't get a chance to say much before we were deposited at the Kaiserman penthouse and two young men in tuxedos took our coats. Ira Aronson patted the hair at the sides of his head, straightened his tie, exhaled in a whistle, and, leaning toward me, said in a low voice, "I used to kid Sandy that you could also love a rich girl. But, Jesus, I never expected anything like this."

You didn't have to be from St. Louis to be impressed. The foyer led directly into a large parlor, along whose walls hung a vast number of nineteenth-century oils. I counted no fewer than six Renoirs and three Monets. I don't know enough about furniture to describe the contents of the room, but the effect was French, suggesting a Louis of not too high numerals. More young

men in tuxedos took our orders for drinks — ginger ale for the
Aronsons — while others passed among us with silver trays laden
with hors d'oeuvres.

"Ah, at last," said a man with powerfully curly black hair and
strong white teeth. He was deeply tanned and beautifully turned
out. "The *machetunim*," he said. "Bernie Kaiserman. Please, make
yourself at home. *Mi casa es su casa*." Kaiserman already had an
arm around Mr. and Mrs. Aronson.

Ira introduced Charlene and me.

"My son-in-law's boss," Bernie said, holding out a hand. "A
pleasure. Tell me, is the kid good at what he does, whatever the
hell it is?" As we shook hands he firmly squeezed my elbow with
his free hand.

"He's very good," I said. "Terrific, in fact."

"Funny he wanted to work for you. No insult intended, but
I could have gotten him a job at one of Sy Newhouse's rags, or
with Time Warner. But he wasn't interested. Independent kid,
your son," Kaiserman said, turning back to the Aronsons. "How
long you folks gonna be in town?"

Apart from Sandy, and now his parents and father-in-law-to-be,
we knew no one else at the party, though a number of the guests
looked vaguely familiar. The apartment felt more like a museum
than anyone's home. At one point, after Charlene deserted me
for the washroom, I found myself in the dining room, its stark
white walls covered with contemporary art. I am no expert,
but I recognized paintings by de Kooning and Rothko, a Robert
Motherwell, a Pollock, an Ad Reinhardt, and a large work in yellow and blue by Helen Frankenthaler. I was standing in front of it
when Kaiserman approached.

"This *chazerei* have any charm for you?"

"Some of it does," I said, "but I can't talk very well about the
pleasure it gives."

"My wife gets more of a bang out of it than me. I don't know the first thing about it. A clever Russian named Sabarsky buys it for us. He tells me that, expensive as it now is, it's going to go even higher. If true, I'll have made my wife happy, earned a few bucks, and covered my walls, all in one shot. A good deal, no?"

Was this a winning absence of pretension, or pure coarseness? I didn't have long to ponder the question.

"Let me ask you something," he continued. "My future son-in-law, what's your true opinion of him?"

"I told you, he's very good at what he does. He's smart and quick and first rate at getting his point of view across."

"How tough is he, is what I want to know."

"Tough?"

"I mean, what's his endurance? How much crap can he take? Has he got any fist?"

"I'd like to help you, but I haven't known him long enough to say," I answered.

"You been around the kid a few months and you still can't tell? I can tell when I'm with a guy for half an hour. And I'll let you in on a little secret: tough is better than smart. Smart guys I can buy all day long, though I prefer to sell them. When I'm acquiring a company, if the head guy comes from somewhere like Wharton or Harvard, I'll almost always give him his walking papers."

A staccato click of high heels on the parquet floor announced the third Mrs. Kaiserman.

"Bernard," she said, pronouncing her husband's name in the English manner, with the accent on the first syllable, "our guests are waiting to hear from you in the drawing room."

Kaiserman introduced me as Sandy's employer.

"Hallo," she said, holding out two cold fingers while looking over my shoulder. "You really mustn't delay any longer, darling."

"Right," he said as Felicia Kaiserman flamencoed out of the room. "C'mon in, watch me play the great patriarch."

✳ ✳ ✳

In the room with all the Renoirs and Monets, Kaiserman stood before an enormous marble fireplace. One of the waiters clinked on a wineglass for attention. The crowd, maybe a hundred people in all, gathered in a semicircle, champagne glasses in hand. I thought I recognized the actor Ricardo Montalban talking with an elderly woman whose nose could have opened a soup can.

"Jenny, Sanford," Kaiserman said. "C'mon up here, please."

Jennifer Kaiserman was small and dark, a female version of her father, without the least trace of shyness as she stood with Bernie's arm around her, Sandy planted on his left.

"Friends, family, family-to-be," Kaiserman began, raising a fluted glass, "this beautiful young woman, my daughter, has brought me nothing but happiness from the get-go. Behind every successful man, the saying goes, there is a woman. In my case the woman is my daughter. My few accomplishments in this world owe more to Jenny than anyone will ever know. What I have built, I built with her and her children-to-come in mind. And tonight she brings me the most happiness of all by allowing me to announce her engagement to a brilliant young man. We're all going to hear fine things about Sandy in the future. So please join me in wishing them health and happiness and a glorious future."

As we all drank, I noticed Mrs. Kaiserman on the rim of our circle, talking energetically to a dowager who, I later learned, was her mother. What had she been thinking when her husband declared his daughter's primacy in his life? What, I wondered, was the relationship between wife and daughter? If Felicia Kaiserman was a stepmother out of Hans Christian Andersen, the young Jennifer Kaiserman did not exactly seem like Snow White. I felt a rush of sympathy for my young associate, who suddenly appeared at my side with his fiancée.

"Michael," he said, "I'd like you to meet Jenny."

"And it's time you met my wife, Charlene," I said before proceeding to tell Jenny Kaiserman that I had found her father a most interesting man.

"Interesting?" she said, raising an eyebrow. "I'd say amazing. It's in the energy, you know. My father has this incredible energy. He sleeps about three hours a night. The rest of the time he's plotting, don't ask me what." She laughed, showing small but perfect teeth.

"After you're married," I said, "don't be surprised if Sandy hits him up for money for the magazine."

"I'd be careful there," she said. "My father is likely to give you a large donation and then find some way to turn around and sell you out to Nabisco. Pretty soon you'll be cranking out a house organ for cookies."

In the elevator going down, we once again found ourselves alone with the senior Aronsons.

"So, whaddya think?" Ira Aronson asked.

"Pretty impressive," I said.

"I told the kid he could also love a rich girl," he repeated himself. "But this is ridiculous. Typical of Sandy, an overachiever if ever there was one."

Arlene Aronson kept her counsel.

Three months later, the wedding took place on the Long Island estate of Jay Gould. Everyone's unasked question was how much it cost. I counted three string quartets, a jazz ensemble, and two dance bands, one for old standards and the other for rock. An eight-course dinner was served to something like five hundred guests, with a new wine for every course. Over the afternoon, Jenny appeared and reappeared in at least three different outfits. By the time a table-hopping Bernie Kaiserman made it over to where we were seated, it was clear that he had quite forgotten who I was, which was fine with me.

Bridegroom and bride took a month-long honeymoon in

Tuscany. Sandy had only two weeks' vacation time coming to him, and when I informed him that he would have to be docked for the other two weeks he pretended to look grave. From now on, there would be a not so vaguely comic aspect to any discussion of money with him. At the end of his first year—a difficult financial period for the magazine—I was able to give him a raise of only a thousand dollars. I considered apologizing for the low sum, especially in light of his stellar performance, but then I just decided to add the money—something on the order of $28, after taxes—to his biweekly paycheck without mentioning the raise at all.

Sandy and Jenny were now living in her place on East 81st Street, off Madison, but as soon as she became pregnant, they bought a house outside the city. When I asked Sandy where it was, he lowered his eyes and said, almost in a whisper, "Westport." I supplied the address to my friend Robert Ginsburg, who lives in nearby Norwalk. "I know the street," he said. "It's waterfront. No houses under two million." Returning from a visit to the Ginsburgs one Sunday afternoon, I made it a point to drive by, and it was a Tudor job of three stories, with an attached garage that held four cars and servants' quarters above, set on a lot of not less than an acre. Sandy, it occurred to me, might be making the salary of one of his gardeners.

In the office, the only visible effects of Sandy's wealth were in his clothes. A careful dresser before, he was now spruce in a quiet but moneyed way. I became a silent student of his shirts, which were made of wonderfully soft cotton and of such subtle blues and creamy whites as I'd not seen anywhere. One day as he was leaving my office, I observed that his thinning hair had been neatly layered in the back.

But his work was as sharp as ever. He had begun writing most of our unsigned lead editorials, and he displayed a distinct knack for understanding and fairly stating rival points of view—and then demolishing them. I would read his flawless, concise arguments on the need for social justice, his calls for the redistribution of wealth, his attacks on unfettered market capitalism, and think of him going home to Westport, to great luxury. And I would wonder, given his talents, the scope of his interests, the ease of his life, why hadn't he left the magazine, gone on to better things? What was he waiting for? Although he could have done my job as well as I did — who knows, probably better — he must have known that I wasn't planning to depart any time soon, though I did take advantage of a colleague's departure to promote Sandy into the job of managing editor (at a raise of all of two grand). I like to know the next man's ambitions, especially when he is working for me. But in Sandy Aronson's case, I really hadn't a clue.

And clueless I remained for the next five years, long enough for Jenny to have a second child and for Bernie Kaiserman to divorce his Argentinean wife and marry a Russian the same age as his daughter. Sandy had by now been working on the magazine longer than any of his less talented predecessors, and his salary had ¡yet to hit the $40,000 mark.

So one day when he invited me to join him for lunch — he was now working partly at home and coming into the city only three days a week — I thought for certain that he was going to announce his long-overdue departure. A new administration had taken office in Washington, and Sandy's father-in-law was a large enough contributor to both political parties to get him an interesting job at State or Defense or even as a White House speechwriter.

I took a cab uptown to the Links, a small club on East 62nd, off Madison. The staff wore green livery. A gray-haired black man led me into a small room toward the back with a single table, where Sandy was waiting, and took our drinks order.

"Look," Sandy said as soon as the man had left the room,

"there are some things I have to tell you, and I wanted to do it in a very private way."

"You're leaving the magazine," I said. "I've been expecting it. I'm lucky to have had you this long."

"No," he said. "I'm not leaving, though I'm going to need a little more free time, at least for a while. My marriage is in serious trouble. It has been for years."

"I'm sorry," I said, not very helpfully. "Can it be fixed?"

"Don't see how," he said. "The trouble, to be embarrassingly specific about it, is that my wife sleeps around."

He paused as a waiter brought in two bowls of dark brown bean soup. "It wouldn't be so bad if she had a single lover," Sandy said when he'd gone, "but there've been a number of them. Just among those I know, there's a local tennis pro, two construction workers, a bartender at the country club in Westport, an airline pilot, and a former point guard for the Knicks — not a very distinguished clientele, I must say."

"With two small kids, how does she find the time?"

"The kids have a nanny. Jenny goes when and where she pleases. Money makes lots of things possible."

"Does she know you know?"

"Yes," he said. "I hadn't the self-control not to confront her with it."

"What did she say?"

"She says if I don't like it, why don't I leave? She's very calm about it. She says she'll be fine without me."

"Does her father know what's going on?"

"I assume he does, but I don't think he cares. He's always been a big player himself. Not exactly a rock of stability, my father-in-law. But I have to assume that, no matter what, he's going to be in his daughter's corner."

"What'll you do?"

"I wish I knew. I may need some time away from the magazine, which is one reason I'm telling you about this disaster."

"But you say this has been going on for a while."

"From nearly the beginning."

"You're too smart not to have considered why."

The waiter appeared with two elegantly presented trouts amandine, from each of which, with long-fingered precision, he extracted the bones. I had barely tasted my soup, which was delicious and which I was sorry to see taken away.

"I wish I could say the problem lies with me. For instance, that I have knotty sexual hang-ups. Sorry to report that in that department we've always seemed to do fine together."

"So what is the problem?"

"The problem is that my wife has adopted the sexuality of a man — specifically, of a single man on the make. If she sees something interesting, she goes after it. Being an attractive woman, her batting average is much higher than a man in a comparable condition. And of course the money makes it easy. She can try anything she likes, and if she falls down, there's a soft golden net to catch her. She can't really lose, and she knows it."

"What about losing you?"

"I don't think she cares."

"And you?"

He inserted a small forkful of trout into his mouth and, after chewing briefly, said in the calmest possible voice, "I have come to despise her."

"So why not leave? Walk away?"

"The children. They're the most important thing in my life. I can't stand the idea of their being brought up by my wife, not to speak of their grandfather lurking in the background, no doubt up to wife number eight by the time they hit adolescence."

"What about a custody fight? Men win custody of their children all the time these days."

"Not against Bernie Kaiserman they wouldn't. With my father-in-law's money behind her, I haven't a chance. If he didn't kill me with sheer legal talent, he'd crush me with the cost of appeals. Michael, please forgive me for dragging you into this, but there's no one else I can talk to. I hate to think of myself as a whiner; it's bad enough thinking of myself as a cuckold. But I felt I had to unload, at least a little, and I'm afraid you're my victim. Sorry."

If Sandy was telling his troubles to me, he must have been lonely indeed. Of course, I could understand his not talking things over with his parents, or with his older sister, married to an accountant in San Francisco. Still, he and I had never shared any intimacies whatsoever, and his unloading, as he put it, suggested a deep friendlessness in the world.

"I may also need to call on you for a bit of help. Would you mind if I brought the kids over every once in a while? Even though I'm living at home, I'm beginning to feel like a divorced father with visiting privileges who gets his kids for the weekend."

I told him I didn't mind in the least. We rode back to the office together, talking about an editorial he was writing on school vouchers. The finished piece, which he turned in later that afternoon, was seven hundred of the most polished, cogent words imaginable.

Another year went by, in which Sandy did not allude even once to our conversation at the Links Club. Then one Sunday morning he called to say that his kids were with him and he was wondering if he could stop by for a half hour. My wife nodded that it was fine, and I said we were looking forward to it.

From our living room window I saw him drive up in a Mercedes SUV. His now six-year-old daughter was riding up front, his three-year-old son in a booster seat in the back. In the eight years I'd known him, I'd never seen Sandy in anything but suits, but today he was wearing tan pants, loafers, a black polo shirt, and a buttery soft suede jacket that looked as if it might cost two months' salary. Walking up to our house, he had his daughter by the hand while carrying his son.

"Hey, Daddy," I said, "who are these beautiful children?"

"This elegant young woman is Caitlin, better known as Catey, or Catey-Bird," he said. "And this gent with his head on my shoulder is Turner, also called Teddy the Bear."

The girl had her father's coloring, fineness of features, and general tidiness of demeanor; the boy was pure Kaiserman, dark, compact, toothy. When I held out my arms to take him from his father, he squirmed in my hands like a ferret or some other small animal that was all muscle. I set him down, and my wife suggested that both children go with her into the kitchen for cookies.

"Thank you, Charlene," Sandy said. "I need a word or two in private with Michael."

I dropped onto the couch; he took a chair on the other side of the coffee table, removing two envelopes from an inner pocket of his jacket and handing them to me.

"One," he answered my unspoken question, "is the editorial on the privatization of Social Security—surprise, we come out strongly against it. The other, I'm sorry to say, is my resignation."

"I'm even sorrier," I said. "Where're you headed? Whoever you're going to be working for is damned fortunate."

"I won't be working, at least not for a while. Where I'm going is to ground. You know that phrase from the old English detective books?"

"It means hiding out, no?"

"It means precisely that."

"What's going on?"

"Jenny wants a divorce. She's found another man. She also wants the children. I've decided not to let her have them. I'm taking them with me."

"Where to?"

"I'd rather not say. Their grandfather is certain to come after me, and it's probably better that you not know."

"I'm sure you've thought this through."

"I've thought about almost nothing else for the past four years."

"You have money?"

"I've been on an allowance of ten grand a month — walking-around money, my father-in-law calls it — since my wedding day, and I've stowed away quite a lot over the years. I've decided to consider it alimony and child support. Money won't be a problem for some time."

"What about the children's mother? Won't they miss her?"

"Probably at first. But I hope they'll get over her."

"Won't she miss *them?*"

"That's unclear. But it's her father I worry about."

"He loves them so much?"

"No, he hates to lose so much — at anything."

Sandy got up, and we walked into the kitchen. At the table Charlene was reading to the children, the boy in her lap.

"We've got to be on our way, kids. Say thanks for the treats."

I walked Sandy to the car and stood while he strapped in his son and set the seat belt around his daughter. We shook hands, and I told him I thought him a remarkable man, adding that if he needed me for anything — anything at all — he had only to call. In the living room, I read his editorial: seamless, beautifully argued, not a word in need of changing.

It was only eight days later that one of our interns buzzed to announce a Mr. Bernard Kaiserman waiting to see me. I suppressed the impulse to respond that I couldn't possibly make time for him without an appointment.

Walking into my office, with its metal desk and shabby furniture, Kaiserman looked around, as if appraising the joint before proposing to acquire it. "I heard you're looking for a new managing editor," he said, taking the seat across from my desk without being invited to do so.

"Are you applying? The pay is low, but the benefits are decent."

"I'm not looking for a job but a son-in-law who's stolen my grandchildren. I wonder if maybe you could help me here."

"How so?"

"When did you last see him?"

"A week ago Friday," I said, lying, "here in the office, when he handed me his resignation."

"Did he say where he was headed?"

"He only said that he wanted some time to consider his options."

"No mention that one of his options was taking my grandchildren?"

"None."

"I see," said Kaiserman, studying my face. "What he's done is called kidnapping, for which he could spend the rest of his life in jail. I suppose, too, that people who withhold information would be considered accessories after the goddamn fact. Have I got that right? I may be a little rusty on my legal phrases. Anyhow, we're talking pretty serious business here. I'm also offering a personal reward of a quarter of a million for any information leading to the discovery of these kids. That have any interest for you?"

Prison and riches, a stick and a carrot, in the same paragraph. It was interesting, watching a real operator at work.

"For business reasons, I'm hesitant to go to the police with this. It wouldn't play well in the press. It might also give some schmuck the idea of stealing my wife's Afghan hound."

"I wish I could help you," I said, "but Sandy never said a thing to me about his plans. I gathered that his marriage wasn't all he hoped for, but I really had no idea it would force him to this."

"Something wrong with him, my son-in-law. I think I sensed it from the first. Low energy. Thin blood. Lives too much in his head. Who knows?"

"How is your daughter taking it?"

"She was planning to divorce him anyway. But right now she's a nervous wreck over her kids."

"You don't think he'd do anything to hurt them, do you? He's not violent or crazy."

"I'm not so sure about the crazy part. Doesn't he know who he's fooling with?"

"My guess is that he probably does," I said. "He's never underestimated you, as far as I could tell. He always thought of you as a very formidable character."

"He'll know how formidable when I catch up with him." With this he rose, took a business card out of his wallet, and placed it on my desk. "Call me if he gets in touch," he said. "I'll make it worth your while."

I walked Kaiserman through the office and into the corridor, waiting with him until the elevator arrived. Back at my desk, I couldn't work. I kept thinking of Sandy and his two children, driving off in who knew what direction or into which sunset. "Drive, kid," I found myself chanting. "Drive. Don't stop. Don't let the son of a bitch catch you."

Life goes on. Two new managing editors came and quickly went. From time to time I would read an item about Bernie Kaiserman in the business section of the *Times,* buying or selling some mammoth enterprise, but otherwise I was shut out from news. Had Sandy gotten away, or had he been quietly apprehended by his father-in-law's private detectives? Was Jenny remarried, with a new set of children? And where was Sandy now? In jail? Remarried? Still on the run?

Until one day, almost four years after his visit to our house, sorting through the morning mail, I came upon a postcard with a scene of mountains capped by snow and clouds, postmarked from a western Canadian province. The message, in a bold printed hand, read:

Dear Michael,
    Kids fine. Things go decently. As Confucius neglected to say, Man who marry rich girl earn every damn penny.

The card was unsigned.

Gladrags & Kicks

T HE RUBINS, BEN AND LOIS, were our neighbors on Washtenaw Avenue in West Rogers Park. We lived on the same floor in a yellow-brick six-flat on a street made dark by elm trees whose branches met in the center of the road and cut off most of the light even on sunny days, which in the Chicago of that time — the middle 1970s — for some reason did not seem plentiful. The Rubins, who were about fifteen years older than my wife and I, were transplanted New Yorkers. Ben was a social worker in the city's welfare department. Lois, who occasionally published poetry in magazines with more contributors than subscribers, stayed home to raise Marney, a child they had had in their early forties and who was now an adolescent. The Rubins cared only for culture and for Marney, for whom they held out very high expectations.

Ben was short, stocky, with a fair complexion, thick sandy-colored hair, and an impressively low hairline. Having lost my own hair in my twenties, I notice such things. He never left for work without a book under his arm, usually a novel; his taste tended toward writers of the realistic school — Balzac and Zola, Dreiser and Gissing. I notice this kind of thing, too, since I'm a high school English teacher, in those days still working on a Ph.D. dissertation that, what with one thing and another, never got written.

That I was trekking down to the University of Chicago for graduate school courses certified me as OK with the Rubins — Lois especially. She was a snob, cultural division. Or at least I used to think so; in time I became less and less certain. When it comes to culture, who knows, I may be a bit of a snob myself. A better word for Lois, I eventually concluded, was "fantast." She was dark, with what my father used to call a chosen nose. A few inches taller than her husband, she was rather matronly by the time I knew her, yet with something fragile or vulnerable about her. I'm sure that she thought of Ben and herself, there in the midst of middle-class West Rogers Park, as living the bohemian life.

In their case, bohemian meant passionately artistic. Lois and Ben had met in high school. As Ben once told me, they fell madly in love from the start — and so they remained. It was as if they had gone out on a first date and the date had never ended. One morning I met a tired-looking Ben in the hallway. "Lois and I were up all night arguing about whether Stravinsky had made a mistake late in his career when he turned to composing serial music," he offered by way of explanation. "Hope the records we played didn't wake you."

The Rubins drove a ten-year-old Dodge, and they didn't seem to care much about clothes or other possessions. Not that it was any of my business, but they seemed to spend a great deal of money on tickets: they were subscribers to the Chicago Symphony, the Lyric Opera, the Ravinia Festival in the summer, the Goodman, and just about every other small theater company in Chicago. They were always going off to a production of Beckett or Ionesco, or traipsing down to the Art Institute or a gallery on Michigan Avenue, or catching some visiting ballet company. They were that couple you see intensely investigating a Cézanne drawing in the museum, or posing a lengthy and altogether too convoluted question at a poetry reading. Ben often brought along a score to follow at concerts.

I was never sure quite how to take the Rubins. Sometimes I thought of them as purely comical. I remember a night they had Carol and me over to dinner; Lois was an ambitious cook, and it was the first time I had ever heard of ratatouille or cassoulet. With the arrival of dessert, the two of them fell into a heated discussion over exactly how long the novels of John Dos Passos were likely to last; at some point my wife and I murmured our excuses and slipped away, with their hardly noticing.

But I also found their dedication to culture impressive. Unlike so many who indulged a pretense in that direction, the Rubins had made genuine sacrifices in their pursuit of the culture gods, living far from grandly and, in Ben's case, deliberately subordinating work and career to what he most cared about. Besides, I was in some ways a member of the same tribe. Unlike most of the boys I'd grown up with, who went for the dough in advertising or law or dentistry or medicine or a family business, had I not chosen to teach high school kids about books because I thought of myself as a missionary of culture?

The trouble was that, for the Rubins, art and culture were good things absolutely and by definition, things of which you could never get enough. This belief, when it came to judging particular works or performances, made them strangely uncritical, and hostage to received opinion. They would eagerly compare the six different performances of *Death of a Salesman* they had seen, beginning with Lee J. Cobb's, or listen with rapt and pristine excitement to old warhorses like Tchaikovsky's *1812 Overture* — or argue over Dvořák's development. What was missing was perspective, discrimination, distance, above all moral judgment.

I once made the mistake of telling them how dreary I'd found Edward Albee's *Who's Afraid of Virginia Woolf?* They reacted as if I had attacked their religion, which, I guess, is pretty much what I had done. And that reminds me of our one serious argument, which was over none other than Mrs. Woolf herself. In doing research for my abandoned dissertation, which was about anti-Semitism in twentieth-century British and American literature, I had discovered how virulent the anti-Semitic strain ran in Virginia Woolf. In her diaries (I had been allowed a look at the manuscripts), few Jews were permitted to pass unspat upon. I supplied chapter and verse to Ben and Lois, who really, I sensed, preferred not to hear it. "And yet," Lois said piously, "her opinions are one thing, her art another. *To the Lighthouse, Mrs. Dalloway, The Waves:* noble books that will live forever."

"Trust the tale, not the teller," Ben put in. "That's D. H. Lawrence's advice."

"Another Jew-hater, by the way," I said.

"And one of the most powerful novelists of the modern movement," Lois replied.

This could easily have turned into one of those relationship-ending discussions, but I wasn't eager to be living next door to people with whom I wasn't on speaking terms. The subject was immensely complicated, I suggested, and let it go at that.

The reason I came to know so much about the Rubins' attending all those plays, concerts, poetry readings, and the rest is that, when they did so during the middle of the week, they would often ask Carol and me to look in on Marney. On weekends they usually arranged to take her with them. What Marney got out of all this I couldn't say. She seemed to go along with the program. Sometimes, when her parents were out during the week, she would study over at our place. Carol, a psychiatric social worker, thought Marney was the indirect victim of parents who loved each other too much — too much, that is, for there to be enough love left over for anyone else.

I myself found it hard to gain Marney's attention. She was never rude or contemptuous toward adults the way teenagers were beginning to be, but something about her always seemed to be elsewhere. Although she went to Mather High, where I taught, she was never in any of my classes. Other teachers told me she seemed bright enough but far from fully engaged.

Short, round-shouldered, rather bulky, with mousy blond hair and dark eyes that never quite looked at you, Marney Rubin, whenever I spotted her in the halls of Mather, seemed slightly lost. She dressed without apparent concern for what she was wearing. Boys seemed to take no interest in her, and in their crude adolescent way no doubt referred to her (I hoped only behind her back) as a dog or a pig. So unexpressive did she seem, so unforthcoming, that one couldn't tell whether she was unhappy or just terminally bored. Not notably cheerful myself, I made an effort to greet her on an upbeat note whenever I passed her at school or in the foyer of our building on Washtenaw. All without much success.

Ben and Lois always spoke of their daughter with an air of promise. They never directly said they hoped she would become an artist, but that is what we assumed. Carol and I had stood by as poor Marney was put through piano and then cello and then flute lessons. "She doesn't have a musical bone in her body," said Carol, who as a kid had studied piano for more than a decade. Then they sent her to drawing classes for children at the Art Institute. Saddest of all was the sight of poor shapeless Marney, in her tutu, being driven by Lois in the old Dodge to ballet class at Miss Olga's, a storefront studio on Devon Avenue near Sacramento.

I've taught lots of teenage girls, and they tend to fall into one of two categories: perky or sulky. Some do perky and sulky both, several times a day. Sulky also comes in two modes, ticked-off and passive. Marney did passive sulky. Even her posture suggested passivity, shoulders hunched forward, eyes down.

The Rubins were one of the few families — perhaps the only one — in West Rogers Park who would have welcomed a struggling poet or painter for a son-in-law. From offhand comments they made, it was clear that they looked down on all those petit-bourgeois Jewish parents longing for sons-in-law who were "professional men." Their own daughter was cut out for something more elevated. I suppose all parents invest in their children the aspirations they themselves have not been able to realize, and in that respect the Rubins were no different from most. I myself imagined Marney going on to a dullish job as a file clerk or an office temp, and with luck marrying an accountant or maybe an insurance man — with luck, as I say.

After graduating from Mather just below the top half of her class, Marney went on to the University of Illinois in Chicago, each weekday morning taking the Devon bus to the Loyola El and then catching another bus to Halsted Street, there to submerge herself in the school's morose gray concrete buildings. When I asked her what she was studying, she said she was an English major.

"An English major," I said. "Really? In what regiment?" The joke elicited a little smile, the first I could recall in all our years as neighbors.

Only in her second year at college did I begin to note a change in Marney. She suddenly seemed, I won't say calmer — she was always a little too calm for my taste — but looser, more relaxed. She began to stand up straighter and even greeted me in the hallway or on our common back porch. These days she was toting around a guitar, her parents' latest musical idea; soon, Carol and I joked, the poor girl would soon be reduced to castanets and a triangle. But Carol also thought something radical had happened in Marney's life; perhaps, she suggested, a boyfriend.

On a snowy night in February, coming back from a late movie at the Nortown, I dropped Carol off in front of our building and went in search of a parking space. It must have taken twenty minutes' looking. As I climbed up the front-hall stairs to our apartment, I couldn't help noticing a couple — Marney and who else? — planted before the Rubins' front door, kissing. It was impossible to avoid disturbing them without walking back downstairs and around to the back of the building, so I soldiered on, making a great throat-clearing noise to announce my presence. Marney and her boyfriend unclenched. Only it wasn't a boy she had been kissing, but a young woman, tall and slender, with black hair cut short, wearing a pea coat with the collar turned up.

I believe Marney said "Good evening, Mr. Greenberg," but I'm not sure about that. I fumbled with my key in the lock and finally made it into our apartment. "Jesus, Carol," I called out, "you aren't going to believe what I just saw."

Carol was in her nightgown and robe. "I can't imagine," she said, "except that you look two steps from a stroke."

"I just saw Marney Rubin being made love to in the hallway by another girl. She's a lesbian, for God's sake. Our little Marney's a lesbian."

Carol didn't seem sufficiently shocked. But then, as a working psychologist, she did not shock easily.

"Really? Are you sure it was a girl?"

"Absolutely sure," I said. "And not too good-looking a one, either."

"I wouldn't worry too much about the looks," Carol said, "since it's pretty clear that *you* aren't going to be asked to sleep with her." She's good at defusing me, my wife.

"I wonder if the Rubins know."

"And if they do? What can they do but accept it? They really haven't a choice."

"I feel sorry for Marney," I said. "If Lois and Ben come crying the blues to us, I can always remind them that Virginia Woolf was a lesbian."

"Try not to add that she killed herself."

Carol had a theory about homosexuality. She thought that gay men were born and lesbians were made. Genetics played an operative role in determining a male's sexual orientation, but it was often life's experiences that most affected a female's. Almost uniformly, it seemed, her lesbian patients had had terrible relationships with men or else thought themselves insufficiently attractive and had given up the battle of the sexes before it really began.

Which, I wondered, was the case with Marney? Although I had watched her growing up, I didn't know her all that well. Falling short of her parents' expectations seemed to me a tough enough life experience already; I hoped she hadn't also been brutalized by boys. Nobody these days, it seemed, got to grow up without lots of complications.

Around ten the next morning, a Sunday, Marney knocked at our front door. When I invited her in, she demurred, saying she just wanted to ask a favor.

"Sure, Marney," I said. "What is it?"

"I'd be grateful, Mr. Greenberg," she said, looking at the floor, "if you didn't mention what you saw last night in the hall to my parents."

"Of course," I said. "You have my word."

"Thanks a lot," she said, and turned away without ever looking at me.

So Ben and Lois didn't know that their daughter, their only child, their great hope in life, was a lesbian. Would they be shocked to learn it? Saddened? Angry? Not in the least displeased? Maybe even a touch delighted, for artistic reasons? Hard to know.

Marney, meanwhile, continued to change her look. From her old drab clothes — ill-fitting jeans, gray sweatshirts — she now turned up in colorful Hawaiian shirts worn with women's pleated slacks out of the 1940s or in print dresses with large flowers. She wore shoes of the kind called wedgies and carried large colorful purses. She dyed her hair ink-black, put on blood-red lipstick, and wore dangling costume-jewelry earrings. It became a point of interest for us to see what she might be wearing on any given day. Carol thought she had a wonderful knack for matching unpredictable colors.

I was emptying the garbage on our back porch when Ben Rubin emerged on the same errand.

"How goes it?" I asked.

"Not so great, Michael," he said. "Marney wants to drop out of school."

"Any reason?"

"The reason is, she wants to go into something called the vintage clothing business with a woman named Donna Salkin, who has a store on Halsted, just off North Avenue near Steppenwolf."

"Maybe she'll get over it," I said. "Nowadays, you know, the kids who leave school call it stopping out, not dropping out. Maybe Marney's just stopping out for a while."

"God, I hope so," he said. "We didn't raise her to sell *schmattes*."

Marney, it turned out, never did return to college. She moved in with Donna Salkin, the woman whom I had discovered her kissing in our hallway, and remained with her for a little under three years.

When Marney finally returned to her parents' apartment on Washtenaw, she was twenty-three, and physically almost nothing about her was the same. She had shed twenty pounds, her old slumping posture was gone, she had a good short haircut, very chic. I was taken by the daily pageant of her shoes, which were always unpredictable and often amusing: for example, she removed the tops from a pair of old Chuck Taylor white Converse gym shoes and used them to cover over a pair of black three-inch heels. Carol learned that she and her partner had broken up, but Marney seemed not in the least troubled by it.

One day the teenage girl who had been unable to look me in the eye rang our back doorbell and asked if we had a free ten or fifteen minutes. There was something she wanted to discuss with us. What she was after, it turned out when the three of us were seated at our kitchen table, was any thoughts we might have about financing for an idea she had.

"What I have in mind is making vintage clothes and shoes, but making them new, and at a very reasonable price," she said. "I plan to call my company Gladrags & Kicks. The market is women my age who find raffish clothes fun. I really think they'll go for it in a big way. I really do, or I wouldn't have come to you."

"What kind of money are you talking about, Marney?" I asked.

"To get off the ground, about a hundred and fifty thousand dollars."

"Have you talked to your parents about this?" Carol asked.

"They think it's a big mistake. They'd like me to go back to school, finish my degree, and after that they want me to go to the University of Florida for a master's degree in arts administration. I can't think of anything that would interest me less."

"I'm sure they intend the best for you," I put in, platitudinously.

"I'm afraid I'm not at all the daughter they wanted," Marney said. "Too bad things didn't work out the way they hoped. It used to hurt me that they didn't."

"We don't have that kind of money," Carol said. "But I have a cousin who's gotten rich in the commodities market. He currently calls himself a venture capitalist, and he's always on the lookout for private companies to invest in. Let me see if he's interested."

"I really appreciate your taking all this seriously," Marney said. "It means a lot to me."

The cousin Carol mentioned was Earle Diamond, her uncle Marvin's eldest son. Not long after dropping out of Roosevelt College, Earle had scared up enough money to buy a seat on the commodities exchange, where he made a killing. He had the confidence — the brashness — that early success often gives a guy. He was also, where family was concerned, sentimental. I always half suspected he couldn't bear the thought that his cousin Carol, whom he was crazy about, had married such an evident loser.

When Carol called, Earle said sure, bring the kid around. At the meeting, she told me later, Earle grilled Marney intensely for more than three hours, and at the end of the session said: "I like this, kiddo. I'm going with it. Give me a day or two to think about the figure." Three days later, he called her to announce that he was in, and not only for the whole amount she was trying to raise, but for more. "I don't think a hundred and fifty is enough," Marney reported his words back to Carol. "I'm going to put up a quarter of a million."

The deal Earle cut with Marney gave him 18 percent ownership of Gladrags & Kicks, out of which he gave Carol 3 percent as a finder's fee.

Marney Rubin, to make a long story short, made a terrific success of her little company. Before she was forty, she sold the business to one of the larger design houses in the country for just over $30 million. And 15 percent and 3 percent of $30 million — I'll let you do the math. Part of the arrangement had Marney continuing to run Gladrags & Kicks, at a very generous salary, for the next decade.

So we all had Marney wrong. She didn't marry the schlubby,

dull accountant I had predicted for her. She didn't become an artist of the kind her parents had hoped. Only Carol, who didn't predict or desire anything for Marney, seemed to have gotten everything right, including the lesbian question. Two years before she sold her business, Marney married a very successful real estate developer in Chicago, a widower with two adolescent kids.

As for Ben and Lois Rubin, they are in their early eighties now, living in a retirement home on Sheridan Road called The Breakers. They have a two-bedroom apartment on the twenty-sixth floor, with views of the lake and the Outer Drive, and from their dining room windows they can see downtown Chicago. Marney pays for the apartment and somehow finds time to look after most of their other needs.

The Rubins haven't lost their passion for the arts. Every Monday afternoon, in one of the common rooms at The Breakers, Ben Rubin gives a little talk for residents on the subject of a great composer, bringing along his violin to supplement his exposition with brief selections from the music. Wednesdays, in the same room, Lois Rubin lectures about and reads from the modern poets — occasionally, I'm told, slipping in a sample of her own verse. Neither of them draws a big crowd, but they don't seem to mind.

On Thursday nights, Marney meets her parents for dinner in the large public dining room. Sometimes, Marney tells Carol, the conversation is easy, sometimes less so. Try though they genuinely do, the Rubins can't ever quite disguise their disappointment at the way their only child's life has turned out.

No Good Deed

SIEGEL PRIDES HIMSELF on taking people as they are, each by himself and one at a time. He doesn't play group favorites — blacks, gays, the handicapped, even Jews. All such claims to special treatment, he happens to think, are so much crap. But that doesn't mean he's heartless. Consider his adventures with Malik Hassan.

Malik stands in front of the Borders bookstore that Siegel passes every morning and evening on his way to and from the Northwestern train station, which is on the way to and from his work at the Chicago Board of Trade. Siegel could drive, but he likes the extra time to read the *Wall Street Journal* on the ride downtown and to decompress, as he calls it, on the ride back.

Malik sells the homeless newspaper, which in Chicago is called *StreetSmart*. Siegel has known him by sight for more than two years. Among his fellow vendors, Malik stands out for not being black or Hispanic. Also, as a man trying to earn his keep out of doors in the tough Chicago weather, for being old. Above all, for being completely unaggressive. Malik is dark. An Indian, maybe, or a Pakistani? Siegel, interested despite himself, isn't sure.

"Help the homeless" is what vendors of these papers usually

call out in a loud voice. But not Malik. He stands on the corner, silent, looking off into the distance, a packet of papers cradled in his arm. Siegel learns that the vendors pay twenty-five cents for each copy of *StreetSmart,* which they sell for a buck. At a suburban dinner party, he suggests that someone wanting to help out one of these guys should just give him a dollar and leave the paper.

Begging is big in the neighborhood. The reason, Siegel has discovered, is that the local churches and synagogues have set up soup kitchens, and one of them provides overnight shelter. As a result of this kindness, you can't walk a full block without getting hit up for your loose change or for the price of a ride on the El. Once, a goofy woman asked Siegel for money to buy a pair of dry socks. "Why dry socks?" he asked. " 'Cause mine are wet, stupid," she said, and walked away.

When it comes to beggars, Siegel has never had a settled policy. He tends to give a dollar for what he regards as unusual requests. Twice a week he forks over a buck to a guy outside the Board of Trade who carries a sign reading, "Help Me Out. I Promise Not to Spend What You Give on Anything but Booze and Cigarettes." Siegel remembers his father being approached by a beggar for a quarter and responding, "Sorry, kid, but I'm working this side of the street." Siegel's father was small — maybe five foot five and no more than 130 pounds — but fearless. Siegel is six one and weighs 220, which, as his wife frequently reminds him, is heavier than he ought to be.

They have a rich variety of beggars in the neighborhood — this much Siegel has to concede. There are the mad ones from a nearby halfway house, many of them white women with pasty complexions and missing teeth; older black men in hanging dreadlocks and clothes that look as if they haven't been changed in a fiscal quarter; and lots of young black guys in NBA or NFL shirts and huge gym shoes, some of whom bring a touch of menace to the job. Once Siegel was stopped, on a sunny afternoon, alone in the middle of the parking lot of the Jewel supermarket, by one of these young guys with felony muscles — muscles gained, he has been informed, by doing endless push-ups and chin-ups while in prison. The guy said he was just out of jail and could use help. Siegel came up with two loose singles and felt he got off cheap.

On his way to the train, Siegel used to pass a large woman in a light blue raincoat sitting on the back steps of the library, three small suitcases in tow, waiting for the building to open. She was missing some teeth but always looked freshly showered and, Siegel thought, hopelessly sad. Greeting him in what sounded like an educated voice, she asked one morning if he'd ever read the short stories of John Cheever. No, he said. Why? "Oh," she said, "you look a little like him." Another morning he offered to buy her breakfast — he was ready to hand her a twenty, she seemed so forlorn — but she said she had already eaten, thank you all the same. Now she's gone: into a madhouse, a pauper's grave, who knows where.

Many of these characters have stayed on the job longer than the young men and women who join and quickly depart Siegel's firm on LaSalle Street. There's the obese black man outside the Blockbuster who says "God bless you" for every handout. There's the young man in a New York Yankees cap, with a mustache and goatee and long thin sideburns; he has the look of an assassin from the time of the Spanish Inquisition. Longest tenured of all — she must be twenty years at her post — is the tall mulatto woman standing by the railing outside the Dominick's supermarket, with her coffee-colored skin, fine features, and toothlessness — Lena Horne in hell, is the way Siegel thinks of her.

Malik seems somehow different — not crazy, certainly not menacing. He stands there in the cold, stoical, something intelligent in his eyes. His hair is steely gray and long in the back. He has a high, thin bridge to his nose and flaring nostrils. There is something majestic about him. He must be Siegel's age, or older.

In winter Malik is layered up in clothes, no doubt acquired from the leftovers of church rummage sales. Sometimes he wears a sweater around his shoulders, like a combination scarf and shawl. Along the way he has acquired a fold-up chair, and in warmer weather he'll sit reading a paperback. He keeps a pencil or ballpoint pen in his hand to make notes.

Siegel first speaks to him on a viciously cold February day as he comes out of Borders into one of those Chicago winds that hit you like a smash in the face, and Malik's papers, maybe a dozen of them, are blowing out of his hand. Malik runs after them in one direction, Siegel in another. Between them they retrieve most of the blowaways. "Thank you," Malik says, "it's murder out here in this wind." He pronounces "out" with what to Siegel seems a slight Canadian burr, and something else not quite definable, a faint, odd rhythm in his voice. He's wearing a watch cap pulled over his ears. His face, despite its dark complexion, is high-blood-pressure red.

"Let me buy one of those from you," Siegel says.

"Sure," he says, "thanks a lot," carefully handing Siegel a *StreetSmart*.

From then on, they exchange friendly nods. Friday evenings Siegel takes to buying a copy of *StreetSmart*. On one such evening, he hands Malik his already read *Wall Street Journal*.

"Thanks," Malik says. "A good paper. Serious. Well written." Siegel begins to make an almost nightly habit of passing his *Journal* to Malik, and two or three times he adds a buck along with it. "Thank you," Malik says, always appreciatively.

"May I ask what you do for a living?" he asks Siegel one day.

"I'm at the Board of Trade," Siegel says. "In futures."

"I thought it must be something like that, I mean with the *Wall Street Journal* and all."

"What'd you do before this?" Siegel asks him.

"A bit of this and that," Malik answers. "I drove a cab for a while, owned by a Syrian gentleman whom I got into an argument with over a time sheet. He joined with the police to make it tough for me to find another driving job."

Siegel doesn't feel it's his place to press further.

"My name's Malik Hassan," Malik says, putting out his hand.

"David Siegel."

"You're Jewish," Malik says, "a fellow Semite." So he's a Muslim, Siegel thinks, although he's not exactly sure how to take the deadpan tone.

As the weeks pass, Malik occasionally asks if he's picked up any interesting information about the economy. Like Siegel, he's a news junkie, and reads two or three real papers a day, which he fishes out of a nearby trash container. Once, when Siegel has been out of town for a few days, Malik asks where, and Siegel says St. Louis.

"Where did you stay?"

The newly refurbished Park Sheraton Hotel, Siegel replies. To which Malik says, very casually, "I once met Hubert Humphrey when he was speaking there." Interesting name-drop, Siegel thinks.

In his political views Malik seems very mild, not angry as you might expect in a person who has been left behind. He isn't, Siegel thinks to himself, one of those types who'll attribute an ice cream headache to the evils of capitalism. They even seem able to talk calmly about the troubles in the Middle East. It could be that he's just being careful, knowing Siegel is a Jew and also that he makes his living as a capitalist.

Siegel remembers sitting at the same table with an Indian couple at his friend Burt Goldman's daughter's wedding. The husband was the Goldman family's internist, and his wife was a radiologist. How like Jews these two seemed, he thought. Years ago, he'd read in *National Geographic* about Indians working as shopkeepers in Africa, the Caribbean, and the far outposts of Latin America; that, too, struck him as very Jewish. Of course, he thinks, they must have been Hindus, and Malik is definitely a Muslim.

Siegel finds himself telling his wife, Julie, that he plans on giving Malik Hassan $50 on New Year's Eve.

"I'm sure he's a nice man and all," she warns. "Just don't get too close to him."

Now they're greeting each other by their first names — Malik asking to be called Mal — and on some evenings Siegel lingers to talk about the news or the economy and to answer questions about the market. Then one day, as Siegel gives him the *Journal,* Malik puts a hand over his face, and when he says thanks his voice is muffled.

"You all right?" Siegel asks. He can see that Malik's lower jaw has dropped, changing the shape of his face.

"I was beaten up and robbed last night, near a mission on South State Street. They broke my lower denture."

"Can you get another one soon?"

"Don't think so," Malik says. "The one they broke wasn't that old. And I've already had my troubles with Medicaid. The cops screwed me up with the bureaucrats down there. Hard to eat without bottom teeth." His speech isn't any too clear. Our looks don't improve much without teeth, Siegel reflects, but Malik, who usually has a sort of natural dignity about him, looks especially pitiful; the missing lower teeth age him by ten years. Siegel gives him $20, suggesting that he get some soft food. "Thank you, David," he says, his hand covering his mouth.

The next morning, without saying anything to Julie, Siegel calls Michael Cantor, his dentist, to ask the cost of a lower den-

ture. If no extractions are involved, Cantor says, he can do it for
$2,400.

That night, Malik looks even more woebegone. Homeless is
bad enough, but now the man is half toothless. "I've been thinking about your predicament," Siegel says. "I have this dentist.
We've been betting on the Bulls for years, and he's into me for
nearly a grand. I've decided to take some of it out in trade. I
called him, and he's agreed to make a lower denture for you. He
says he can rush it through in less than a week. You can pay me
back whenever you like."

"That's very good of you," Malik says. "But why would you
want to do this for me?"

"Among other reasons," Siegel says, "because this is probably
the only way I can get this guy to pay up on part of his debt. I'll
call him tomorrow and let you know when he can see you."

"I'm very grateful, David."

When he calls for the appointment, Siegel tells Cantor that
Malik Hassan is homeless but gentle, and in no way disruptive.
"He's seen better days," Siegel says. "But he's clean, doesn't smell,
usually shaves. I think he's a decent guy. He leads a hard life."

Why is Siegel doing this? The only explanation he can come
up with is, why shouldn't he? Maybe he likes the idea of actually
seeing his charity at work, one on one, instead of giving money
to organizations that do God knows what with it. And then Malik
is, as he himself said, a fellow Semite — maybe in some weird
way there's something to that. With Muslims at war with Jews
everywhere, here they are, the two of them, getting on so well.
Another thing is that Siegel has made more than half a million
this year, and his house, bought ten years ago for $700,000, has
doubled in value. He's been on a pretty good roll. Somewhere he
read that the real test of generosity isn't what you give but what
you have left over after giving it. A lot to that, Siegel thinks. What

will it hurt him to help out Malik Hassan? He doesn't mention it to his wife.

On a cold Saturday, long after the denture has been replaced, Siegel exits the CVS drugstore and sees Malik at his usual post. He has galoshes on his feet and looks as if he's wearing three sweaters under his ill-fitting trench coat. His watch cap is pulled over his ears, but he's wrapped another sweater around his face and tied it under his chin, which makes him look like one of those women — babushkas, if Siegel remembers the term — who sweep the snow off the streets in Moscow. Malik wears no gloves.

"Brutal day, David," he says.

"Got time for lunch, Mal?" Siegel asks him. "You look like you could do with a bowl of soup. It's on me."

They walk across the street to Panera, a franchise joint with decent food. Malik orders vegetable soup served in a bowl made of bread, a turkey sandwich, and a large coffee around which he warms his hands. He keeps his coat on, and eats every scrap.

"This reminds me of the sandwiches at the Montefiore Club in Montreal," Malik says. "Have you ever been there?"

"Can't say as I have."

"It's the Jewish city club in Montreal. It's like the Standard Club here, but Canadian-style. Some of my father's wealthier customers took us there, usually on Friday nights when they had this fantastic buffet. Everything tasted wonderful. Jewish clubs always seem to have good kitchens. I mean that's what they're really about, the food, right?"

"What did your father do in Montreal?" Siegel asks.

"Men's shirts. He owned a factory with his older brother. Our family in India were always merchants. When partition came in 1947, they chose not to live in Pakistan. They sensed what was coming, got out before the slaughter, and settled in Canada. I was still in grade school when we left.

"In the clothing business, my father and his brother dealt mostly with Jews. They had houses on the same block in Westmount. That's the wealthy Jewish neighborhood in Montreal, or at least it was in those days. I don't know how they afforded it. But they always felt comfortable around Jews, and nobody ever bothered them."

"What made you leave Canada?" Siegel asks.

"My father and my uncle had a big falling-out. They went to their graves without speaking to each other for twenty years. It was over me, actually. My father was hoping I'd take over the business. His brother's wife couldn't have children. I left McGill after two years to work for them, but I was a wild kid. During my twenties I was girl-crazy. I did a lot of drinking, too, despite what Islam says. I'd disappear for two or three days at a time, sometimes holed up with a young woman. It drove my uncle mad; he was very devout. My father tried to defend me. A defense of the indefensible, I'm afraid. They split up the partnership. My uncle took the business, and my father invested his half of the money in real estate. It went bad."

"And then?"

"At first my father had me help run a few of his buildings. When that went sour, so did my job. I sold men's clothes for a while. Kicked around. I decided that Canada was too tame and came to the States when I was twenty-five. I'd always wanted to live here, ever since I was a boy and my father took me with him on his business trips. And I did fairly well. But I couldn't hold a job. I had a real patience problem. Now I've finally learned patience. Too late to do me any good."

Siegel doesn't know how to respond. He asks Malik if he wants dessert.

"Thanks," he says, "but I'd better get back out there. I've got my expenses to make. I need to clear twenty-five dollars a day. I can get by on that."

Siegel wonders what his expenses might be: food, shelter, razor blades? On some nights he sees Malik headed toward the El with his bags — going where, he has no notion — so there's his fare to worry about, too.

"Usually make your twenty-five?" he asks.

"Usually, yes, if the police leave me alone. I have my regular customers. People who buy a paper and hang around to talk. They like the idea of chatting up a homeless man. Makes them feel better about themselves. By putting seventy-five cents in my pocket, they think they're doing a mitzvah, as your people say."

Siegel is dying to ask what he'd done in all the missing decades of his life, how he'd happened to meet Hubert Humphrey in St. Louis, what had finally driven him out into the streets, why he couldn't get himself into shape to do work of some other kind. Instead he thinks about the fact that the men who sell *StreetSmart* have to pay a quarter for it, which means that the guy who's printing it must be showing a handsome profit. So many years at the Board of Trade have given Siegel a low view of human nature. For a long time now he's been waiting for a scandal to break about the huge fortunes a small number of people must be raking in from the recycling game.

Outside, the cold hasn't let up. Siegel makes a mental note to find a pair of old gloves he can pass along to Malik.

"Thanks for the lunch," Malik says.

"Enjoyed it," Siegel says. Leaving him in the cold wind, he goes home, where, a blaze going in the fireplace, he watches the Illinois-Indiana game.

Malik makes it through the winter — something Siegel isn't sure he could do in his place. He judges Malik to be in his late sixties: no sprung chicken, as Siegel's mother's Russian dressmaker used to say. He must have some terrific inner toughness. Maybe it comes from not having much choice, of having to either accept life on the terms in which he finds it or die. Stark but simple.

So many mornings, when he first awakes, Siegel feels a sense of doubt: time is running out, he thinks, am I doing the right thing with my life, does anyone but my wife and two daughters really give a damn if I'm dead or alive? He supposes Malik never gets around to such questions. If it isn't raining, or the wind isn't whipping his face, or the cold numbing his hands and feet, or the sun boiling down on him, that must be gift enough.

Lunch with Malik is never repeated. Siegel gives him another $50 at New Year's Eve, continues to pass along his *Wall Street Journal,* each time with a buck in it to help him cover his daily expenses. Malik is beginning to look even older. Schlepping to the El with his heavy plastic bags filled with extra clothes, bits of reading, razor, and toothbrush, plus his fold-up canvas chair, he has begun to stoop badly, to shuffle as he walks. His greasy gray hair, straggling out of his one-size-fits-all baseball caps, flows down his neck.

During a rare trip to the library on a Sunday afternoon, Siegel spots Malik in a chair against a far wall, asleep with his mouth open. He wonders whether, in whatever shelter he finds himself in, Malik sleeps in his clothes, or sleeps at all. He must have to worry about other homeless characters stealing his few worldly goods. When does he have a chance to shower or shave? Does he miss many meals? What will he do if he gets sick? How does he keep things going? What stops him from throwing in the towel?

Not long after, as Siegel hands over his *Wall Street Journal* with the dollar bill on top, Malik, instead of exchanging a greeting or launching a discussion, takes the paper, mumbles his thanks, and turns away. The same thing happens the next night, and the night after that. Finally Siegel asks him what's wrong. Has he said or done anything to offend?

"You know what's wrong," Malik says, sudden anger on his face. "That conversation we had in the library last week. You reported the whole thing to the police. Those sons of bitches think they can mess with Malik Hassan, they've got another think coming."

"Mal," Siegel says, "we never had a conversation in the library. And even if we did, why would I want to report it to the cops?" But Malik turns away.

Paranoia. Of course, it has to be that. This isn't the first time Malik's complained about the police fouling up his life. Siegel has put it down to a tic of sorts; it's hard to believe the cops would spend much energy on an old homeless guy. Maybe Malik has been a little crazy all along; if not, his unbearably hard life could easily have driven him into madness.

But why should Siegel, of all people, have become his enemy? He can't help thinking about the $2,400 he put out for his denture. Would an enemy have done that? Or is there something to the old saw that no good deed goes unpunished?

The next time Siegel passes by, Malik looks away with a particularly sour expression on his face. Does he know where I live? Siegel suddenly wonders. Is he, possibly, dangerous? Is he goofy enough to attack someone on the street? Siegel decides to stop his forays to Borders, except after dinner or early on Sundays when Malik isn't on the street. He changes his route home from the train, noting with resentment that the move adds a wintry extra two blocks to his walk.

After a month or so he says screw it. He's done nothing wrong, and he won't go out of his way to avoid some sad, broken-down old homeless guy. He resumes his old route. When he passes by, Malik pretends he doesn't exist. Well, Siegel can live with that, though he can't help half hoping that Malik will call him over one evening and say, "David, I don't know what got into me, I just can't explain it, but I'm really sorry to have offended you, of all people." But months go by and Malik never says anything of the kind.

A year or more later, around nine o'clock one night, Siegel picks up the phone and hears Malik Hassan's voice: "If you and the police think you can run me out of town, forget about it. It is not going to happen. I know all about people like you. I've dealt with them all my life. If I were you, I'd be careful who you're fooling with."

Siegel tries to answer, urge Malik to come to his senses, convince him it's all a mistake. But before Siegel can say a word, he has hung up.

Siegel doesn't tell Julie about the phone call, but less than a month later she shakes him out of a deep sleep. Someone is rumbling around on their front porch. It's nearly two in the morning. Sure enough, when he goes downstairs, Siegel sees Malik Hassan, bundled up in his winter clothes, trying to pry open a triple-track window and making a bad and noisy job of it. Siegel isn't sure what to do. He's certain he can overpower him, but who knows? He might have a knife or a lead pipe on him. So he does what Malik, in his paranoia, would guess he'd do. He calls the police.

Within five minutes they arrive and very efficiently drag Malik off, struggling and screaming: "Fucking cops, fucking Jews." Talking with one of the policemen, Siegel learns there isn't much they can do about a guy like Malik unless they catch him assaulting someone or actually destroying property. At the moment, the only charge Siegel can file is for trespassing. He sees no point in that, and the cop agrees. At most, Malik would get a week or so in jail.

Malik is still working the corner in front of Borders, still facing away when Siegel passes. Siegel wonders how many more winters he has in him. And here is something he feels strongly but is ashamed to admit: he hopes it's not too many. For reasons he can't quite explain to himself, he finds Malik Hassan to be an affront, a deeply personal affront, and would like him to disappear so that he'll never have to think about him again.

But he won't. No, Malik will not go away.

The Philosopher and
the Checkout Girl

EARLY ON A TUESDAY morning at Dominick's super-market on Broadway, Howard Salzman, retired professor of philosophy, emptied his cart onto the conveyor belt in the express lane, FIFTEEN ITEMS OR LESS. "Fewer," he noted to himself, not "less." He set out six cartons of fat-free Lucerne yogurt in assorted flavors, two bottles of San Pellegrino water, a half pound of turkey pastrami, a package of six Bay's English muffins, three Granny Smith apples, four Anjou pears, a loaf of rye bread, and a jar of Grey Poupon mustard.

"Excuse me," the checker said, "you look familiar. Didn't you used to shop at our Evanston store?"

"I did," Salzman said. "The one on South Boulevard."

"I used to work there," she said. "I thought I recognized you." Her nametag identified her as Irene. She was small, dark, with heavy lipstick and thickish auburn hair. She was in a black T-shirt and jeans.

"I believe I remember you, too," Salzman said, not sure he actually did. "Nice to see you again."

"Good to see an old face," she said as she ran his groceries through the scanner. "A familiar face, I mean," she corrected herself, smiling and touching his wrist. She bagged his groceries. He paid, took his change.

"Enjoy your day," she said. "See you again."

"Thanks," he said. "Be well." It was a phrase his father had used regularly; now he was using it all the time. Behind the wheel of his Volvo, before starting the engine, he looked at himself in the rearview mirror. "Good to see an old face," he muttered. The beard he had grown in the early 1980s had come in salt-and-pepper but had long since turned completely white. His eyes, when he removed his glasses, were rimmed in red; his face seemed pallid. Maybe not so good, he thought, turning the key.

At home, as he put away the groceries, Salzman's thoughts strayed to the woman at the checkout. He did remember her. Fifteen or so years ago he had been in her line at the South Boulevard Dominick's and she, behind the counter, had tears in her eyes. He'd asked her if everything was all right. She answered that she'd be fine in a minute and continued to check him through. His wife, Marcia, now seven years dead, may have been with him, but Salzman couldn't recall.

Today Irene looked much the same, maybe a little fuller in the face. She was a pretty woman. American life is predicated on progress, Salzman thought, and here she is still working the same job and clearly not making all that much. He tried to remember if she'd been wearing a wedding ring.

Not long after Marcia's death, Salzman had sold their house in Evanston and moved into Chicago, taking a two-bedroom apartment overlooking the lake on Sheridan Road. He used one bedroom as an office, though in retirement he found he really hadn't much need for it.

His specialty had been analytical philosophy. Once he had found it elegant and exciting to work out the subtle language games and problems the field presented; it was like playing a form of high-speed verbal Ping-Pong with A. J. Ayer or J. L. Austin, even if he was finally unable to score any points against them. Today it seemed to him arid and empty. Analytical philosophy encouraged his detachment, which was probably the last thing he needed.

As he headed toward his seventieth year, the tempo of Salzman's days was *adagio molto*. He awoke early, usually around six, wrote in the diary he had kept for nearly forty years, filling more than fifty notebooks that his daughter, Connie, would have to get rid of after he died, took his hourlong walk along the lakeshore. Occasionally he would meet a former colleague for lunch before doing his bits of shopping and then cooking and eating his simple dinners while watching the news broadcast on PBS. He read biographies of composers and musicians, the occasional nineteenth-century novel; went to concerts, mostly chamber music; every once in a while took himself to a play at the Goodman or a foreign movie at the Fine Arts. Days passed without his seeing anyone, but he didn't mind the solitude. If anything, the days seemed to whir by all too quickly.

Salzman didn't miss teaching in the least. Although he had published a number of articles, some of them thought to be important in their day, and although he held a named professorship — the Edward Padnos chair — he didn't kid himself that anything he had done in philosophy was likely to be remembered. In the end he was just another kibitzer, staring in at the edge of the crowd. The only colleague whose company he had genuinely enjoyed was a working-class Englishman named Paul Wilson, a specialist in German philosophy who had a strong taste for harsh statement, and who died the year after Marcia.

Marcia he did miss. She had been a good wife, though he came to recognize this rather late. She had put up with his brooding nature, his penchant for sequestering himself in his home office for days at a time. She had bravely gone through the horrors — mostly boredom, he supposed — of being an academic wife. It was Marcia, really, who did all the work of raising Connie, their only child; she was brokenhearted when, after her divorce, Connie announced she was moving to Seattle with her two young children. Marcia died of leukemia, which took her in less than a year.

Permanently settled in Seattle, Connie taught mentally handicapped children in the public schools. At first Salzman had traveled three times a year to visit his grandchildren, but as they grew older and seemed less in need of his attention, he cut the trips down to twice and then once a year. Connie, no great beauty, was, Salzman thought, unlikely to remarry.

For himself, remarriage was something he had never considered. He saw no women after his wife's death. Some men, Salzman thought, seemed to regard themselves always as husbands; he had begun to wonder whether he, married for nearly forty years, wasn't one of nature's true bachelors. Through much of his life with Marcia, he now felt with a stab of guilt, he had been an absentee husband and father even while, technically, never leaving the premises.

He also figured himself for a low-libido type. During the late sixties and early seventies, when his colleagues were jollily bonking (the phrase was Paul Wilson's) their students, Salzman steered clear. Now he had lived into the age of Viagra, when men in their eighties were walking around with grins on their faces. But during his marriage and afterward he had felt no strong need to pursue women. "The screwing I get," Paul, a lifelong bachelor, would intone in his harsh working-class accent, "ain't worth the screwing I get." Paul was also fond of quoting the poet Philip Larkin to the effect that sex was too good to share with anyone else. Salzman took this to heart. The truth was that he had long since ceased to regard himself as being of any possible interest to women. He had lost most of his hair and he had a slight slouch, the product of too many years bent over too many books. Although he made a serious effort to stay tidy, he was well aware that being reasonably kempt had nothing to do with making himself sexually attractive. But he had dropped out of the sex game, and he believed for good.

If so, why were his thoughts turning to the checkout girl at Dominick's? Something about this Irene he found attractive, though he couldn't say what. He could only guess at her age: late thirties, maybe, or early forties. He didn't know her last name; her darkness suggested she might be Jewish, but then again she could as easily be Greek or Italian or even Lebanese. Years spent working in a supermarket bespoke neither a college education nor an easy life. He thought about taking her to a play or dinner; he thought about making love to her, tried to imagine her body naked. What he couldn't imagine was his own aging body in the same bed.

Four days later, against his more reasonable self, Salzman returned to Dominick's at the same hour. In his cart he had orange juice, Twining's Earl Grey tea, angel-hair pasta, more San Pellegrino and yogurt. She was there, in the express lane. The store was quiet, no one was in line behind him, and he noticed that she wore no wedding band. But she did have a ring on the thumb, index, and little finger of each hand, plus a watch on each wrist. She was wearing jeans and a white T-shirt that, in red letters, proclaimed, "I Am Woman, I Am Strong, I Am Invincible, I Am Tired."

Ahead of Salzman in line was a black kid, seven or eight years old, one of those forlorn, seemingly unattached children he saw a lot of in the neighborhood. Irene had rung up a Pepsi, a box of doughnuts, and a package of red licorice — breakfast, Salzman assumed. But the boy didn't have enough to pay for his purchases.

"You need another dollar sixty-five," Irene said.

"This all I got," the boy said, uncomprehendingly.

Irene looked at him, sighed, reached below her counter, and from her change purse added $1.65 to the boy's coins.

"Go to school," she said, caressing his cheek as she handed him his food in a plastic bag.

Salzman watched but said nothing.

"How're you today?" she said, checking him through.

"Not bad," Salzman said. "And you?"

"Hangin' in there," she said. "No other place to hang, you know."

"I wonder if you'd like to meet one day for coffee," Salzman blurted out.

"You're not married?" she asked.

"I'm a widower," he said.

"I'm a divorcée," she said. "Same result, different method. Sure, I'd be happy to. I'm off on Tuesdays and Sundays. My number's in the book."

"What's your last name?" Salzman asked.

"Lawrence," she said, "Irene. I live in the neighborhood, three blocks from here, on Winthrop. What's yours?"

"Howard Salzman. I'm at 5901 Sheridan. What's a good time to call?"

"At night, any time between six and ten."

An elderly woman hunched over with osteoporosis appeared behind him and began setting her groceries on the belt.

"I'll call you soon," Salzman said, amazed at his temerity.

He forced himself to wait two nights before phoning, and they agreed to meet the following Tuesday afternoon at the Java Corner on Broadway. She signed off saying, "Look forward to it, honey." Honey? thought Salzman, hanging up the phone; what's this honey business? He was feeling a little edgy about the whole thing.

When they met, she was wearing a bright red sweater and black pants. She had a nice figure, still youthful. Her hair was swept back off her face in a ponytail. She wore large hoop earrings and even more makeup than on the job.

"So what do you do for a living, Howard?" she asked after he had brought their coffee and biscotti to the table.

"I was a college teacher, now retired. Philosophy."

"Sounds heavy," she said. "I went to Oakton Community College for a while, but it didn't do much for me. I got married when I was twenty and dropped out."

"You probably didn't miss much," Salzman said. "College education is highly overrated. Take it from a man who dispensed it."

She sipped her coffee, bit into her biscotti. "Has it ever occurred to you," she said, "that biscotti are just stale *mandel* bread?"

"You're Jewish?" he asked, the word *mandel* starting memories of his mother's kitchen.

"Very," she said. "Maiden name Kaplan. Grew up in West Rogers Park. Went to Mather High School."

"Was your husband Jewish?"

"Yes," she said, "but his real religion was gambling. He was very observant. Our marriage broke up over his gambling, mostly on ball games, but birds flying off fences would do in a pinch. It's the worst, the gambling jones. Better to be married to an alcoholic. At least they pass out."

It occurred to Salzman that he had never been in the company of a woman who talked with such candor or knowingness; but it was the absence of irony, that staple of academic conversation, that he found riveting.

"In the old days one wasn't supposed to ask this of a lady," he said, emboldened, "but may I inquire how old you are?"

"Forty-nine," she said.

"You look much younger. Forgive me, but that's not meant as a compliment. It just happens to be true."

"So did my mother, right up to the day she dropped dead at fifty-three. I figure that a clock is running on my life. That's why I wear two watches. So I'll always know what time it is." She held out her wrists.

Salzman told her he was sixty-eight, and she answered without flinching that he looked it. "If I were doing your makeover," she said, "I'd tell you to lose the beard. A white beard is maybe the unsexiest thing going. I'd also maybe suggest you wear brighter colors." He was in his usual getup of brown tweed jacket, white shirt, black knit tie, gray trousers. "Bright colors liven us up, you know."

After two hours of filling each other in on their pasts, Salzman supplying information more circumspectly than Irene, he returned to his apartment exhausted but oddly exhilarated. This woman was beyond anything in his experience. She said things never dreamt of by Wittgenstein — whose philosophy, when Salzman came to think of it, had a very low dream content. They had agreed to meet again, though when was left open.

The following morning, brushing his teeth, Salzman considered his beard. Although he tried to keep it trimmed, the whiteness made it appear scraggly. He had grown it after acquiring a terrible windburn on a trip to Scotland, where he had given a paper at the University of Edinburgh on the Vienna Circle. Not shaving for a week or so relieved his skin, and Marcia liked the effect, or at least never said anything against it. But now, without giving the matter any more thought, he proceeded to take a razor to it, remembering what Henry James wrote to his brother William when he shaved off his own beard in his late fifties — that, afterward, he had felt "forty and clean and light."

Looking at his beardless face in the mirror, Salzman wished he could say the same. Instead he noted the things that time had done to his face while it lay hidden beneath its white shrubbery. His skin sagged at the cheeks; his lips were thinner than he'd remembered; two deep lines jutted down his chin from the corners of his downward-pulling mouth. His was the face, he thought, of a disappointed man.

That night, he called Irene with an invitation. He had two tickets to Music of the Baroque at the Methodist church in Evanston on Sunday at three. Would she like to join him?

"Music of the what?" she asked.

"Of the Baroque," he said.

"I thought you said Music of the Broke, a poverty group, maybe," she said with a laugh. "I'm not much for longhair music, Howard. Broadway show tunes and Barry Manilow are more my kind of thing. But sure, why not? Let's do it."

On Sunday, getting into his Volvo, she looked at his face. "It's an improvement," she said, adding hesitantly, "I think. It'll take some getting used to."

The concert took place in the main chapel. Looking around, Irene said: "Is this your crowd, Howard? You know, I was a little worried about what to wear this afternoon, but these people, with their cataracts, probably can't see me anyhow." She had on a rather tight yellow sweater that emphasized her breasts, blue pants that stopped just above the calf, and shoes with heels that made her almost as tall as Salzman.

She was right; funny he hadn't noticed before, but now, looking around the room, Salzman saw nothing but aged specimens, several pulling themselves behind walkers. Lots of bald heads, plenty of mottled skin. For the first time it occurred to Salzman that what most of these people were looking for in chamber music was consolation—consolation for not being beautiful, or rich, or somehow better equipped for life, or for the terror of approaching death. Was he here for the same reason?

"I'll say one thing for this audience," Irene said. "It makes me feel young and full of energy, like I could dance Gene Kelly's big 'Singin' in the Rain' number."

"They are pretty elderly," Salzman agreed.

"Howard," she said emphatically, "this is no matinee. This is a graveyard special."

At the intermission, standing outside, she reached into her purse and withdrew a pack of Marlboros. "Hope you don't mind," she said almost as an afterthought, lighting up before Salzman could answer.

"Are you enjoying the music?" he asked.

"I've had worse times at the dentist," she said. "Mostly I'm looking at the big lips of the guy playing the violin on the far left. Also his stomach. His front footage, as my dad used to call it. He looks like he gets a lot of pleasure out of life. I like these hardy types with an appetite."

Salzman decided not to put her through the torture of the final item on the program, an oratorio by Handel. Instead he proposed a walk and then an early dinner at a Chinese restaurant.

"The walk part sounds fine," she said. "But how about we stop and buy something I can fix us at my place?"

They walked east to the lake. A warm day, sunny; everyone they saw seemed youthful to Salzman. Fit-looking young women jogged past, ponytails bobbing out of the backs of their baseball caps. A large man with weightlifter muscles was promenading a small white dog with black button eyes. Salzman felt a wave of depression wash over him.

They bought two salmon steaks, broccoli, and the makings of a salad at Whole Foods before returning to Salzman's car. Irene lived in a dark building on Winthrop, off Catalpa. Three Mexican boys walked by in baggy jeans low on the hips, unlaced gym shoes, and baseball caps worn backward.

"What do you suppose this backward-hat business means?" Salzman asked.

"I don't know," Irene said. "Maybe the kids don't know how to wear them. Maybe the hats should come with instructions."

The apartment was small—a living room, a bedroom, a little kitchen giving onto a dark back porch. The furniture was a hodgepodge. There were old-fashioned venetian blinds on the windows; colorless curtains hung limply. No books were in evidence, though there was a television set.

"Hope you like my furniture," Irene said. "It's Salvation Army colonial."

She suggested that Salzman sit on the sofa while she went to prepare dinner.

"I don't have anything like Going for Baroque, but how about a little Louis Armstrong?" She extracted a CD from a small pile on a coffee table.

Listening to trumpet music with a background of kitchen noise, Salzman, a late-afternoon napper, fell asleep. He dreamed about his own memorial service at the university. In the dream, every speaker was someone he had considered oafish or clownish. Their comments were entirely irrelevant. Marvin Citterman, the Spinoza man, invoked Salzman's facility in long division. Jacob Lerner, a Neo-Platonist, compared his penmanship with Leonardo da Vinci's. Nancy Weiss, a phenomenologist and the department feminist, spoke exclusively about herself and the difficulty of her adolescent menstrual cycles. What did all this have to do with him? Salzman was wondering, when he felt Irene's hand gently on his shoulder, announcing dinner.

He stepped into the bathroom to wash his hands, splash some water on his face. A cramped room, it had no medicine chest. All of Irene's pills, makeup, lotions, and feminine things sat on two shelves over the toilet. Difficult to imagine two people living in this apartment; it wasn't all that convenient for one.

In the kitchen, she invited him to remove his jacket and tie, which he did, placing them over the back of his chair. She had opened the door leading onto the back porch to release the heat from the oven.

They ate at a Formica table of the kind Salzman remembered from his mother's kitchen, on Kimball Avenue in Albany Park in the late 1940s. The two kitchen chairs didn't match. The refrigerator and stove both looked more than thirty years old.

Irene must have noticed him taking inventory.

"My original plan didn't call for living like this, you know," she said, setting their salads on the table. "It called for a large house in Highland Park or Glencoe. Which is why I married a man just out of law school. My mistake was not knowing that he couldn't stand to hold on to money. He preferred to donate it to bookies and other creeps."

"How long have you been divorced, Irene?" Salzman asked.

"It'll be fifteen years in December," she said.

"You're an attractive woman. No one else has asked you to marry?"

"You may not believe this," she said, "but Richard — that's my ex — has kept me in shell shock. I've had a few gentleman friends, but when things get tight, I get going. I'd rather live like this than have another disastrous marriage. Ready for the salmon?"

Salzman generally cared little about food, but the salad was good, the salmon seemed excellent, and the broccoli was cooked to the right degree of crispness. Irene had made him a Scotch and water, then a second. She kept pace with him. Over dinner they talked more about their pasts. He told her about his daughter and grandchildren in Seattle. She told him about her painful relationship with her father, who had wanted her to leave her husband much sooner than she did. He, unlike her mother, had never approved of the marriage to begin with, which didn't make things easier, her father being, as she put it, "an I-told-you-so kind of guy."

Instead of coffee, Salzman had a third and then a fourth Scotch, eliminating the water and ice cubes. Irene smoked her Marlboros. Not normally a drinking man, he found himself saying things to her that until now he had hardly said even to himself. He told her that he wasn't much of a husband, that his mind had always seemed to be elsewhere. He told her of his feeling an increasing detachment from life. He told her he thought he would die unmourned, that he worried about dying alone in his apartment, his body undiscovered for weeks afterward. The worries, the fears, the terrors poured out of him.

Salzman didn't believe that telling your troubles helped make them better, which was why he had never undertaken psychotherapy. But here he was, jabbering away to a woman he barely knew. He couldn't say why, but he found he could talk to her in an unguarded way, dropping the heavy, strangling, Count of Monte Cristo mask of irony he had acquired early in academic life and worn through all his years in the university. Apropos of nothing at all, he protested — to himself? to Irene? — that Karl Popper was right about Freudian analysis: no discipline deserved to call itself scientific if it could not provide the means of its own refutation.

That was his last conscious thought before the sun came into Irene's small bedroom and woke him, alone in her bed, in his underwear. He turned and found a note on the nearby pillow:

Don't worry, your virginity is still intact. You fell asleep talking at my kitchen table, and I was able to drag you into the bedroom and get your shoes and pants off. I had to be at work by seven this morning. Your clothes are in the living room. There's a jar of instant coffee on the gas range and orange juice and bread for toasting in the refrigerator. Help yourself.

Irene

Later that morning, back in his own apartment, surrounded by his books, Bach cantatas sounding from his expensive stereo equipment, Salzman asked himself what had driven him to become so confessional. Yes, such thoughts had clearly been preying on his mind, his subconscious. But that they should have found their release in a hot, dark kitchen with the smell of broiled fish clinging to the walls, in the home of a grocery checker from a world utterly different from his own, was not so easy to explain. Could this very difference be the reason he was able to talk so freely to Irene? Or was it because her world was the same lower-middle-class world in which he, too, had been raised, but from which he had determined to become as greatly distanced as possible some fifty years ago?

Salzman had spent much of his early adult life in that concentrated effort, desperate to escape the deep — and to him deeply depressing — philistinism of his family and especially of his father, a jobber of women's handkerchiefs and table linens. And escape he had; meeting Salzman, you would spot him as Jewish, certainly, but you wouldn't be able to tell his social class or geographical origin. He had fled his past and all the traps it had set for his future, fled it decisively, profoundly. But into what?

Bach in the background, Salzman was vaguely pleased that nothing had happened when Irene dragged him to bed. He could all too easily see himself drunk, ineptly passionate, groping and grasping, in that claustral bedroom. But why was she so kind to him, and why did he crave her company? Idiots would place the blame on a midlife crisis, but Salzman didn't believe in midlife crises. Besides, nearing seventy, he was too old for one. What he had was something much more serious: a late-life crisis, the one, he thought, that occurs when, in the face of approaching death, a person realizes that his regrets greatly outweigh his achievements and there isn't enough time left to do much about it.

In the credit-and-debit department, Salzman was clearly in the red. True, on the credit side, he had radically changed himself, made himself into a man once taken seriously — see, e.g., the winter 1982 letters column of *Mind* — by the likes of W. V. Quine. But on the debit side, he had written no lasting books, given his name to no useful theories, made no real difference to the life of anyone, even, terrible to tell, his family. He had never known the pleasure of guileless behavior, of saying precisely what he felt and acting upon those feelings. He had lived his life at a second, perhaps a third, remove. And now the clock was ticking, insistently, incessantly.

And Irene? She, obviously, was his ticket to life, his way back into the fray. But why should she be interested in him, almost twenty years older than she, nothing much to look at, decently well off but hardly wealthy? Maybe he qualified in her eyes as mildly exotic, a man interested in things about which she had probably never heard. He was certainly not aggressive, sexually or in any other way, which she might or might not find to his credit. He hoped that in their few meetings he had shown his gentleness, assuming — by no means a safe assumption — that this was valued by a woman like Irene. The fact was that Salzman didn't know much about what Irene or any other woman wanted in a man. But he did sense, among so many inchoate feelings swirling about in his usually orderly brain, an urge to protect her, maybe make her life a little better — he could, at a minimum, get her out of the supermarket if that was her wish, though he had no notion that it was.

But surely all this was sheer sentimentalism, if not outright fantasy. Irene was honest and unselfconscious, and right now everything she said seemed of interest to Salzman. Soon enough, though, she was bound to become tedious. What could they possibly talk about? And who the hell *was* Barry Manilow anyway? Salzman had meant to find out but had forgotten.

He might just neglect to call Irene again; or he might call to apologize for getting drunk and thank her for taking care of him, saying that he would be in touch and then doing nothing further about it. Instead he phoned that afternoon to make a date for Sunday evening dinner at the Greek Islands.

"Opa!" yelled the Greek waiter as he squeezed lemon juice over the flaming cheese dish served at the table behind them.

"Did you notice," Irene said, once they'd been seated on the small upper floor of the crowded restaurant, "that the car in front of us and the car that pulled in behind us were both white Lincolns? What is it with Greeks and white Lincolns? Wonder why they're so nuts about them."

Salzman had not noticed. What he did notice was that she always managed to pick up on things that sailed over his head. He knew phemes and rhemes and how to spot illocutionary speech acts, but Greeks in white Lincolns went right by him. Which, he asked himself, was the more useful sort of information? To his chagrin, knowledge of Greeks and white Lincolns seemed to him to win hands down.

"You know," she said, looking at him like a portrait painter, her head bent slightly to the right, "maybe you should let the beard grow out and consider dyeing it black. Or maybe you should go for just a mustache."

"I'm afraid I'm beyond repair," Salzman answered.

"Don't worry about it," Irene said. "A woman doesn't want to be seen in the company of a man more attractive than herself. I always distrust a couple where the guy's hair is more carefully coifed than his girlfriend's." Looking around, Irene motioned Salzman to observe a blonde, young and quite beautiful, accompanied by a dark grizzled man who looked as if he had to shave right up to his eyeballs.

"God," Irene said, "women will do anything."

"Not all of them," Salzman said. "My guess is that you wouldn't."

"I've come pretty close a time or two," she said.

"Which reminds me," Salzman said. "I remember once seeing you in tears when you were working at the Dominick's in Evanston. It's none of my business, but what was that about?"

"I don't remember. But I went through a really bad phase right around the time I kicked my husband out for good. I realized I wasn't going to be one of those lucky women who have everything taken care of for them by their husbands, which was the life I had planned on. And I don't mind telling you that it sent me into a real shlunck, maybe for six months. I'd cry at work, sitting on the toilet, waking up in the middle of the night. The tears would just flow and there wasn't anything I could do about it."

"What brought you around?"

"The realization that I really was one of the lucky ones. I was healthy. I could earn my living. Being alone, I didn't have to kowtow to anyone. A lot in life — food, music, watching other people — gave me real joy. And I decided then and there not to live for a grand future but for today. Does this sound stupid?"

"Not at all," Salzman said, and then he suddenly started explaining his notion of the late-life crisis to her, the crisis he was suffering from.

"I don't buy it," she said. "Most of us are going to leave life with more regrets than what you call achievements. Make that *all* of us, even the winners. We regret we didn't have our mother's boob longer, we didn't get a chance to sleep with Cary Grant, we're not sitting beside our own Olympic-size swimming pool, we aren't two dress sizes smaller. Regret's easy, friend, and maybe a little cheap."

"Cheap?"

"I guess I mean common," she said. "Life can't be about feeling sad for the things we didn't do or couldn't do. At least it better not be."

Their dinners arrived: lamb chops for Irene, roast chicken for Salzman, large side dishes of green beans and rice in tomato sauce, glasses of Roditis. They concentrated on their food. She ate, Salzman noted, with an energy close to passion, at one point excusing herself for picking up a lamb chop and gnawing the meat off the bone. She ended the meal with two espressos and a baklava. Salzman settled for a decaffeinated American coffee.

"Some nice-size boys in this room," she said, looking around as Salzman signed for the check. "I like a restaurant with lots of overweight men. It's an indication that good food's being served."

When they arrived back at Irene's, he parked the car and walked her to the door of her apartment. She asked Salzman if he would like to come in. "You have my word that I won't open the Scotch and take unfair advantage of you."

"You know," Salzman said, once again surprised at what he was about to utter even while realizing he couldn't hold it back, "I'm afraid of you."

"What on earth for?" she asked.

"I'm not used to living life so directly."

"You ought to try it," she said. "Dive in. The water's fine."

"I won't drown?" he asked.

"I won't let you go under. I promise." She stood there smiling, holding the door open for the Edward Padnos Distinguished Professor of Philosophy Emeritus, dry of throat and full of trepidation, to step through.

What Are Friends For?

THIS RESTAURANT, Weinstein sensed immediately, was a mistake. M. Henry, it was called, the M. apparently standing for Monsieur. He had driven past it many times, so he thought he might as well give it a try when his friend Buddy Berkson called to set up one of their regular monthly lunches. The restaurant was crowded, mostly with women and gay men, and noisy, very noisy. Seated, given a glass of water and a menu, Weinstein quickly noted that there was nothing here for him to eat: mostly ornate salads, sandwiches ruined by various cheeses, and vegetables and herbs he had never heard of. Men don't like complicated food, Weinstein thought, at least he didn't.

Awaiting the arrival of Buddy, contemplating this impossible menu — what the hell, under Seafood, was alphonsino? — Weinstein looked across the room and saw Linda Berkson, Buddy's wife, her hand interlaced across the table with that of a large man with a graying ponytail, gazing into his eyes in a way that suggested much more than a business relationship or even friendship. Weinstein felt a surge of panic. Must get out of here before Buddy shows up. He set a five-dollar bill on the table and quickly walked out of the restaurant, hoping Linda didn't see him.

"It's crowded and noisy in there," Weinstein said when, five or so minutes later, he met Buddy outside the restaurant, "and nothing to eat but female food. Not our kind of place."

They walked a few blocks south on Clark Street and settled on a restaurant called Hamburger Mary's, where the music was louder than Weinstein liked, but there were things on the menu he and Buddy could eat. They talked about sports, about the stock market, about people they had seen from high school days, which Buddy always referred to as "the old country." They distinctly did not talk about what Weinstein had just witnessed at M. Henry.

They had known each other since seventh grade at Daniel Boone School, Phil Weinstein and Buddy Berkson, when the Weinsteins moved from Albany Park to West Rogers Park. Buddy was the best athlete at Boone: the quarterback, the shortstop, the playmaker guard. He was small, wiry, fearless. He would crash into a wall to catch a fly ball, was ready when necessary to fight boys thirty or forty pounds heavier than he. Everyone admired Buddy. Along with his athletic prowess, he had a sweetness of temperament, behind which the thirteen-year-old Phil Weinstein sensed a good heart. One sign of this was that Buddy befriended Weinstein, who wasn't an especially good athlete and who had always felt himself, until Buddy took him in, a natural outsider.

The girls all adored Buddy. He had black hair and a great smile. He had no awkwardness around girls — or, for that matter, around anyone. He had a natural charm, which seemed to work on everybody, including grownups. "That's a nice kid," Weinstein's father, who could be very critical, said of Buddy when Phil first brought him around. "I like that boy."

What Buddy saw in him, Weinstein didn't know. He was awfully glad, though, that he saw something. Being Buddy Berkson's friend made life easier all around. At Senn High School, Buddy arranged for him to get into the Ravens, one of the best of the many clubs and fraternities in the school, the semester after he himself became a member. Weinstein was good at school, and in sophomore year he and Buddy had the same geometry class, with a small, serious woman named Mrs. Hackman, and most nights Buddy, who was not so hot at math, walked the three blocks over to Weinstein's and they did geometry homework together. Geometry was the one subject that genuinely pleased Weinstein; he liked its orderliness, its having rules and laws that tidily solved all the problems the subject presented. Geometry, with its clear and clean solutions, gave him his first inkling of the way his own mind worked.

In high school, guys used to tease Weinstein about his relationship with Buddy. They'd call him his tool or his valet or joked that he was queer for him. In fact, they misunderstood the nature of the friendship. Nobody knew it, but Buddy got as much out of it as Phil. Buddy felt the depth of Phil Weinstein's loyalty — it was, he rightly understood, complete — and he never underestimated the value of that. Although Buddy continued to be immensely popular in high school, was second-team All-North section in basketball his senior year, with his pick of the prettiest girls in the school, a boy outwardly successful in every way, he was also vulnerable, given to dark moods, which nobody knew about but Weinstein, in whom he confided. Phil did what he could to console Buddy and protect him against his inexplicable attacks of sadness.

They went off to the University of Wisconsin together. Both pledged Pi Lamb, the best Jewish fraternity on campus; another case, Weinstein knew, of his coming in on Buddy's coattails. They were business majors. Like so many Jewish boys from Chicago whose parents didn't go to college, they wanted to show their seriousness and so put themselves through four years of mostly useless courses in accounting, economics, corporate finance.

Senior year they moved out of the fraternity and took an apartment together.

After college, Buddy was going to go into his father's business, bar and restaurant supplies, everything but the linens, which the Mafia in Chicago controlled. Buddy's father, Lou Berkson, was a calm man who had built up this business, and was pleased at the thought of one day turning it over to his only son, whom he loved without complication. Weinstein's father was a salesman; he sold watchbands for Speidel in a territory that included Illinois, Iowa, and Indiana, and had no business to offer his son, and so Phil thought he would go to law school. He'd try for Northwestern, and also apply to DePaul as a fallback position. As it turned out, he got into Northwestern.

Just before midterm of their first semester in the apartment, Buddy was hit by one of his bouts of depression, a particularly rough one. He couldn't make himself get out of bed for class, or for anything else. Weinstein didn't know what to do. He reminded his friend of all that was good about life, and his, Buddy's, life in particular. Buddy told Weinstein that he would never understand how dark and hopeless the world seemed to him, with nothing good, nothing the least promising, in it; today seemed terrible to him, tomorrow even worse. Weinstein worried that when he went off to class he might come back to find Buddy had killed himself, and twice he took the two sharpest kitchen knives in the apartment off to class with him in his book bag. He wondered at the strangeness of the world; here was his dear friend Buddy, good-looking, a good athlete, everywhere much liked, and yet, owing to who knew what little jingeroo in his brain, under the lash of such deep depression.

All that week Weinstein did Buddy's homework for him. He took it to Buddy's professors, telling them that Buddy had the flu. He brought in food and served his friend in the bedroom; he stayed near and held Buddy's hand and rubbed it gently, trying to calm him as his friend drew one bleak picture after another of the world as he saw it.

Buddy emerged from this depression, as he did from two others over the course of the year he and Weinstein lived together, returning to his usual self. The two boys never discussed these episodes. Weinstein wasn't sure that Buddy had told his parents or anyone else about them. Buddy never thanked Weinstein for his help, and, Weinstein felt, no thanks were required.

After college, life pulled them apart, at least a little. Weinstein was in law school, and Buddy joined his father in the family business, on Jefferson Street just off Roosevelt Road. At least once a week, the two friends telephoned each other. His last year in law school Weinstein had a call from Buddy asking him if he'd like to share a half-season's ticket to the Bulls games with him, it would be Buddy's treat. When, four years out of school, Buddy married Linda Hoffman, Phil Weinstein was his best man. Three years after that, Buddy performed the same service for Weinstein, when he married his wife, Elaine Becker.

Over lunch at Hamburger Mary's, Buddy told Weinstein that his psychiatrist had taken him off Prozac. Twice he had had his dosage of Prozac increased, and there was nowhere further to go with it. He was now on something called Zoloft.

"Betcha didn't know there's something called 'Prozac poopout,'" Buddy said.

"I didn't," Weinstein said. "But I've heard of Zoloft. What're the side effects?"

"The usual: nausea, diarrhea, headaches, insomnia, and the always delightful disappearance of erections. No one ever said it was easy being nuts."

Weinstein thought of Buddy's wife and the guy in the ponytail.

Buddy's business seemed to be holding up nicely, with new

restaurants opening regularly in Chicago, which was undergoing a youth boom of sorts. Weinstein, whose legal specialty was estate planning, had done his friend's will and knew Buddy was a wealthy man. How easy his friend's life might have been had he not had this odd glitch in his brain chemistry, but he had it, and he was paying for it. Nobody but nobody, Weinstein's father used to say, gets off this earth without *tsuris.*

That night, near ten-thirty, Weinstein and his wife were in bed, the lights off, when the phone rang.

"Philly, it's Linda, Linda Berkson." Weinstein asked her to hold while he took the call downstairs.

"Sorry, Linda," Weinstein said. "What can I do for you?"

"One thing you can do," she said, "is forget you saw me today at M. Henry. I take it you did see me. I saw you walk out."

"I'm afraid I did see you," Weinstein said.

"And I also take it that I am not likely to convince you that the man I was with is a long-lost cousin, or my new decorator, or someone like that."

"It would be a hard sell," Weinstein said.

"Do you want an explanation?" she asked.

"None required," he answered.

"All I can tell you is that life isn't easy living with Buddy and his pills and his depression."

"I'm sure it isn't," Weinstein said, "but you two have been together for more than thirty years."

"Patience wears out," she says. "It's complicated."

"What do you want me to do?"

"Very simple," Linda said. "I want you to forget that you saw me with Ted — that's his name, Ted Olevsky, he's a painter — this afternoon."

"I'll do my best," he said.

"It's important, Philip," she said.

"Let's talk about it," Weinstein said. They made a date to meet for lunch later in the week.

Weinstein found it hard to get back to sleep. Linda was right, of course. The easiest thing was for him to forget he saw her with this guy in the restaurant. Just block it out. God knows, he blocked out lots else: the unethical behavior of clients, his children's flaws, his own weaknesses. Just pretend he never saw it. He asked himself what Buddy would have done if he had seen Weinstein's wife in similar circumstances. Would Buddy have told him? Would he have wanted him to? Weinstein liked to think himself prudent, and wouldn't prudence call for him to keep his own counsel, forget about what he had seen, and go about his business? For every other man he knew, this is what he would have done, no hesitation, forgot the whole thing and moved on. But all the other men he knew weren't Buddy.

Linda and Weinstein met in another Andersonville restaurant, this one called Taste of Heaven. Linda was there when Weinstein arrived, seated at a table along the wall, under a small sign that read, "What If the Hokey-Pokey Really IS What It's All About?" The place was less noisy than M. Henry or Hamburger Mary's; no music was playing, people were modestly dressed. Linda, in her casual chic outfit, almost looked to be slumming.

Linda Berkson was always a knockout, and now, in her early fifties, her good looks were of the mature, I've-been-around-the-block-a-time-or-two kind. She was, Weinstein thought, as sexy as ever. True, she seemed a little hard, a touch too much in the know, but this may have added to her sexiness. Weinstein could never have married such a woman. Not that Linda Berkson would for a moment have considered Phil Weinstein a possible husband.

Small, with streaked blond hair, Linda managed a year-round tan without any of the accompanying leathery look. She wore smart clothes — very expensive, according to Elaine Weinstein — with simple gold jewelry. She used to say that she hated diamonds, but she said it with the easy confidence of a woman who could afford lots of them. She was the granddaughter of the biggest Chevy dealer in Chicago; her father had been a periodontist, very successful. She grew up in Highland Park, and went to Sarah Lawrence College.

She offered Weinstein her cheek to kiss. "Andersonville's filled with good restaurants," she said when he had sat down in a chair across the table, facing her. "This is because of all the gays and lesbians who live in the neighborhood. In the bad old days, when Jews or blacks moved in, people would say, 'There goes the neighborhood.' Now, when gays and lesbians move in, they say, 'Here *comes* the neighborhood.'"

"What do you eat here?" Weinstein asked.

"The omelets are wonderful, never greasy," she said. "So, too, the soups and sandwiches. Everything's very fresh. I'm for an omelet."

After they had ordered, Linda, leaning in, said, "I seem to remember from college days a Greek play, I don't remember which one, where the messenger bearing bad news has his eyes put out."

"Meaning?"

"Meaning that Buddy might not want to hear what you have to tell him about my gentleman friend and me. He may find the news crushing, and despise you for life for bringing it to him. Would you want him to tell you something similar about Elaine?"

"I would hate it," Weinstein said, "but I think I would rather know than not."

"I take it, then, that you don't believe the old adage about what you don't know won't hurt you."

"Lots of things we don't know can hurt us," Weinstein said. "Diseases in your body, fraudulent business practices, a huge pothole ahead in the road. I myself want to know everything, even the worst."

"Would everything include my side of the story?" Linda asked.

"Of course," he said.

"Your friend Buddy and I haven't had sex in almost four years. It's those fucking pills he takes for his depression — or perhaps I should call them those antifucking pills. I don't pretend to speak for you, Philip, but I happen to enjoy sex."

"I like it, too," Weinstein said. "I think it's a great indoor sport. But if someone told me I couldn't bowl or play basketball anymore, I don't think I'd put my marriage in jeopardy because of it."

Their food arrived. The omelets looked great. Weinstein's was with mushrooms and fontina cheese, fried potatoes on the side. The coffee was strong, the cream rich.

"That's what sex is to you, Philip, an indoor sport?"

"I said a *great* indoor sport. I know people risk a lot for it, but, sorry, I don't happen to think it's worth risking an otherwise good marriage. We are talking about spasms here, are we not?"

"Philip Weinstein," Linda said, "you astonish me! You really do. You're a much colder fish than I had ever imagined."

"Cold fish isn't bad," Weinstein said. "Think smoked salmon. Think sturgeon."

Linda's eyes became watery, which Weinstein hadn't expected, and she abruptly excused herself to use the ladies' room. He thought about the preposterousness of this meeting with his best friend's wife, airing his views as he had been doing on sex, friendship, and the rest. None of this was his style. Meeting with Linda was not, he concluded, such a hot idea. What had Weinstein thought would come out of it? An apology? A promise never to betray his friend again? Who was he to exact such a promise? Was the whole thing any of his business? And yet somehow he couldn't turn his back on it.

"Maybe this meeting was a mistake," Linda said after she returned. "I thought I could make you see my side of things. Guess I was wrong."

"I'm glad we met," Weinstein said. "Really."

"So where do things stand?" she asked.

"The truth is, I wish I'd never gone into that damned restaurant in the first place."

"Sounds as if you actually do believe that not knowing at least some things can't hurt you."

"Maybe. Except once you know some things, the world has changed for you, unalterably sometimes."

Weinstein paid the check, and they stepped out onto Clark Street. Linda was parked around the corner, on Balmoral, and he walked her to her tan Mercedes convertible. After she had opened the door, she again offered her cheek.

"Try to remember," she said, "that doing absolutely nothing is also an option."

Weinstein squeezed her arm gently, reassuringly, though he offered no other reassurances, as she slipped behind the wheel of the car. When she pulled away from the curb, it occurred to Weinstein that she might one day break down and tell Buddy about this meeting. The worst thing would be for Buddy to know that he, Weinstein, knew what was going on and had never told him.

Until now Weinstein had said nothing about Linda Berkson and her friend the painter — what was his name, Olevsky? — to his wife. But the subject was so much on his mind that he brought it up that night at dinner, even though he hadn't intended to. Elaine, for some reason, didn't seem at all shocked at the news that Linda was a player. He explained the effects of the antidepressant pills on Buddy's libido.

"What a funny word, libido," Elaine said. "First time I heard it, I thought it was one of the Balaban and Katz movie theaters of our youth. Like, what's playing at the Libido this weekend?"

"I guess that's Buddy's problem," Weinstein said. "Nothing's playing at his libido. But what do you think? Is Linda justified in hunting up a love affair to make up for his deficiency?"

"Lots of people nowadays couldn't even begin to understand why she wouldn't be justified."

"But we're not lots of people. Buddy's not lots of people."

"I'd have to say that it all depends on how other things are going in the marriage," Elaine said. "And marriages, I don't have to tell you, dear husband, are among the most mysterious things in the world. Lots of married couples don't always know what's going on in their own."

"Still, if I were — what the hell's the French phrase? — you know, out of action, would you feel justified in having a love affair?"

"*Hors de combat* is the phrase, sweetie, *hors de combat*. You should have taken French instead of Spanish in high school. So much more useful for discussions like this. The answer is no, I don't think it is justified. If I were in a similar condition — with a grave illness, say — I would expect fidelity from you. But I'm not Linda Berkson, and you aren't Buddy. Incidentally, if you ever are interested in 'a little on the side,' as I believe you boys call it, go ahead and try your luck. But do know that if I catch you at it, you're a dead man."

"Noted," Weinstein said.

"Two things you might consider here," Elaine said. "First, if you tell Buddy, you may lose him as a friend. Bad news, even coming from dear friends, is still bad news, and leaves a sour taste in the mouth. The second thing is that telling him about his wife's love affair might just increase his depression. How couldn't it."

"I've considered both things. But what do I have to gain by telling him?"

"What *you* have to gain isn't really at issue here. But since you bring it up, I suppose all you have to gain is your friend's reinforced knowledge of your loyalty, which, my guess is, he's fairly confident of in any case. The real point, I'd say, is what Buddy gains by such knowledge."

"He gains awareness. And that's a lot. It's one thing to be a cuckold, but another to walk around not knowing you're a cuckold."

"If you really believe that," Elaine said, "then you probably have no choice but to tell Buddy what you know."

"I don't think I have much choice, either," Weinstein said. "But I was hoping you could find a solid excuse for me not to have to do it."

The following Monday, Weinstein called Buddy at work, telling him that he needed to meet with him fairly soon on some important business. He didn't specify. Buddy said that he had a crowded week, but they could meet for a quick lunch on Wednesday, preferably in the neighborhood of his place of business. They settled on Manny's Delicatessen, at noon.

Weinstein hadn't been to Manny's for a long time — since, in fact, several years ago when he was warned that his cholesterol number was in the mid-200s. The restaurant's two large unadorned rooms were filled with bulky customers clearly not there for reasons of social status. Standing near the entrance awaiting Buddy, Weinstein stared down the cafeteria line, at the middle of which a man rhythmically adept with his knife was cutting corned beef, pastrami, and brisket sandwiches of a staggering height. Heavy soups, thick kugels, stroganoffs, and rich brown stews were also on offer. Not a place, Manny's, where one was likely to get a good alphonsino, Weinstein thought.

When Buddy arrived and they took trays and began their way down the line, Weinstein decided to have a corned beef sandwich on a kaiser roll, which came with an enormous latke and a large dill pickle. He picked up a can of diet Dr. Brown's cream soda. Here goes two months' allowance of cholesterol, Weinstein thought. Buddy, who worked out at the East Bank Club before going to the office in the mornings, still looked youthful and in terrific shape, and took a pastrami sandwich, with the latke and pickle, a rice pudding, and a Pepsi for good measure. They found a table near the windows in the second, larger inner room of the restaurant, among beefy cops and many others who had long ago chosen gluttony over pride as their favorite deadly sin.

"So what's your important business?" Buddy asked after they had removed their food from their trays. "Hope you're here to tell me you've found some large loophole that will result in my getting a six-figure refund on my past five years' tax returns."

"Wish I were," Weinstein said. "Nothing so profitable, what I have to say."

"What is it?" Buddy asked.

"Very complicated stuff, Bud, something I've struggled about telling you at all."

"I think I know," Buddy said. "You're leaving Elaine for the man who cuts her hair."

"That would be easier to tell you than what I have to tell you, which is that I caught — I guess caught is the right word — Linda with another man."

Buddy didn't seem moved by the news. He had a mouthful of pastrami. He chewed it slowly, then said: "Was it the painter, this guy Olevsky? If so, I've known about him for the last two months. I've even gone to an exhibition of his work. If he's screwing my wife as badly as he paints, she won't be with him long."

Weinstein didn't know how to respond. "How long've you known about this?" he asked.

"Not from the very beginning, but soon after it got going. I also knew about my wife's affair with the guy from Charles Schwab, the tennis pro at Briarwood, also her psychotherapist, guy name of Leonard Dopkin . . ."

"How did you find out about all this?"

"Initial suspicions. Too much free time unaccounted for. Finding her unreachable too many times during the day. So I hired a detective," Buddy said. "He's building quite a file on the woman I've already begun to think of as the first Mrs. Berkson."

"How come you never mentioned it?"

"Because it's damn embarrassing. Some things you don't want even your best friend to know."

"You have a plan?"

"Yep. To divorce Linda. To see that she leaves the marriage with only her suntan. I would do it now, but Sherri is only sixteen and seeing a therapist as it is, and I don't think she's ready to be put through the stress of a divorce. I can wait. Everything's on my side." Sherri was Buddy and Linda's third and youngest child.

Weinstein wasn't any longer sure whom to feel sorry for: Buddy, who had been cheated on, or Linda, who would before long be crushed by Buddy's revenge. His old friend's taste for retribution was an element in Buddy that Weinstein hadn't known about until now. Doubtless it was a sign of how much he had been hurt by his wife's betrayal. You never know everything about anybody, Weinstein thought. You often don't know even the most important things about them.

"Shouldn't be a total loss, as our people say," Buddy said, "your seeing Linda out with her lousy painter will make you a great witness in a divorce proceeding."

"I'd like to think about that one," Weinstein said.

Weinstein himself, in the glare and clatter of Manny's, felt muddled, rudderless, sad, so much so that in the remaining conversation, in which Buddy set out how he planned his divorce attack on his wife, he neglected to eat more than a few bites of his corned beef sandwich, which he took back to his office in a Styrofoam box.

Back on LaSalle Street, Weinstein told his secretary to hold his calls. At his desk he ate the rest of his sandwich and pondered the strange way the world worked and his own inadequate understanding of it. What, as his dear mother would have said, was any of the Berksons' marital problems his business? But without meaning to, he had made it so. Go then and explain why, after having finished his sandwich, swept the crumbs from his desk into his wastepaper basket, Weinstein found himself calling Buddy to tell him that when the time came he would of course serve as a witness in his divorce case, and for that matter he'd be glad to do anything else required of him. What, after all, are friends for?

Danny Montoya

BAFFLED IN THE large section of the Home Depot devoted to lighting fixtures and bulbs, Jerry Mandel has spent the past six or seven minutes trying to find small frosted 40-watt bulbs for the fixture over his wife's and his bathroom mirror. Finally he asks a young guy with a shaved head and a complicated tattoo on the left side of his neck, wearing an orange Home Depot apron, for help. "Mr. Montoya is the lighting guy," he says. "I'll call him over."

A minute or so later, a short man, dark, bald, chunky, wearing black-framed glasses and with a walk that has a bounce to it, arrives to ask Mandel what he's looking for.

"Sometimes they hide these things pretty effectively," he says after Mandel tells him. "But we'll find 'em for you." The nametag on the pocket of his apron reads "Daniel." Mr. Montoya. Daniel. Daniel Montoya. Danny Montoya. It takes a moment for it all to register.

"Danny! Danny Montoya!" Mandel says. "Are you the same Danny Montoya I played tennis with back in the early fifties at Senn High School?"

"I did play tennis at Senn," he says. "Sorry, but I'm not sure I recognize you."

"That's all right," Mandel says. "These days I often don't recognize myself. I'm Jerome Mandel. Me. Jerry."

As Danny Montoya stares at him, Mandel can see that he still hasn't picked up on his name. "Oh, yeah," Danny says at last. "It's been a long time."

"Only half a century or so." Mandel puts out his hand, and Danny Montoya shakes it. "What've you been doing?"

"Long story," Danny Montoya says. "I've got a break in roughly half an hour. What say I buy you a cup of coffee at the lunch joint at Target next door? We can catch up then."

"I'll meet you there," Mandel says.

"Meanwhile, let's find you those bulbs," says Danny, which he quickly proceeds to do.

Fifty years ago, Jerry Mandel would have traded his life for Danny Montoya's without a second's hesitation. Danny was the number-one-ranked boys-fifteen-and-under tennis player in Chicago and its suburbs. The suburbs are important to mention, because tennis in those days was very much a suburban game, dominated by country club kids with names like Vandy Christie and Gaylord Messick. Nationally, most of the main figures in tennis had names like Gardnar Mulloy and Bill Talbert and Hamilton Richardson, though the two Panchos, Gonzales and Segura, were also on the scene. Like the Panchos, Danny Montoya, too, was everywhere taken for Mexican — or so at least Mandel thought before he first saw him. In fact, Danny's mother was Irish and his father, who worked at the post office, was Filipino. He was a city kid — inner city, we would now say — and played most of his tennis on public courts. His coach was his father.

Danny was small and quick, graceful and savvy, knowing how

to get the most out of his game. He had dazzling footwork and nearly flawless anticipation, so he always seemed in the right place, his Davis racquet perfectly positioned to slap home winners with an ease that encouraged a sense of hopelessness in his opponents, making them wonder if learning how to play tennis in the first place had been such a great idea. He made his half of the court seem no larger than a Ping-Pong table, his opponent's side the size of a football field. He was always in complete control; he never beat himself.

This was in the days before carbon-fiber racquets and tank tops and baseball hats worn backward, and Danny, like everyone else then, wore all-white tennis clothes, which made his dark skin stand out all the more vividly. He had fine features, a winning smile, glistening black hair that he brushed straight back. Mandel remembered Danny standing at the baseline, awaiting service, how he would twist his racquet, sometimes giving it a double flip by slapping it at the grip, the way a cowboy might twirl his pistol before returning it to its holster. He'd shuffle his feet, seeming just a touch bored, and then take a high-bouncing serve and flick it crosscourt with his amazingly accurate backhand or slash it forehand down the line for another winner. Without breaking into a smile, he would do another double flip of his racquet and walk over to take the serve in the ad court.

Haughty didn't describe Danny on the court so much as jaunty. He commanded the court, floating, gliding, seeming to dance — an intricate smooth Latin dance of his own devising — over to whack the ball precisely where he wished. He had textbook-perfect strokes and all the shots, including a drop shot of such delicate deceptiveness that his opponents often never saw it coming, and those who did weren't able to get anywhere near it before it died after a spirit-deflating low bounce. His topspin lobs left opponents at the net feeling pure dejection as they watched the ball sail over their heads. His serve wasn't overpowering but always well placed, and he never double-faulted. He appeared to be without sweat glands; in his combination of nonchalance and authority on the court, he was aristocracy in motion.

Jerry Mandel discovered that he and Danny Montoya were born two months apart, and Mandel, as a boy tournament player who usually went out in the first or second rounds of local competitions, watched Danny with an admiration bordering on worship. Mandel had taken up the sport at thirteen—much too late, as he would discover—and for the next three years found that playing tennis was all he really wanted to do. He longed to be brilliant at it. Mandel was well coordinated, with a strong instinct for imitating style. Sports was all that was on offer when he grew up in West Rogers Park, and like all the boys in the neighborhood, from the age of ten or so he played the current seasonal sport—baseball, football, basketball—and played them reasonably well, but none dazzlingly.

Indian Boundary Park, six blocks from the Mandels' apartment, had four concrete tennis courts, lined up vertically, each enclosed in a chain-link fence, and one day Mandel and his friend Harvey Resnick, who lived a block from the park, walked over to swat a few balls. Mandel didn't own a racquet—this was his first attempt at tennis—and used Harvey's older sister's. They played in gym shoes and jeans.

Mandel wasn't particularly good at the game that day, but he watched some older boys rallying the ball back and forth with smooth powerful strokes and thought this was something he would be able to do. He liked the rhythm of the game, the sound of the ball against the racquet when it was hit solidly in the sweet spot, the clothes, the graceful elegance that went along with playing well. There may also have been an unconscious social motive behind the thirteen-year-old Jerry Mandel's ardor for the game.

Tennis, with its British, Waspy feel, suggested a significant jump from his own lower-middle to the upper-middle class, from the Jewish to the Gentile world.

Harvey and Mandel played a few more times and then Mandel bought a racquet of his own and a pair of Jack Purcell tennis shoes. He would wander down to Indian Boundary on weekends and watch the better adult players. He concentrated on picking up technique: their serving motion, the way they positioned their bodies before striking the ball, the short blocking stroke of the volley. He began to acquire a sense of the angles of the game. He absorbed the chatter—"Let, take two," "Add out," "Too good"—the hand movements, the various ways to pick up a loose ball from the ground with one's racquet without having to bend down for it.

One day early in the summer of his fourteenth year, Mandel took the El to play with a friend on the clay courts of Northwestern University. The clay was a café au lait color, freshly rolled and re-lined every morning by a man who looked as if, in another life, he might have been a hard-drinking naval chief petty officer. In the small clubhouse, where they assigned courts, collected rental fees, strung racquets, and sold equipment, a sign read PRO'S HELPER NEEDED. Mandel inquired about the job. What it entailed was going out with the pro, who was also Northwestern's tennis coach, and collecting the balls he used when he gave lessons to children and housewives. The pay was $1 an hour, and you could use the courts for free, and you got a 10 percent discount on tennis clothes and equipment. Mandel applied for and got the job.

The pro was a heavyset man who in the late 1920s had had a national ranking. He had a gruff voice and a kind heart. Mandel went out with him four or five times a day as he gave his half-hour lessons, collecting the loose balls, picking up what he could from the fairly fundamental instruction: forehand, backhand, volley, half volley, three kinds of serve: American twist, flat drive, slice.

After a few weeks, the pro used Jerry to demonstrate the strokes he taught.

When Mandel wasn't shagging balls and demonstrating strokes, he played with people whose partners were late or failed to show up. Sometimes he hit balls with older guys who played on the Evanston Township High School team. He saved his small earnings and used them to buy a new Jack Kramer model Wilson racquet, a few white Lacoste shirts, tan Fred Perry shorts.

Mandel began to expand his repertoire of shots, hit a harder second serve without too often double-faulting, developed a stronger backhand. Each night he took the El back to Chicago, a fine brown clay dust on his Jack Purcells. Daydreaming, he imagined himself brilliantly winning the fifth and deciding match of the Davis Cup for the United States or playing on Centre Court at Wimbledon. He must also have been undergoing a sexual awakening at this time, but now, in his memory at least, thoughts of tennis crowded out all others.

That same summer Mandel began to play in local tournaments, in the public parks as well as at tennis clubs in Oak Park and River Forest. He didn't have much success. He might win a round or two, but even players of lesser skill than he — who had less stylish strokes, less of a feel for the game — often defeated him. Mandel was too enraptured by his own fantasy of style. He wanted above all to be an elegant player; his opponents were content merely to win.

That summer, too, Jerry Mandel first saw Danny Montoya, of whom of course he had heard; with fewer sports on offer in those days, the Chicago papers covered prep and other junior sports more thoroughly than now. When he saw Danny — in a tournament from which he, Mandel, had been eliminated in the first round at the River Forest Tennis Club — he recognized the game he himself longed to have. Danny had the style Mandel dreamed of, though in Danny's case style didn't keep him from winning.

Danny won that tournament, beating a kid named Esteban Reyes, who had come all the way up from Mexico, 8–6 in the third set. Danny met Reyes at the net, shook his hand cordially, flashed his brilliant smile, and walked over to his father, a small pudgy man, who looked a lot like the Danny Montoya that Mandel had met fifteen or so minutes before at the Home Depot.

Mandel played on his high school tennis team, which was no big deal, for tennis in the Chicago public schools in those years was strictly a minor sport, like fencing or speed skating. The good junior tennis players were at New Trier or Evanston Township or from the western suburb of Hinsdale, where Claire Riessen, the father of Marty Riessen, who was later nationally ranked and would play Davis Cup, was the coach. Mandel played number-four singles in his sophomore year, and most of the kids he played from other schools — Roosevelt, Sullivan, Fenger on the far South Side — wore black sneakers and white gym shorts with their boxer underwear sticking out at the bottom; black socks under Keds were not uncommon. All this was a long way from Centre Court at Wimbledon.

Senn High School had a tennis coach who worked summers as the pro at the River Forest Tennis Club, a tall, white-haired, pink-faced, taciturn man named Major Singleton, known to everyone as Maj. Rumor had it that he had been a young flying ace in World War I. (Mandel's friend Barry Grolnik, in later years trying to describe him to a group of people who hadn't gone to Senn, said, "You have to imagine a Gentile John Wayne.") The coach's own tennis past was a bit unclear, though everyone who played tennis in the Midwest seemed to know Maj Singleton. One afternoon decades later, Mandel heard Tony Trabert, on television, remarking that Stephen Singleton, in the umpire's chair, was the son of Major Singleton, "one of the great gentlemen in the game."

Maj Singleton must have been the reason behind Danny Montoya's transferring from Crane Tech, in the middle of the city, to Senn High School, on the Far North Side, his junior year. The Montoyas lived a few blocks south of Madison near Western Avenue, a tough neighborhood even then, and it may have been that Danny's parents were worried about their son's going to a school where gangs had begun to form and violence was more and more part of daily life for adolescents. Crane had no tennis team but was noted for its black basketball players, one of whom, Leon Hillard, had recently replaced Marques Haynes as the dribbling wizard of the Harlem Globetrotters.

"Jerome," the Maj said to Mandel one day in his office, "Danny Montoya is transferring to Senn. When he arrives, I want you to keep an eye out for him."

"I'll do everything I can, sir," Mandel said. He played tennis for three years for Maj Singleton, and this may have been Maj's longest speech to him, though once, in a doubles match against two kids from Roosevelt wearing brown Keds, he gave Mandel and his partner, a boy named Mickey Hoffner, some advice having to do with the wind; neither of them heard what Maj said, and both were too daunted by him to ask him to repeat it.

Senn High School was roughly 60 percent Jewish, 40 percent working-class Irish, Germans, and Swedes, with six or seven black kids and no Hispanics at all. Mandel didn't think of Danny Montoya as particularly ethnic — the word was not then in use — but chiefly as an amazing athlete. But that morning, even as Maj Singleton introduced them — "Jerome Mandel, Danny Montoya. Jerome here's going to show you around" — Mandel sensed that Danny wasn't going to be happy at Senn.

Danny was wearing rust-colored pants with outer stitching and severely pegged at the cuffs, a shocking-pink shirt with a Mr. B collar (Mr. B being the singer Billy Eckstine, "That Old Black Magic" man), and square-toed blue-suede loafers. His hair was heavily pomaded, and swooped into a duck's ass at the back. The clothes had been bought at Smokey Joe's, a zoot-suitery on

Halsted, off Maxwell Street. If Maj Singleton bothered to notice Danny's clothes, he gave no sign. This getup may have worked among the black kids at Crane Tech, but for Senn every item was wrong.

Mandel used to eat lunch outside, at Harry's, where the more with-it Jewish kids hung out. He didn't fancy taking Danny out there with him, at least not in those duds. He walked him to his first class and told him that he'd meet him for lunch fifth period at the entrance to the school's cafeteria.

In the cafeteria, Mandel asked Danny how things were going.

"OK," he said. "Not bad."

"Anything I can do to smooth the way, let me know. I'm glad you're here."

"Thanks," Danny said. "But do you think I can get something better to eat than this gunk?" He pointed at his lunch tray, which had the sandwich called a sloppy joe on it and some gloppy macaroni and cheese.

"Tomorrow I'll take you to a better place," Mandel said. "Don't be offended, but maybe you aren't wearing exactly the right clothes. We dress a lot more casual here."

"Yeah," Danny said, smiling, "I noticed. I feel as if I'm dressed for maybe the wrong play."

"Where did you get your backhand?" Mandel asked, changing the subject. "I'd kill a guy for your backhand."

"Everything I know about tennis I know from my father," Danny said. "He worked as a locker room valet at a ritzy tennis club in Manila — that's in the Philippines — and picked up the game on his own. He spent a lot of time teaching me, beginning when I was three or four. I've got a brother, Bobby, he's only five now, you should see him. He figures to be a lot better than me."

The next afternoon, Maj Singleton called a practice at Indian Boundary to introduce the team to Danny. Everyone paired up afterward to hit some balls, and Danny and Mandel hit together.

Rallying balls back and forth, Mandel felt himself getting into Danny's rhythm. And how satisfying that rhythm felt! *Whap* went the balls Mandel hit, *pock* came Danny's returns, all right at Mandel, so he scarcely had to move to return the ball to him. *Whap, pock, whap, pock,* Mandel could have stood on that court all night, so fine did he feel rallying with Danny.

When Mandel came to the net, Danny provided him precisely placed lobs so that he could hit practice overheads. He fed him volleys to his forehand and backhand sides. Mandel felt the level of his own game rise just by being on the court with Danny. They played a set, which Danny won, 6–2. Mandel wasn't quite sure how he got the two games, but was very pleased he did. At the end, meeting at the net, Mandel was breathing like someone who had just completed a marathon. Danny was cool and smiling.

On another afternoon, Mandel and Danny played doubles together against two other boys on the team, Tim Ritholz and Dicky Simpson. Danny was the perfect partner, unselfish, backing up Mandel whenever necessary, cheerfully congratulatory whenever he scored a winner. Danny made difficult half volleys look easy. His sense of the angles of the doubles court — and doubles, he taught Mandel without having to say a word about it, was essentially a game of angles, geometry in motion — was unerring. Like all really good athletes, Danny had mastered form and yet was ready to abandon good form when winning the point required it. In the few autumn practices the team had, Mandel, warming up with Danny, playing doubles with him as his partner, felt he was playing well over his head; and it occurred to him that exactly there, over his head, was the best of all places to play.

Mandel and Danny had no classes together, but they met every day for lunch. Mandel never took him to Harry's but instead to other places a little farther from school. Sometimes, when he had the use of his mother's car — a 1953 Chevy Bel Air, cream-colored with green trim — Mandel would drive to Morse Avenue and they would have lunch at Ashkenaz Deli. Danny had long since changed his Smokey Joe's wardrobe and now came to school, like everyone else, wearing Levi's and a V-neck sweater over a white T-shirt. If Danny made any other friends at Senn, he never mentioned them to Mandel; whenever he saw Danny in the halls between classes, he walked alone. The darkness of his skin, made even darker by his long summers on the tennis court, made him a fairly exotic figure. Mandel once asked him if he wanted to meet any girls, and Danny told him thanks, but he already had a steady girlfriend in his neighborhood.

Danny's happiness at Senn wasn't a question Mandel felt he ought to ask about. He wasn't sure Danny had been all that happy at Crane Tech, either; at least he never spoke fondly about missing it. With a Filipino father and a white mother, Danny would always, Mandel supposed, be without any definable group he could easily slip into. What went on in the classroom was of less than minimal interest to him. At their lunches together, Danny and Mandel talked chiefly about sports, girls, offbeat places in the great city in which they had both grown up. Danny never rationed his marvelous smile; his walk had a natural spring to it; he had enormous cordiality. If Danny was unhappy, he kept it to himself.

When the tennis team held one of its autumn practices, Mandel usually drove Danny to the Loyola El station afterward. One night Danny had dinner at the Mandels' apartment, and afterward he drove him home. Dropping Danny in front of his building on South Hoyne, he was reminded of the toughness of the neighborhood in which the Montoyas lived. Mandel had begun reading the popular novels of the day, many of them set in slums: *The Amboy Dukes, A Stone for Danny Fisher, The Hoods, Knock on Any Door,* books that, as he would later understand, eroticized the lives of the poor.

One Saturday afternoon in November, Mandel picked up Danny at his apartment. In the entryway, two mailboxes, sprung from their hinges, hung open. Unappetizing food smells — cabbage maybe — clung to the air. When he rang the bell, Danny came down, wearing a dark brown leather jacket, in which he looked great. He told Mandel that his parents were out back, and they walked around to the rear of the building, where Danny introduced him to his mother and father.

Danny's mother was hanging wash on a line in the concrete backyard. She was shapeless and not wearing any makeup. Her hair was stringy. She wore a gold cross over a housedress. She seemed worn out, though she was probably not much older than forty. She said only that she was pleased to meet Mandel, and went back to hanging her laundry.

Mr. Montoya, who was handing his wife clothespins, stopped to shake Mandel's hand with enthusiasm.

"Nice to meet," he said in choppy English. "Danny tell all about you. How kind you are to him. His mother and I grateful for this."

The neighborhood, which seemed so menacing at night, in daylight turned out to be chiefly dilapidated. Windows on a number of buildings were boarded up. A six-flat on Danny's block had had a fire, and no attempt was apparently being made to repair the damage; the charred ruin just stood there, like a blackened tooth in an already unattractive mouth. A few blocks to the west, across Western Avenue, skid row began, with red-faced drunks wandering the streets.

Danny and Mandel drove two blocks over to Bell Avenue, where Danny's girlfriend, Claire, was waiting for them outside the bungalow that she and her five brothers and sisters lived in with their widowed mother. Her father had been a Chicago cop, killed four years ago, as Danny had earlier explained, in the line of duty while chasing a drug dealer down an alley off Wilson

Avenue on the North Side. Claire went to Immaculata High, was Irish, and Danny's age. She was small, a dishwater blonde, and was wearing jeans and a sweatshirt; young as she was, there was already something a little tired-looking about her eyes, or so Mandel thought.

The three of them drove to Maxwell Street. The day was crisp and sunny. Maxwell Street was humming. Older men grabbed their arms, telling them that terrific bargains were to be had inside their dark clothing shops. Carts in the middle of the street were loaded with fake Zippo lighters, neckers' knobs for steering wheels, playing cards with blurrily photographed naked women on them, eight-battery flashlights, French ticklers. A butcher sold live chickens. An ancient-looking black woman was seated on a kitchen chair hovering over a blanket on which she displayed dishes, some of them chipped, that she offered for sale. A Gypsy family sat before its doorway, hawking fortunetelling and suggesting that more than mere fortunes could be obtained within. The smell of fried onions and Polish sausages on the open-air vendors' grills suffused everything.

Danny, as always, seemed completely at ease. He bopped along with his jaunty walk, very much with the show, laughing at the young black guy who stopped him in the hope of selling him a gaudy wristwatch. Claire, less confident, clung to Danny's arm. Mandel didn't say much to her after Danny introduced them. He felt she looked on him as a rich (by her standard, anyway) Jewish boy from the Far North Side, possibly slumming, which, though he preferred not to think so, he may well have been doing.

Danny bought Claire a necklace with a St. Christopher medal. They walked to Roosevelt Road, where Mandel showed Danny that he could get Florsheim plain-toed cordovans, factory seconds, for $10 at a place called Wolinsky and Levy. They stopped for hot dogs at the Vienna Sausage outlet store on Halsted. They looked at the wild clothes on display in the windows at Smokey

Joe's. On the drive home, the three of them sitting in the front seat — this was before the age of bucket seats — Claire fell asleep on Danny's shoulder, continuing to clutch his arm. "She's not been feeling so good lately," he told Mandel.

Danny Montoya never actually played for Senn. A week or so after the Christmas vacation he didn't show up at his and Mandel's usual meeting place for lunch. The next week Mandel asked Maj Singleton if he knew anything about Danny's absence. The Maj told him that Danny had decided not to return to Senn, but said nothing more. Mandel was disappointed but not completely surprised. Danny had no known social life at the school apart from him, which, for a naturally gregarious kid, must not have been easy. He got no real coaching from Maj Singleton, nor did he need any. Maybe he just became bored with the long bus and El rides up and back to school.

Mandel felt he ought at least to call Danny to ask what was going on. His father's name (Gustavo Montoya) was in the book. He twice left messages with Danny's mother, and only a week or so later did Danny call back.

"Jerry," he said. "Got your message. What's up?"

"Nothing much. What's up with you?"

"It's complicated," he said. "I'm getting married. Two weeks from next Saturday. Claire's pregnant."

Mandel didn't know what to say. Congratulations, maybe? God, how terrible, maybe? He felt a combination of pity for Danny's situation and a touch of admiration for his entering adulthood so calmly. Mandel asked Danny if he was planning on going back to school anywhere else.

"Don't think so," Danny said. "Nothing much there for me. School's not my best game. Don't think I'll miss it much. I've got a job. I'm working at Claire's uncle Matt's grocery right now till something better turns up. Gotta run. Stay in touch, OK?"

They didn't stay in touch. Once married and working for a living, Danny, Mandel assumed, must have quit tennis, because his name no longer appeared in the papers in connection with local tennis tournaments that spring and summer or anytime thereafter. Danny slipped prematurely into an adult world, and Mandel was allowed to remain a boy for another five or six years, still searching for the perfect backhand, which he never found. He never learned what became of Danny, and though he may have had a stray thought or two about him over the years, Danny otherwise disappeared from his mind, until twenty-five or so minutes ago when he saw him working the floor at the Home Depot.

Mandel arrived at Target first. Then Danny came over; under the orange Home Depot apron he'd shed, he had on a pair of khakis and a blue polo shirt. His hair, unlike Mandel's, is still dark but thin in front. Mandel searches for the face of the boy in the man, but has difficulty finding it. Danny, he notes, seems to be doing the same to him.

"Can I get you a coffee? A hot dog or something?" Danny asks.

"A coffee will be great," Mandel says.

"Maybe I'll have just a coffee, too," Danny says, touching his paunch.

"It took me a minute or two to bring you back to mind," he says when they return to the table with their coffees. "You went out of your way to be nice to me during the time I transferred to Senn. I don't think I ever thanked you for that."

"More like I was sucking up to you," Mandel says. "I admired tremendously the way you played tennis. I can still picture you, like Muhammad Ali, floating like a butterfly, stinging like a bee. You were amazing."

The man across from Mandel flashes that great smile and something of the boyish Danny Montoya returns. "I had a few good moments back then. Tennis was the only game our old man let my brother Bobby and me play. Baseball, football, basketball, everything else he put off-limits. Concentrate on one sport, he used to say; be really good at one thing. He wasn't someone you defied. Not in those days anyhow. You still play?"

"I stopped not long after high school. My ambition was a lot greater than my talent, and since I could never shake off the ambition, I just quit playing."

"What do you do? I mean for a living," Danny asks.

"I teach biology," Mandel said, "at Loyola University. I mainly teach future high school biology teachers."

"Where did you get an interest in biology?"

"From not getting into medical school, to tell the brutal truth. After not being accepted to med school, I graduated from the University of Illinois with a degree in zoology. Having nothing better to do at the time, I went on to get a couple more degrees in the subject. But what about you? What've you done all these years?"

"I've mostly been a salesman. I was seventeen when my first daughter was born. Claire and I had three kids, all daughters. I nearly drowned in estrogen. Did you ever meet Claire, my wife? She died two years ago, lung cancer."

"I met her once," Mandel says, thinking it not worth reminding Danny of their day on Maxwell Street. "I'm sorry she's dead."

"Anyhow, after a bunch of odd jobs, I got into selling cars. Then I worked at selling home improvements, which I did for more than thirty years. I did all right at it. I'm semiretired. I'm working here at Home Depot part time. I live with my second daughter, Jackie, in Buffalo Grove. She's divorced with four kids of her own. I help out a little, financially and with babysitting. I have a daughter fifty-two years old. Jesus! Tell me, please, how the hell that happened."

Mandel fills Danny in on his own family life, his two sons and his five grandchildren, his two marriages.

"Do you ever think about tennis?" Mandel asks Danny. "Do you ever play it? Do you watch it on television?"

"I don't think about it or play it or watch it."

"You were really good, you know, amazingly good."

"Nice to hear that, but if you think about it, there wasn't anyplace for me to go with it. If I'd come along twenty or thirty years later, maybe my father would have sent me to one of those professional tennis camps where they take kids at seven or eight years old. Maybe then things would have been different. But I probably got about the most out of the game I could. I was never a hard hitter. I could never have been a big-time player."

"I recently read a book by an English mathematician," says Mandel, a little worried about sounding pretentious, academic, "who, attempting to justify his own career in mathematics, says that only a tiny minority of people can do anything really well. When you were out on the tennis court you qualified as one of those people."

"It wasn't a very important thing to do," Danny says. "It was tennis, only a game."

"That it was just a game doesn't matter. I've never come close to doing anything in my entire life as well as you played that game."

"Come on! You teach at a college. I'll bet you were a pretty good father, right? That's not nothing. I'm a lot prouder of my daughters than I am of winning a few tennis trophies when I was a kid."

"There're lots of good fathers, good husbands, good teachers. But I never saw anyone fly over a tennis court as beautifully and happily in command of things as you."

"Forgive me for saying so, Jerry," Danny says, "but I wonder if maybe you're not laying it on a little thick. You're not planning to sell me life insurance before I get up from this table, are you? You wouldn't try to sell an old salesman, would you?" He flashed the great smile.

"All I'm saying is that for a brief stretch of time you belonged to a small but elite club of people who did something magnificently well. Maybe it didn't have world-shaking significance, but it was pretty damn rare."

"Sorry, but I don't quite see the point," Danny says, glancing at his watch. "Hey, I better get back to work." He stands up and drains off what is left in his coffee cup.

The two late-middle-aged men walked the sixty or so yards from Target back to the Home Depot.

"Good to run into you," Danny says.

"Same here," Mandel says. They shake hands. Neither says anything about getting together again.

Driving home, Mandel realizes that what he couldn't get across to Danny is that, though his life has been easier than Danny's, though most people might think the work he does is more useful, Danny, for a few brief years, because of his magical talent, was able to soar, while his, Mandel's, life, lucky though it has been in many ways, has been spent entirely on the ground.

That night, his wife asleep beside him, Mandel lies on his back and tries to put all his problems out of mind: small money worries, squabbles in the department at the university, the news that his grandson may be dropping out of Yale because of depression.

Mandel is back at Indian Boundary Park, where he is sixteen and playing doubles with Danny Montoya as his partner. The sun is high in the sky, the grass outside the courts is dark green and dewy after a light rain, the balls make a crisp sound coming off the strings of their wooden racquets. The partners work a complex switching maneuver at the net that sets Mandel up for an easy overhead smash. Out on that court Danny Montoya's skill has, somehow, rubbed off on Mandel. His strokes are wonderfully smooth and his shots deadly accurate; he can make the white tennis balls do anything he wants. "Good serve, Jerry," Danny says, smiling as he looks back from his position at the net after Mandel has served an ace, *pow!,* straight down the center service-court line. Danny double-flips his racquet, walks over to the deuce court, crouching, a few feet behind the net. "Do it again, kid," Danny says, looking briefly over his shoulder. And Mandel does it again, and again and again, over and over, again and again. Even in the midst of this dream, he realizes he is dreaming, and already feels a tinge of regret that he will have to wake.

Under New Management

I WAS IN EIGHTH GRADE, and because it was raining that afternoon I didn't hang around the schoolyard playing softball as usual but came straight home. My mother was out shopping. The phone rang. "Is this the home of Marty Abrams?" a man with a gruff voice asked. I said Marty Abrams was my father, but he wasn't in at the moment. "Tell that son of a bitch that Jim Shanahan called," the man said, "and if he doesn't give me back my four hundred bucks for his piece of shit car, I'll kill him."

Just before dinner, I told my father about the call, leaving out the "son of a bitch" and "piece of shit" parts. He smiled.

"Aren't you worried about this guy's threat, Dad?" I asked.

"Nope," my father said. "I see it as a chance to take back the car and put him into an eight-hundred-dollar one."

This was in the early 1950s, which will explain the prices. What isn't so easily explained is my father's high spirits. In those days, they were invariably high. Had he gone to a psychotherapist, who knows, he might have been diagnosed as borderline manic. I myself think he was just an optimist. When he heard the word "no" from a customer, however emphatic or repeated, he took it only to mean "not yet."

My father never had more than fifteen cars scrunched into his sixty-feet-across-the-front used-car lot on Broadway, between Thorndale and Ardmore. The office felt overcrowded with only him in it. He would have done OK except that he had no talent for keeping anything resembling careful books, let alone paying his taxes on time. If it wasn't an irate customer calling, it was the IRS or the Illinois Department of Revenue. My father fended them all off cheerfully. He didn't live long enough to hear the phrase "no problem" come into vogue, but if he had, he might have used it as a personal motto. For him, nothing seemed to be a problem.

He used to say that his best piece of luck was finding my mother. He adored her. She was beautiful and goodhearted and, as I only later came to understand, had a wonderfully even temperament. He was always bringing home flowers and boxes of candy; she had a weakness for the chocolate-covered orange peels made in Chicago by the Dutch Mill Company. With a pal named Izzy Levinson, who ran a pawnshop on the edge of the Loop, my father arranged complicated swaps that occasionally yielded diamond earrings or tennis bracelets or pearl necklaces. "Genuine simulated mother-of-pearl," I remember him saying once, with a wink in my direction as he fastened a clasp around my mother's long and slender neck.

She loved him. He was good-looking, with black hair and blue eyes, the graceful muscles of a former athlete — in his youthful glory days he'd played shortstop for Midland Motors in the Windy City softball league — and a great smile and spirit of adventure. I never heard them argue. Who knows how many times my father's wild schemes, frequent job changes, and gambling nature sent her to bed filled with anxiety? But so far as I know she never complained. She listened raptly to his accounts of the cupidity and transparent slyness of his customers. She always spoke of him, in the way all husbands wish to be spoken of, with a combination of deep affection and unshakable respect.

✳ ✳ ✳

We lived in a one-bedroom apartment in a courtyard building on Sheridan Road, between Lunt and Greenleaf. My parents gave me the bedroom, and they slept on a studio couch in the living room. The small bathroom had a tub but no shower. Ida Kaplan, a sister of the former welterweight champion Barney Ross, and her husband, Irv, lived across the courtyard. A family named Glick, second cousins to the comedian Morey Amsterdam, lived in the apartment beneath us. A furrier named Max Fineman, who had a gap between his front teeth and a beaming smile, lived upstairs with his blond wife, Pearl.

In her late thirties my mother was found to have breast cancer. My father borrowed a few thousand dollars from friends and took her on a shopping spree — a vote of confidence that she would beat the disease. Max Fineman let him have a mink jacket at cost. My mother lived less than a year. Her last weeks were the first time I ever saw my father look defeated by life.

I was fifteen when my mother died. I won't go into the pain I felt. We never talked about this, my father and I, but I knew that his desolation couldn't have been less than my own. My mother's sister Florence and her husband, Ben, a dentist, suggested that I come live in Highland Park with them and their two daughters, one my age, one five years younger. My father didn't go for it. He didn't much like his brother-in-law. "He's a safe player, your uncle Ben. He's made a lot of dough, sure, but look what he had to do to get it. Dig around in people's mouths. He's a small-advantage man, the kind of guy who shifts his savings account from one bank to another in order to get a free electric blanket. I hope you don't ever come to think that's any way for a man to live."

Without my mother around, our life lost not only the softening feminine note but what we nowadays call structure, though we did keep to an odd regularity of our own devising. By then my father had given up his used-car lot and was working for an outfit called Royal Lumber, selling roofing, siding, and garages, chiefly to Czech and Polish families on the Far Northwest Side. Most of his calls were made in the early evening. He left me money to eat out or bring something home. On nights when he had no potential clients to see we had dinner together, usually at Ashkenaz Deli on Morse Avenue, with its great clatter of dishes, talk of deals being made, and, on the walls, signed glossy photos of Shecky Greene, Jack E. Leonard, Shelley Berman, and Jerry Vale.

I suppose some people must have felt sorry for me. I missed my mother a lot, but I also liked the freedom of being by myself most evenings. Besides, my father was usually home by nine-thirty or ten. Mornings he woke me for school, made breakfast, and sent me off with a peanut-butter-and-jelly or salami sandwich, a piece of fruit, and my allowance for the day. He put another bed in the apartment's single bedroom and we slept there together.

He did his best to keep up a respectable housekeeping standard. We made it a rule never to leave the apartment without making our beds; no dirty dishes were allowed to pile up in the sink for more than a day; a black woman named Emma Simpkin came in to clean every second Tuesday. I did the shopping, what little there was of it — orange juice, milk, bread, butter, eggs, canned soups and tuna, fruit, sandwich makings from the Kroger's on Morse Avenue — and every five or six days I would run down to the basement to toss in a load of laundry.

When it came to school I was an uninterested student, and my father was an equally uninterested parent. He hardly looked at the C's and occasional D's on my report cards before signing them. He had barely gotten through Marshall High School — he found it excruciatingly boring — and going to college in the teeth of the Depression was never a serious option. School was for dentists like his brother-in-law Ben or for what he called bullshit lawyers.

I waited up every night for my father to return from his calls and, as my mother must have done, sat with him while he ate and told me about customers or new leads. He had endless stories about the tricks salesmen would pull to close a deal. A guy named Wesley Demanos, for example, with whom he had gone to high school, was in the television repair business. He used to offer free roofing estimates, then, once up on the roof, his men would break the television antenna; the next day he would send a different salesman offering a low rate on new antennas. The name Wesley Demanos stuck in my mind; twenty or so years later, he turned up as the sole owner of the Milwaukee Bucks.

From my father's stories there emerged the picture of an amusing but slightly dangerous world. Sharks, wolves were out there; I mustn't let this frighten me, but I mustn't ever forget it, either. Proceed carefully was his implicit message. Oddly, he never suggested that the world was divided between winners and losers and that I had better decide which I wanted to be. Nor did he brag about his own prowess as a salesman. It's possible, I suppose, that he really put the screws to some guy in a bungalow in Jefferson Park, or lashed a widow to five years of installment payments, or padded a bill on a black family in Brownsville. I don't really know; I prefer to think he never did.

He did talk a lot about the disorder, financial and otherwise, in so many of the lives he came in contact with. We talked about politicians (they were all crooks, some worse than others). We talked about money (very good to have, but plenty of things not worth doing for it). We talked about sports. He used to take me to the Golden Gloves at Marigold Arena, and one night we went to the Chicago Stadium to see Ezzard Charles quickly KO a local heavyweight with a glass jaw named Bob Satterfield. We had seats fifteen or so rows from ringside, and I remember how many of the old-timers seated around us seemed to know my father; most of them, remembering his softball days, called him Lefty.

One of the things my father and I never talked about was women. When I was sixteen, he said he assumed I was already too old for him to fill me in on the birds and the bees. "You know that old joke, don't you, Artie?" he said. As a salesman, he knew all the jokes. "It's the one where the Polish count is walking around his estate with his fourteen-year-old son. And he says to the boy that it's time he learned about the birds and the bees. 'You remember, André,' the count says, 'what we did last week with those two beautiful peasant girls we met on this path? You should know that the birds and the bees do it, too.'" That was it for the subject of sex, which was fine with me.

My father never spoke of the sadness or disappointments in his life, and only once, two or so years after her death, did he say he missed my mother. He was forty-one when she died. He was an attractive man. I had no idea whether he was seeing women; if he was, it must have been during the day, because he always came home at night and never failed to make my breakfast and see me off to school. Not that I would have minded; the subject just never came up.

I was in my senior year when, one afternoon, returning from school, I found a note from my father on the kitchen table. "Come to Miller's at 7:00. Someone I want you to meet."

Miller's was a steak house on Lunt and Western. Fred Miller, the owner, had sold furnaces and air-conditioning systems until he made enough to start a business of his own. He did so well that he bought this restaurant, which gave him, a bachelor, a place to go in the evenings to see his pals. A small man, bald, with rimless glasses, Fred Miller had what my father called "the touch." He used to bet the daily double, using combinations that added up to thirteen, and won a disproportionately large number of times. My father never showed the least envy of Fred Miller and his great good luck. Envy didn't seem to be in my father's makeup.

Miller's had an air of prosperity about it, its parking lot filled with Fleetwood Cadillacs, Buick Roadmasters, Chrysler Imperials, Olds 98s. My father's own taste ran to flashy cars. At the time, he was driving a year-old Oldsmobile Starfire convertible with a red and white paint job.

As I came into the restaurant that evening, Marcy, the hostess, sexy in an I've-been-around-the-block sort of way, showed me toward the back. There was my father, leaning across the table and talking earnestly to a dark-haired woman, her chin resting in her hand, who seemed to be listening to him with amusement.

"Artie," my father said as I approached the table, "there's someone I want you to meet. Suzanne, this is my son, Arthur. Arthur, meet Suzanne Chang."

"How nice to meet you," she said. "Your father talks about you all the time."

"Sit down, kid," my father said. "Sit down. We didn't order till you got here. Hungry, I hope."

Was this woman a customer of my father, now a salesman for something called SeeThrough Awnings? Her saying that my father spoke about me all the time suggested a longer acquaintance. Suzanne Chang looked to be roughly my father's age — that is, in her middle forties. Her Chinese features were refined, elegant in a slightly severe way: high cheekbones, a solid chin, good teeth, small ears, black eyes that seemed not to miss much.

Before dinner, she grilled me lightly, like the steaks at Miller's. What was I studying in school? What was I reading? Did I know any foreign languages? ("Spanish," I said in answer to this one, failing to add that I knew it only at the level of *El burro es un animal importante.*) Where did I intend to go to college? What did I want to do with my life?

Until then I hadn't thought very much about any of these questions. I assumed that I would go to college, maybe the University of Illinois at Navy Pier or possibly Wright Junior College. As for what I wanted to do with my life, I hadn't a clue. I said I thought I might become, like my father, a salesman. (His only advice to me on the matter of occupation had been to do something I loved, as he loved closing deals.) To my ears, everything I said sounded forced and unconvincing.

She was, I later learned, Mrs. Suzanne Chang, divorced, no children, the daughter of a man who in his day had had the license to sell all the Philip Morris cigarettes in Mainland China. Her parents had sent her, their only daughter, to a finishing school in Geneva. When Mao and the Communists took over, her parents and her two older brothers were killed, and she was forced to evacuate to Taipei, where she lived with an uncle and aunt until her marriage. Following the divorce, she lived in London for a while, then moved to Chicago and obtained American citizenship. She spoke an educated English without any trace of a Chinese accent.

Lest I look too crude, I did not order my usual that night at Miller's, the full slab of ribs; in front of Suzanne Chang, I didn't want to eat with my hands. Instead I had a strip steak and listened closely to make out what I could about the relationship between this woman and my father.

He did most of the talking, saying that he suspected he would soon need to find a new job. SeeThrough Awnings were selling well enough, but the place, my father felt, was badly run. The owner, a man named Morty Schulman, had begun to buy stakes in prizefighters, and guys from the Syndicate were occasionally spotted on the premises. The whole operation seemed very shaky.

Suzanne Chang was a salesman, too — of real estate. "You're really selling the women," I recall her saying. "The key is to direct your attention to the men but always watch the eyes of the women." My father said he thought real estate would be too slow for him; he preferred quicker action, bang, in and out, close that same night.

A woman with a natural formality, Suzanne Chang called my father Martin, a new one on me: to everyone else he was Marty or Lefty. She paid the most careful attention to everything he said. Although their conversation was mainly shoptalk, I wasn't in the least bored by it. After dinner the three of us walked out to the parking lot. Suzanne Chang was tall, maybe five foot seven, which, in her heels, made her roughly the same height as my father. He hugged her lightly before she got into a black Lincoln. "Goodbye, Arthur," she said to me. "I hope we shall meet again with a chance to talk much more." She blew a kiss to my father as she drove off.

Back in our apartment, my father and I went through our nightly ritual. We had some coffee, listened to the ten o'clock news, washed and dried the breakfast dishes. Only afterward, in our beds, with the lights out, did I ask, "What's with you and Mrs. Chang, Dad? Is she a business acquaintance or something more?"

"Something more. Actually, she's a lot more. We're thinking about getting married, Artie."

"How come?" I asked.

"Because," my father said, "she's an attractive woman. She's very smart. And I think maybe it wouldn't be such a bad thing for the two of us to have the regular company of a woman. It'll civilize us a little, if you know what I mean."

At that instant I felt a gate close on our life together. I also made the decision right then to go away to school, to the University of Illinois in Champaign, where they had to take state residents no matter how poor their grades in high school. I didn't want to live with my father and Suzanne Chang, or with him and any other woman. I wanted him to myself, at least to the extent that I had had him to myself since the death of my mother. Let him see all sorts of women, sleep with the lot of them if he wanted, but I didn't understand the need to bring one permanently into our lives.

"You all right with this?" my father asked in the dark. "I think you'll come to like Suzanne a lot. Give her a chance, kid."

"Sure, Dad," I said.

"Sleep well, kiddo," my father said. But I didn't.

Roughly four months later, in the study of a compliant Reform rabbi on Pratt Avenue, with me as best man, my father and Suzanne Chang married. The following day I went off to the University of Illinois and they took a two-week honeymoon in Hawaii. Earlier Suzanne had found a spacious three-bedroom apartment on Pine Grove, off Lake Shore Drive, four or so blocks east of Wrigley Field. One of the bedrooms, Suzanne instructed me, was mine, to furnish as I wished. I had helped them move into the new apartment and done my best at feigning pleasure in their happiness. I really wanted to like her, if only for my father's sake.

While I was away my first year of college, coming home only for Thanksgiving and Christmas and spring breaks, my father left SeeThrough Awnings and started a real estate agency with his new wife. They opened an office on Fullerton, near Lincoln Avenue. Suzanne did the inside work, which meant the details, my father most of the actual selling. She must have taught him patience, because he soon became terrific at moving real estate. Occasionally, when an especially good thing came on the market, they bought it for themselves.

"*Tsigl,*" my father said to me, "Yiddish for brick, kid. The old

Jews used to say that brick, by which they meant real estate, was better than diamonds, cash, stock, or any other form of wealth. *Tsigl* remains *tsigl*. It stays in place. Everything else fluctuates."

Along with his work and his address, my father's wardrobe had also changed. He used to go around in slightly emphatic sport jackets, with gray trousers, tasseled loafers, colorful ties. Now he wore only gray or blue suits, white shirts, dark ties with subdued patterns, black shoes with a raised line running across the toe. He began having his nails manicured. When I remarked on his nails one night at dinner, he smiled and nodded toward Suzanne. "I'm under new management, kid," he said.

The two of them branched out from sales into management. When the owner of a sixty-eight-apartment building on the corner of Sheridan and Glendale went bankrupt, they bought the building at a distressed price. This was the time in Chicago when condominium fever was kicking in, and after doing minimal rehab, they turned the apartments into condos and made out handsomely. They proceeded to buy two other large buildings — one on Marine Drive, the other on Cornell Avenue in Hyde Park — evidently making a nice bundle on these, too. Under his second wife's management, my father was becoming a wealthy man.

I worked hard at my freshman-year classes, if only to avoid humiliating myself by flunking out. The feeling that failure would have made me seem disgraceful in Suzanne's eyes may have been an added impetus. In time I found that I wasn't bad at school; I even enjoyed it. In my senior year I wrote a thesis in sociology with the title "The Ethos of the Modern American Salesman." The professor for whom I wrote it was so pleased by it that he offered to arrange a fellowship for me to stay at Illinois and do graduate work under his supervision. But I decided that I wanted to become a high school teacher, and I turned him down.

Home in Chicago was no longer an apartment on Pine Grove but rather a co-op on the tenth floor of 3920 North Lake Shore Drive, overlooking the Outer Drive and Waveland golf course. My father was more and more preoccupied with his deals.

Suzanne and I grew no closer, though we never argued. What I took to be her air of superiority began to get on my nerves. During semester break in my junior year, she had asked me what courses I would be taking in the spring semester. "Interesting," she said after I had told her, "but you know, when I was a girl of fifteen, in Switzerland, we read Montaigne, Molière, Montesquieu, Madame de Staël, Benjamin Constant. All in French, of course."

Suzanne and my father were no longer salesmen or managers but now officially known as developers. Along with rehabilitating old buildings and selling them as condos, they had put up a cluster of new houses in Buffalo Grove, one of the new suburbs beyond O'Hare Airport, and another in the southwest suburb of Oak Lawn. The money, I assumed, was rolling in.

I was home less and less, but when I was around I noticed that my father talked a lot about stocks and Treasury notes and government bonds. He and Suzanne had a full-time maid. They were thinking of acquiring a large summer place on Lake Geneva in Wisconsin. Marty was now permanently Martin, and Lefty was long gone. I missed those guys.

When we were alone, my father and I still spoke about some of the same old things: the pennant race in the National League, or the Bears, for whose home games he had acquired excellent season tickets. But his mind was elsewhere, or so I felt — in Buffalo Grove, maybe. No longer a man who took things as they came, he had become a man who checked the progress of his investments at the end of the day. Who knows, he may have gone off to sleep figuring his net worth, which by then must have been well into the millions. I had to wait until my twenties to acquire a father like everyone else's: a man distracted, concentrated on moneymaking, with less and less sense of the everyday adventurousness of life. I blamed Suzanne Chang for that.

In fairness, if my father was pulling away from me, so, without meaning to, I was doing the same from him. Around the time that my father and Suzanne acquired their townhouse on Astor Street, I rented an apartment in Hyde Park, on Dorchester, to be near the atmosphere of the University of Chicago, for I was thinking of going to graduate school, and within striking distance of the high school where I was teaching history.

On a summer evening during a Shakespeare festival at the university's outdoor Court Theatre, I spotted Suzanne with two other women. She introduced me as her stepson — always a cold word, I thought then, and still do.

"My father with you?" I asked.

"He's at home," she said, adding, "*The Tempest* is not for Martin."

Sorry, but no *Tempest* for you, Dad, I thought. If my father was even aware of his wife's condescension, he didn't seem to mind. Much as I wished it were otherwise, I couldn't help recognize how much he loved this woman. She had channeled his energies, made him a rich man. But what he felt toward her wasn't anything like gratitude. He was just pleased to be around her, pleased that she had chosen him for a husband. He was nuts about her.

I sometimes wondered if my father still thought of my mother, who loved him without qualification and saw no need to put him under any management whatsoever. My mother was gentle and beautiful, while Suzanne was hard-edged and handsome. With her new wealth, she carried herself as if she were an empress; her name began to appear among the heavy contributors to local cultural institutions — the Art Institute, the Chicago Symphony. I began to think of her as Madame Chiang Kai-Abrams.

✳ ✳ ✳

A year or so after this meeting, my father called to inform me that he had just received a diagnosis of prostate cancer, already in an advanced stage. I gulped when he told me. I didn't know what to say. My father always seemed invincible. Although I was seeing less and less of him, I wasn't ready to handle the world without knowing he was there in the background if I needed him.

"Some things we need to talk about, kid," he said. When I asked if Suzanne would be along, he said, "No, just the two of us. How about tomorrow? You know the Tavern Club? 333 North Michigan. Noon OK?"

When I arrived the next day, a woman at the desk said that my father was waiting in the bar.

"How go things, kiddo?" my father said, coming forth to shake my hand. Not yet sixty, he was still handsome, still had a full head of dark hair, still carried himself well, with no sign of the deadly disease inhabiting his body.

"I'm fine, Dad," I said. "What about you? How're you feeling?"

"Apart from dying I'm in pretty good shape," he said. "You know this joint?"

He gave me a brief tour, the best part of which was a room done in red wallpaper with, my father explained, two famously fake Matisse paintings on the entrance wall. I was a little surprised to learn that my father knew the name Matisse. The windows looked straight down Michigan Avenue to the north, with a grand view of the Wrigley Building, the Tribune Tower, and all the shops along what a real estate operator named Arthur Rubloff once dubbed the Magnificent Mile.

"Some magnificence," my father said. "It's just about money, and money isn't always that magnificent. Sometimes it isn't even a lot of fun. You always have to be watching over the goddamn stuff, making sure it's producing on its own, that someone isn't making a tenth of a percentage point more than you, which leaves you feeling like a schmuck. This is not a problem I expected to have."

"Most people would call it a happy problem, Dad."

"One of life's little surprises, kid. This cancer is only the latest. The way the doctors talk about it, it might also be my last surprise."

"The prognosis is bad?"

"Using my best high-pressure methods, I got the oncologist at Rush to handicap my chances of survival at twenty-to-one against. For Suzanne's sake I've agreed to put myself through the full chemo treatment. But what I really wanted to talk with you about now is money."

"It's not a subject I know a lot about," I said.

"Here's all you need to know: I'm holding, as they used to say at the track when I was a kid. I'm a rich man — that is, Suzanne and I together are rich. At the moment we're rich mostly on paper. In the neighborhood of roughly twenty-five million, but most of it is tied up in development deals still in the works. I take it you have no interest in going into the real estate business."

"None."

"You'll have to work all this out with Suzanne, 'cause if I die within the next six months or so it would be unfair to her and all that we have going on to pull out my half of the business to pay over to you. That's the way things are divided: half of what I'm worth goes to her, half to you. But it's all corporate and complicated, and you'll probably need a very smart and expensive lawyer to work through the details. Meanwhile, do I have your word that you'll be patient?"

"Of course. But I'd much rather you stayed alive than I get to worry about what to do with your money."

"I take it you're not too crazy about Suzanne, even though she's the one really responsible for your one day becoming a rich man."

"It shows?"

"Never try to sell an old salesman, kid. Suzanne noted it right off. Her thought was that you didn't want her replacing your mother."

"Closer to the truth to say that I didn't want her to take you away from me. When she came into your life, I sort of dropped out of it."

"You never lost me, Artie. I'm proud of you, kid. I think, though, maybe you've been too tough on Suzanne. Cut her some slack. Remember that they murdered her family in China. She's been through a lot more than both of us put together."

"I've thought about all this, Dad, believe me I have."

"What she saw in me I still don't know," my father said. "But I'm glad she saw what she did. Without her, I'd probably be selling air conditioning to Eskimos. I've been damn lucky in my two wives, Artie."

We went through the rest of our lunch together as if my father weren't being stalked by death. We talked about our food, about sports, even about his new business deals, as if a long future lay before him. He was making it easy on me, diverting me from the only subject that was on both our minds. On the street, I offered him a ride home, but he said he'd rather walk. We're not huggers, my father and I, and we didn't hug there on the sidewalk. We shook hands. He didn't have to tell me that he loved me, nor I that I loved him. We both knew.

"Stay in touch, kid," he said. He pulled up the collar of his double-breasted blue cashmere overcoat, belted in the back. He looked great in it, I thought, watching him walk into the wind as he crossed the bridge over the Chicago River.

The next day, I called Suzanne at the office. "My father told me about his cancer yesterday," I said. "He also said he promised to undergo chemotherapy because you want him to. I'd be grateful if you released him from that promise."

"Why?" she asked.

"Because I love him," I said, "and I don't want him to suffer."

"I love him, too," she said, "as much as you do. I want him to live a lot longer. He is still not an old man, your father, and he is my husband."

"He tells me the odds are strongly against a cure."

"Whatever they are, they are better than nothing."

"Not if he has to spend his last days suffering."

"Forgive me," she said, "but I have another call I must take," and she hung up. Which I took to mean, Sorry, Charley, case closed, you lose. Thank you, Suzanne. Bitch.

My father went through a stringent regimen of chemotherapy and died in three rather than the five or six months he had mentioned at our lunch at the Tavern Club. He had the death we all live in terror of, ending up hairless, weighing less than a hundred pounds, tubes stuck into him every which way, lying in a cold white hospital room attended by strangers. This particular tempest, I thought looking down on him, I wished Martin had been able to avoid.

Toward the end, the last week or so, Suzanne and I took shifts at the hospital—I during the day, she at night—sitting beside his bed. His final three days he was in a coma. On a sunny May afternoon, a Wednesday, a great closer was closed by an even greater closer. I called Suzanne at her office to tell her. She gasped, then I heard her begin to weep just before she hung up the phone.

At the cemetery, Suzanne and I stood together in the sunshine over my father's grave. Long ago he had acquired three plots: one for my mother, one for him, and one for me. Standing at the graveside, listening to a rabbi who never knew my father intoning Kaddish, I heard Suzanne sob quietly. This was the moment when I should have put my arm around her shoulder, or at least clasped her hand in mine, but I was unable to do either. She loved my father, I knew that, just as I knew he loved her. What did it matter what I felt about her?

As we left the cemetery, driving off in the funeral home's limo, I told her I wanted her to have the third cemetery plot, so that my father could be buried surrounded by the two women in his life he loved dearly. Sorry, Dad, I really wish I had been able to say or do more, but it was the best I could come up with.

Beyond the Pale

I LEARNED YIDDISH from my grandfather, who came from Montreal to live with us in Chicago for the last four years of his life, after his health failed and he could no longer stay alone. These were the years, just after World War II, when I was between fourteen and eighteen—not a bad age, really, for absorbing a new language. A small and somewhat foppish man, my grandfather began each day by wrapping himself in a prayer shawl and *tefillin* for his morning devotions. After bathing, he would dress in one of his five suits, tailor made and very well cut, which he maintained with great care and wore in rotation. His shirts were white and starched, his neckties dark. A thick gold watch chain depended from his vest. When he died he left the watch to me, and also, I would later come to realize, a certain standard of seriousness.

In Montreal, where he had spent much of his adult life, my grandfather had been a leading figure in Hebrew education. Old-timers in that city still remember Raphael Berman as a man of deep learning and wide culture. Living with us in Chicago must have marked a sad coming-down for him. Immaculate was the word my mother always used to describe her father-in-law; he, for his part, worried about her following the laws of *kashrut,* previously foreign to her. After more than eighty years of keeping kosher, he feared falling off the wagon at this late stage of his life.

My grandfather had strong memories of pogroms in his childhood shtetl, a few miles outside Odessa. He told me how his parents had managed to smuggle him out of Russia to avoid conscription into the czar's army. Although he never said so aloud, he must have been disappointed that none of his four sons — of whom my father, a successful retail furrier, was the youngest — had turned out to be in the least scholarly or even mildly bookish. There was only me, his grandson: a last chance to impart to another generation his love for Hebrew and above all for Yiddish, his sweet, endlessly subtle *mama-loshen.*

Patiently he taught me Yiddish grammar, syntax, vocabulary, the semantic intricacies of a language whose every word — including, my grandfather joked, the prepositions — seemed at least a triple-entendre. Once we had run through the few available lesson books, he led me gently into the great storytellers: Sholem Aleichem, I. L. Peretz, Mendele. Together we also read David Pinski and Chaim Grade and Abraham Reisen, even the problematic Sholem Asch.

At sixteen, I may have been the world's youngest reader of the *Jewish Daily Forward,* still sold in those days at the newsstand at Devon and California, four blocks from our apartment. It was in the pages of the *Forward* that I first came across the stories and serialized novels of Isaac Bashevis Singer, published, in their Yiddish versions, under the name Bashevis. And it was there, too, that I first discovered Zalman Belzner, a writer who interested me more than Singer.

Belzner wrote of the struggles of young Jewish Communists in the early days of the Russian Revolution, and of the plight of young men caught between the traditional Judaism in which they had been raised and the lure of Haskalah, or Jewish "enlighten-ment" and secularization, in its various early-twentieth-century permutations. Belzner wrote about these things in the most vivid detail. He achieved realism, I remember my grandfather saying, rather cryptically, with none of its accompanying vulgarity.

I was still a kid, had not yet been exposed to Tolstoy or Dostoyevsky, Proust or Thomas Mann, but in Zalman Belzner I already sensed that I was encountering literary writing built to last a long time. Such writing, it seemed to me then, was the ex-clusive province of the dead, of whom I assumed Belzner was one. "Oh, he's very much alive and kicking," my grandfather in-formed me when I inquired. "I believe he lives in New York, with his second wife, a story in herself, if you'll pardon the expres-sion." My grandfather chose not to tell that story, at least not to an adolescent boy, but I could read a fair amount in his raised right eyebrow.

My grandfather died the year I went off to college. There were not all that many Jewish students at Yale in the early 1950s, when strict quotas were still in effect, and those few among us did not exactly advertise our Jewishness. I studied English; after my grandfather's influence, I wasn't really good for anything but literature. In the fashion of the day, I was taught to unpack the meanings, often Christological, hidden in English lyric poems, and to comb and curry the symbols from the brooding works of American fiction, an exercise for which, after extended exposure to the power and charm of the great Yiddish writers, I hadn't much taste.

The study of English at Yale convinced me that I did not want to teach, and so, upon leaving New Haven, I took a job at *Time* magazine, where Yalies in those days, even Jewish ones, had an inside track. The work paid well, and many interesting characters were on the premises, drawing large checks and full of contempt for their jobs, their boss, and the society that forced men of their talent to slave at infusing the trivia of the news with interest and dash. I myself felt lucky to have the job. And then, too, I met Naomi, my wife, at *Time*, where, after graduating from Radcliffe, she had been hired as a researcher.

Living in New York I began to read the *Forward* again, every so often buying a copy from the newsstand at 79th and Broadway, not far from our apartment. In the *Forward* I came upon a notice of a reading by none other than Zalman Belzner at the Rand School, downtown near Union Square. Since Belzner was in his early eighties, and would live who knew how much longer, I felt I couldn't miss it.

Including the rickety woman on two canes who introduced the guest of honor, there were seventeen of us in the audience that Thursday night, twelve women and five men. I must have been the youngest person in the room by fifty years. The crowd reminded me a little of the one that had gathered on a cold February evening in Chicago to mark the death of William Z. Foster, who in 1932 had been the Communist candidate for President of the United States. I no longer remember why I attended that event, but like the American Communist Party, Yiddish literature in the 1950s seemed to me another, if much more gallant, lost cause.

Zalman Belzner was given an introduction in which he was at one point called the Homer, and at another the Shakespeare, of twentieth-century Yiddish literature. As he slowly approached the lectern, one could see that he was near the end of his trail. He was a large man and must once have been very handsome. His skin was wrinkled but pinkish, his hair white and still plentiful; in fact, he was in need of a haircut. He had big, fleshy ears, which stuck out. His features, as sometimes happens with people in old age, had become a bit blurry, as if someone had fooled with the contrast button. His hands were large; lifting them seemed to require an effort. His breathing carried a low rasping sound.

Yet as soon as he began reading, passion kicked in and Belzner's age dropped away. He began, in Yiddish, with a series of five poems, recounting the cycle of Jewish hope and disaster that was the great revolution in Russia. He next read, also in Yiddish, from two welcoming letters sent to him by Sholem Aleichem upon his first publications. Next, in somewhat stilted English, he read from what he called "a work in progress," a section from a new novel about a young yeshiva student in Vilna whose ardor for a beautiful young leftist catches him up in the intricacies of revolutionary politics. Belzner's strong greenhorn accent made what he read seem all the more powerful. At the end of this excerpt he thanked his wife, Gerda, for her work on the translation.

Applauding, everyone turned to look at a woman sitting in the row in front of mine and a bit to my left. Gerda Belzner looked to be in her late fifties, at least two decades younger than her husband, small and very thin, with fine bones and emphatic features and hair dyed henna red. She sat with an impressive uprightness; deep pride showed in her bearing. She took the applause, I felt, rather as if she were not the translator but herself the author.

A reception had been set up that reminded me of the small spread after Shabbos services at Ner Tamid Synagogue, where I used to accompany my grandfather. Slices of sponge cake and small glasses of Mogen David wine plus, in this case, a samovar with glasses for tea. Belzner was standing near the samovar. Supported by a cane that he hadn't used at the lectern, his wife holding his other arm, he was talking to three admiring elderly women. After they wandered off, I went up to him.

"Mr. Belzner," I said, "my name is Arnold Berman, and I work for *Time* magazine, and I just wanted to tell you that your writing has meant a great deal to me, and I want to thank you for it."

"No, no," Belzner said, extending his hand, "it is I who must thank you. All that a writer can ask for is intelligent and generous-hearted readers. And in you, young man, I seem to have found such a reader. I am most grateful to you." I felt my hand disappear in his large padded paw.

"If you don't mind my asking, Mr. Berman," said Mrs. Belzner, "how did you come to learn about my husband's writing, a man so young as you?" She was less than five feet tall, and her eyes, more black than brown, shone fiercely. Her accent was as strong as her husband's, but metallic and harsh where his was warm and caressing.

"Through my grandfather, who taught me Yiddish."

"And for *Time* magazine," she said, "what exactly, if I may ask, it is that you do?"

Don't ask me why, but I lied, or at any rate exaggerated. "I write about culture," I said, "mostly things in what we call 'the back of the book.'" In fact, in those days I chiefly wrote the squibs, in the section of the magazine called Milestones, about recent births and deaths and divorces of celebrities.

Two other women had captured Belzner's attention, and he was expending his charm on them, but Mrs. Belzner stayed with me. "You would like a piece of sponge cake or a glass tea?" she asked.

"Thank you, no," I said. "I really must be going, but I didn't want to leave without telling your husband how much I admire his work."

"He is a great writer, Zalman Belzner," she said, fire in her eye, "and if he wrote in any other language but Yiddish, the world would long ago have known it."

I told her I thought she was absolutely right about this, and excused myself.

The next afternoon at the office, just after I returned from lunch, the receptionist called to say that a large package had been left for me. When I picked it up, I discovered that it contained three of Zalman Belzner's books in Yiddish, all inscribed to me, and a copy, in manuscript, of his wife's translation of *Beyond the Pale*, the book from which he had read the night before. It also contained no fewer than thirty reviews of Belzner's work, almost all of them from the Yiddish press, and, in an emphatic hand, a four-page letter from Mrs. Gerda Belzner.

I'll spare you the florid *politesse* of her opening and closing paragraphs, which could only have been written by someone whose first or second or even third language was not English and were in a style more appropriate to the eighteenth century than to our own. The main point of her letter was, as she put it, "a simple but felicitous idea" — namely, that *Time* put Zalman Belzner on its cover, with a story, to be written by me, about his travails as a great Yiddish author. She, who knew Zalman Belzner's life better than anyone in the world, would be pleased to fill me in on the facts, perhaps over lunch at the Belzners' apartment on West End Avenue at, she wrote, underlining, *"your earliest permissible convenience,"* adding: "maybe next Tuesday." She also noted that she would appreciate my comments on her translation of *Beyond the Pale.*

I waited until the next day to call.

"Mrs. Belzner," I said, lying again, "I talked over the idea of a cover story about your husband with Mr. Luce, our editor in chief, and he said that while he thought the notion had much merit, perhaps the timing was wrong. In any case, we've already run three covers on writers within the last fourteen months. He asked me to thank you for your interest and to congratulate you on the translation of *Beyond the Pale.*"

The truth was that I had never met Henry Luce, having been in the same room with him only once and then was too nervous to introduce myself. Except as the wildest comedy, I certainly could not imagine discussing with him, or with any of the senior editors, a *Time* cover on Zalman Belzner.

"You'll maybe forgive my saying so, Mr. Berman," she said,

"but this man Mr. Luce must be an idiot. Zalman Belzner is probably the greatest writer in the twentieth century, and hardly anyone knows about it. *Time* is a newsmagazine, no? If this isn't news, what, if I may ask, is?"

"You're probably right, Mrs. Belzner," I said, "but it's Mr. Luce's magazine, and what he says goes."

"Like I say, an idiot," she said. "But you'll come to lunch anyhow?"

"I'll be happy to," I said.

"Next Tuesday at one-thirty is good. Zalman Belzner writes from ten till one. You have the address?"

The Belzners' building, at 420 West End Avenue, was not all that far from where Naomi and I lived, but in certain respects it seemed a different world. Although the West Side was entering a decline that would only get messier and more dangerous as the sixties wore on, most of the large buildings on West End retained their air of solid if shopworn gentility. The side streets were another matter; the thought of the shaky Zalman Belzner on his cane walking those streets was not pleasant to contemplate.

An elderly doorman in a shabby maroon coat, hat slightly askew, informed me that the Belzners lived on the sixth floor. Someone had scratched "Up Yours" on the inside of the elevator door. The interior halls were gloomy and gave off a cabbagey smell. When I knocked, Gerda Belzner came to the door.

"Mr. Berman," she said, "I'm sorry to have to inform you that Zalman Belzner, because of poor health, will not be able to join us for lunch today."

"Nothing serious, I hope," I said.

"With Zalman Belzner, everything is serious," she replied. "He is a sick man."

"What's wrong?"

"The aftereffects of tuberculosis, which, not helped by smoking for so long, have turned into emphysema," she said. "Another gift from Mother Russia, the tuberculosis. Zalman Belzner, you should know, is a writer who has been a guest at the Lubyanka prison under two regimes, the czar's and the Communists'."

I hadn't known. Nor did I know, as I would soon discover, that Belzner had been acquainted with Babel, Pasternak, Akhmatova, and the Mandelstams. His second wife filled me in on these and other matters. Belzner's first wife, according to Gerda Belzner, was a maniacal Communist. She had tried to persuade him to write in the style of socialist realism, to desert Yiddish for Russian, and, later, to take up the editorship of the Yiddish magazine *Soviet Homeland,* which was devoted to the lie that Jewish culture in the Soviet Union was thriving. When Belzner was able to flee the Soviet Union, she chose not to go with him. She was said to have died in the Gulag in 1950, three years before the death of Stalin.

While telling me these stories, Gerda Belzner would frequently interrupt to go to the back of the apartment — to minister to her husband, I assumed. At each return she took up the conversation without missing a beat. She told me that she had met Zalman Belzner after he had defected; he lived briefly in Paris before moving to New York. She was herself originally from Warsaw, a refugee from Hitler. As a young girl, a member of various Jewish literary societies in Warsaw, she had of course read Belzner and admired him greatly. When she met him in New York she was immediately swept away. "He was," she said, "an even more handsome man than he is today."

"You understand, Mr. Berman," she said, "my life is devoted entirely to the work of Zalman Belzner. It has no other meaning."

She didn't really have to say it. Everything about her underscored the point, not least her inability to refer to her husband except by his full name, as if she were reading it off a title page.

Gerda Belzner served me a bowl of cold and not very good borscht, a platter of cold tongue and hard salami, rye bread, a sliced onion, a tomato, some too-strong coffee, with grapes and an overripe banana for dessert. None of the food seemed quite fresh. But, then, neither did anything about the dark and dusty apartment, whose every available flat surface was covered by Yiddish books and newspapers. The windows had not been cleaned for a long time, and the light coming in felt crepuscular even though it was midday. Every so often I would hear a weak but racking cough from the back. I imagined poor Belzner, sequestered in his room in an old woolen bathrobe in a bed with less than clean sheets. A homemaker Gerda Belzner clearly was not.

"And so, Mr. Berman," she asked, "have you had a chance to read my translation of *Beyond the Pale*? And if you have, what, if I may ask, do you think?"

"It's a wonderful story," I said, "and the translation is excellent, fluent, only a few rough spots."

I was truthful about the story but not about the translation, which was stiff, overly ornate, studded with odd bits of immigrant English, its syntax hopeless, sometimes bordering on the comic. The Yiddish of the Zalman Belzner I remembered from my grandfather's *Forward* was straight, delivered with power and unshowy verbal agility, in staccato, machine-gun-like sentences. Only well after you read a passage did it occur to you to wonder how, in so few strokes, he had managed to bring off the astonishing effects he did. His skill as a pure storyteller deflected your attention from the style that gave his tales their magic.

"I have now sent this translation to nine American publishers, none of whom has expressed any interest whatsoever," she said. "What do you make of this, Mr. Berman?"

"I'm not quite certain what to make of it," I said, "except perhaps that there may be limited interest in your husband's subject matter. We live in sensationalist times. Everything is geared to the contemporary."

"Then how do you account for the success of that pig Singer?" She did not so much pronounce as spit his name.

I. B. Singer was just then beginning to catch on with a large American audience. "Even for Singer I'm told it hasn't been so easy," I answered. "I've heard that when Knopf brought out *The Family Moskat,* they cut the manuscript substantially. It's a hard world, the world of American publishing, with very little sentimentality."

"May I ask you a very great favor, Mr. Berman? May I ask you to go over my translation once more, with an eye to eliminating the rough spots you mention, and then maybe to think about where next to send the book? More than anything in this life, I want *Beyond the Pale* published while Zalman Belzner is yet alive."

Careful, Arnie, I said to myself. This woman can only be trouble. Besides, I had quite enough going on in my life. There was my job at *Time,* up whose masthead I had only begun to climb — I was now an associate editor and had become the magazine's third movie reviewer. My wife was pregnant with our first child. I had writing ambitions of my own; I was on the lookout for a good subject about whom to write a biography. To take on the polishing of this wretched translation — polishing, hell, a full retranslation was required — was not exactly a good career move.

Of course, there was Belzner himself to consider. However reduced his circumstances, he was a great writer, of that there couldn't be any doubt. And my grandfather, I thought, would have been pleased that his grandson was putting his training to such high purposes. The manuscript of *Beyond the Pale,* in Yiddish, ran to 460-odd pages. A fair portion of it was in dialogue. If I could do two pages a night, with perhaps a little more on weekends, I might have the whole thing done in less than six months. Gerda Belzner set off all my warning signals — dangerous, nutty woman, *beware*—but her husband's situation was serious and sad. Never suffocate a generous impulse, my grandfather used to say.

"Let me give it a try," I said. "Working at a full-time job, I can't promise to have it done too quickly, Mrs. Belzner. But maybe, just maybe, I can smooth out the rough spots and make the novel a bit more attractive to an American publisher."

"Tank you, Mr. Berman," she said, failing to pronounce the *h*, "and I know that Zalman Belzner will want to tank you, too, and will do so in person once he is again up and around. We are both most grateful to you, please never to forget that."

Leaving the Belzners' apartment, the Yiddish manuscript and Gerda Belzner's translation in a Klein's shopping bag, I thought, Well, kid, you're in the soup now, up to your lower lip. Out on West End Avenue it had begun to rain. On the side street to Broadway a young guy in a tweed jacket three sizes too big for him, a crazed look in his eyes, approached.

"Hey, buddy," he said, "can I have all your change?"

Caught off guard, I reached into my pocket and gave him what must have been nearly two bucks in silver.

"Thanks, pal," he said. As he walked away I noted a large tear in the seat of his pants.

This, apparently, was my big day for charity.

After my second session with *Beyond the Pale,* I dispensed altogether with Gerda Belzner's translation, which was, as I discovered on closer scrutiny, crude beyond retrieving. The novel, however, was Zalman Belzner's masterpiece. It recounted the life of a boy, Eliezer Berliner, brought up in strict religious observance, a star pupil at one of the great yeshivas in Vilna, with all the potential to be a great scholar and rabbi, who runs off to Russia, lives among revolutionaries in Moscow, where Jews were not allowed, is captured and imprisoned in Lubyanka, rejoins his comrades on the eve of the Russian Revolution, only to be jailed again two years later by the Soviet secret police, and finally flees to Paris, where he hopes to devote his life to poetry. Belzner had supplied brilliant cameo roles for Lenin and Trotsky, Bukharin and the young Stalin. In his taut narrative, Belzner took on the emptiness of formal religion, the hopelessness of radical politics, the vanity of all art that does not ultimately turn one back to religious contemplation, if of a vastly different kind from that ever dreamed of by the Vilna rabbis who trained his protagonist.

Belzner's method in telling Eliezer Berliner's story was pointillism of a sort, a careful setting down of dots, one after another, of precise and synecdochical detail. So perfectly had he linked these dots that one read with the intensity of a dying man racing through a book prescribing hitherto unknown cures for his disease. As a boy, I had done translation exercises of a page or two for my grandfather, but nothing so extended as this. I found myself working four hours a day on *Beyond the Pale* — two hours in the early morning before going off to *Time,* another two after Naomi, tired from her pregnancy, had gone to bed. I thought about it at work, in my mind revising English phrasings that weren't quite adequate to Belzner's powerful text. I lingered over it before I fell off to sleep, reformulating sentences, my arm around my wife and my mind in Moscow with the young Eliezer Berliner.

It was only a translation, but I found an immense excitement in the task. By now I knew that in my own life I would never attain to truly creative work; toiling on Zalman Belzner's manuscript was as close as I was ever likely to come to the thing called literature. In getting things right, a great deal — everything, really — was at stake.

I finished two months earlier than I planned and sent the work, along with Gerda Belzner's version, to the apartment on West End Avenue. Four days later she called.

"Mr. Berman," she said, "Zalman Belzner has read your translation of *Beyond the Pale* and would like to meet to talk with you about it. When, if I may ask, are you available?"

We settled on Thursday. She suggested lunch at their apartment, once again at one-thirty.

This time Belzner himself answered the door. His largeness filled the doorway. He was wearing unpressed gray trousers, a rumpled white shirt with an ink stain near the pocket, and at his neck a skimpy paisley ascot with a maroon background. His eyes looked more tired than I remembered from our previous meeting at the Rand School.

"Ah, Mr. Berman," he said, full of bonhomie, "is good to see you once more. Do come in. Do come in."

The same table was set — once again for two — in the small living room.

"My wife will not be joining us today," he said, "which is perhaps just as well, since it is about her that we must talk, at least in part."

The meal, already on the table, turned out to be exactly the same as the one Gerda Belzner had served me roughly four months earlier, from borscht to the grapes and overripe banana. Belzner questioned me a bit about my grandfather and his origins. When I said he came from Odessa, Belzner smiled and said, "Ah, the city of Jewish violinists and Benya Krik, the great Jewish gangster." He told me about his meeting with Krik's creator, Isaac Babel, also of Odessa, and about Babel's craze for literary revision: forty or fifty times he would rework a simple three-page story.

Over dessert our conversation began in earnest. "I wish to speak to you, of course, about your translation of my book. My English is less than perfect, as you can hear even now as I talk to you, but your translation seems to me excellent, highly excellent really, and I am most grateful to you for the care you must have put into it. For a writer in Yiddish, as you must know, a good translator into English is not important merely — it is everything."

"I'm pleased you think well of it," I said, genuinely delighted.

"I think very well of it, but I couldn't help noticing you seem not to have made much use of my wife's work as first translator of the book. Is this not correct?"

"Correct," I said. "I felt it was better to begin from scratch."

"Yes," he said, "from scratch." He stopped to think about an American idiom that was evidently new to him. "From scratch. I see what you mean. What I wonder now is whether I can convince you to share the credit with Mrs. Belzner as cotranslator of the book. It would mean a great deal to her if you were to do so. Meanwhile, in recompense, I am sure some royalty arrangement on the translation could be worked out in your favor."

"It's a little irregular," I said.

"I'm sure it is," Belzner said, "but as you may have noticed, so is life, and so especially is Mrs. Belzner a little irregular. She is not an ordinary woman, my Gerda, as you will have noted."

"It would be difficult not to note it," I said, trying to sound neutral.

"She, I fear, has maybe a greater investment in her husband than is perhaps normal. But I owe her everything. More even than I am able to explain to you. She has saved my life, and continues to save it every day that remains to me. Without her, please believe me, I would long ago have been dead." Belzner took a soiled handkerchief out of his back pocket and dabbed at his flushed face.

"I told Gerda," he continued, "that your translation was built on hers, that it was, in the highest sense, a collaboration between two good minds. To do otherwise, you understand, would have been very cruel. And you don't seem to me a cruel man, Mr. Berman."

"I hope not," I replied.

"Excellent," Belzner said. "When my wife returns I shall tell her that, if we are able to get an American publisher, the title page will read 'Translation by Gerda Belzner and Allan Berman.' She will be pleased."

"Arnold," I said.

"I'm sorry?" he said, cupping his right ear.

"My name is Arnold, not Allan."

"A thousand apologies," he said. "Please to forgive."

Zalman Belzner walked me to the door. He moved as if in slow motion; his footfall was heavy; I could hear his every breath. As we parted, he grasped my hand in both of his and said, "I am more in your debt than you can ever know. I thank you, Mr. Bergman."

Through a connection at *Time,* I was able to get my translation into the hands of Ben Rayburn, a small publisher interested in things Jewish, who quietly brought it out eight months later under his Horizon imprint. I was unable to attend the publication party for the book. A page-three, highly laudatory review by Irving Howe appeared in the *New York Times Book Review,* with a brief paragraph toward the end commending the "stately translation" of Gerda Belzner and Arnold Berman. *Beyond the Pale* had a modest sale of some 2,700 copies.

I never saw a penny in royalties, which was all right with me. I hadn't done it for money. I did it for Zalman Belzner; I did it for my grandfather; who knows, maybe I did it for myself. In any case, it was over, and I went back to my regular family life and to my job at *Time.*

Roughly eighteen months after the publication of *Beyond the Pale,* around eleven-thirty on a Tuesday night, I stumbled out of bed to answer the telephone.

"Mr. Berman," said Gerda Belzner in her unmistakable accent, "my husband Zalman Belzner is terribly ill and needs to be driven to Florida — tonight. Can I count on you to help me drive Zalman Belzner to Miami? We need to leave immediately, within the hour."

"Mrs. Belzner," I said, "can't this wait till the morning?"

"No," she said, "Zalman Belzner must leave for Florida now. There is no time to lose. Can you help me drive him to Florida or not?"

"Mrs. Belzner," I said, "I have a pregnant wife and a young child to worry about. I have a job. I can't take off for Florida at midnight on such short notice."

"Very well," she said. "Thank you anyhow."

"Mrs. Belzner . . ." But she had hung up.

Two days later, I read the six-inch obituary of Zalman Belzner that ran in the *New York Times*. It announced that he had died, of congestive heart failure, on Monday, the day before Gerda Belzner's call, and that he was being buried that day in a private ceremony.

From my office at *Time,* I called Gerda Belzner.

"Mrs. Belzner," I said, "I see in the *Times* that your husband's funeral is today, though no address for a funeral chapel is given. Where is it to take place?"

"I am sorry, Mr. Berman," she said, "but you are not invited. No one is invited who refused to drive Zalman Belzner to Florida with me."

"But Mrs. Belzner," I said, "unless I'm mistaken, when you asked me to drive your husband to Florida, he was, according to the *New York Times* obituary, already dead."

"That," she said in a cold voice, "is none of your business. You were unavailable when needed. I am inviting to the funeral only those friends of Zalman Belzner who were willing to drive him with me to Florida. Thank you anyhow for asking." She hung up.

I stared into the phone. What was going on here? Another

Jewish test? Our religion, after all, almost begins with a test, when God commands Abraham to sacrifice his son, Isaac. But this test of Gerda Belzner's, driving a man already dead to Florida, at midnight and on a moment's notice, provided a new twist — this was nuts. In any case, I had failed the test.

But my Belzner connection was not permanently broken. A few months later, Gerda Belzner called again. She wanted another meeting. She suggested a dairy restaurant on Broadway near 86th Street. I wanted to say no, but somehow I couldn't bring myself to be cold to this woman, who was now, for all I knew, absolutely alone in the world.

I arrived fifteen minutes early. The crowd in the restaurant was made up chiefly of elderly Jews, most of them immigrants, to judge by their speech and dress. The majority must have escaped Hitler or Stalin; some may have had to escape both. They had seen the devil up close. I felt callow in their presence.

When Gerda Belzner walked in, she was wearing a black cloth coat with a black dress underneath, boots with high heels, her henna-colored hair swept up in a bouffant, her makeup at maximum strength, leaving her sharp features in something approaching boldface. She seemed a small, possibly predatory bird. Yet there was also a touch of the regal in her appearance. She was, after all, now the widow of Zalman Belzner.

Along with her purse, she was carrying another of her shopping bags from Klein's. I rose and waved from my table. She saw me and walked over.

"Well, Mr. Berman," she said, "we meet again."

"I thought perhaps we had seen the last of each other."

"Why would you think that?"

"It's been a while," I said, choosing not to mention the funeral from which I had been excluded.

We ordered vegetarian cutlets, small salads, tea. The waiter, an older man, flatfooted, a slightly dirty towel over his forearm, looked and sounded like something straight out of a classic Jewish vaudeville routine. ("Vich of you gentlemen vanted the clean glass?")

"Mr. Berman," she said, getting right down to business, "I have today a proposition to make to you."

"What might it be, Mrs. Belzner?"

"I want you should translate with me six of my husband's as yet untranslated novels. My plan is for us to do them together, as we did with *Beyond the Pale*. I would give you a third of the royalties on each of the books." She passed her shopping bag over to me; it contained copies, in Yiddish, of the books.

"Forgive me for saying so, Mrs. Belzner, but that doesn't finally come to a lot of money. I have a wife and child to support, and another on the way. You realize you're asking for a commitment here of several years on my part."

"Which reminds me," she said, "please give my very best wishes to your Mr. Luce. All right, then, how about half the royalties?"

"That's very generous of you. But the objection remains the same. The truth is, I couldn't afford to do it for all the royalties. Money isn't really the main point here, Mrs. Belzner."

"Then what is?" she asked.

"The main point is that I have to get on with my life. There are literary projects of my own that I would like to work on."

"I don't know what these things might be," she said, "but how can they be more important than seeing that the books of Zalman Belzner, a man who belongs to world literature, find their rightful readers? Let's not kid ourselves, Mr. Berman. What you are going to write for yourself cannot compare with the writing of Zalman Belzner."

This was an argument I had no way of winning—at least not with this intense little woman sitting across the table from me. I told her I would have to think it over. We had rice pudding and coffee. Mrs. Belzner was without small talk, or at least any that she wished to expend on me. She repeated the urgency of getting all of Zalman Belzner's works into good English-language editions as soon as possible. She went into a brief tirade against Isaac Bashevis Singer, who had been so fortunate in his translators but whose filthy writings could not compare with those of her husband.

"Zalman Belzner is a very great writer, as you know maybe as well as anyone in this country, present company excepted," she said. "Someday, with God's help and yours and mine, Mr. Berman, he will have the readership he deserves." She touched my hand as she said this. I looked into her eyes and saw, for the first and only time in all my days, what it meant to have a true mission in life.

When we parted outside the restaurant, I told her I would call her within the next few weeks. I had agreed to take one of her husband's novels home to read, and I now shifted it to my left hand in order to shake her own small, bony, and dry hand. I watched her walk off down Broadway, her thin legs in high-heeled boots, swinging her Klein's bag before disappearing amid a wild assortment of scruffy kids, elderly Jewish couples, failed hustlers, and doubtless many others with spoiled ambitions and busted dreams, none of whom had ever heard or could possibly ever hear of Zalman Belzner.

I had already made up my mind at the restaurant not to take on the translation of any of these novels. The whole thing was hopeless. At *Time* I had been made a general editor. I was doing the occasional book review and was called in to help edit the magazine's larger culture stories. One of the senior editors let me know that the magazine was soon going to need a new theater critic and asked if I had any interest in the job. In short, it was no time for me to be spending all my free hours sweating over books about old Jews cavorting around Eastern Europe in a culture that had long since been wiped out.

In a cab on the way back to the Time-Life Building, I thought I would write Gerda Belzner a letter in which I would set out my responsibilities to my career, to my family, and to myself, and how I must give these priority. Even she could see that first things came first — that the living have a greater claim on us than the dead. And if she couldn't see it, well, too damn bad.

I didn't have much luck with the letter. I intended it to be less than a page, but it kept running on, in one version to five full pages before I even got to my wife and family. I attempted a second draft, and then a third, both unsatisfactory.

A couple of weeks after our lunch, Gerda Belzner phoned.

"Mr. Berman," she began, "I have called to report to you that Zalman Belzner's reputation is in peril."

"In peril?" I asked. "How in peril, Mrs. Belzner?"

"An essay on Yiddish writers appears in a Philadelphia Jewish paper, the *Investigator* — maybe you know it? It pretends to discuss Yiddish literature and yet it makes no mention, none whatsoever, of Zalman Belzner. Mr. Berman, it is incumbent on you to write a strong letter of complaint to the editor. It wouldn't be such a bad idea to do it on your company stationery. In this letter you might say that the failure to mention Zalman Belzner in such an article is not an oversight but an outrage, which no serious student of Yiddish literature can be expected to tolerate."

"Mrs. Belzner," I said, "the absence of mention of your husband is a serious mistake, I agree, but it is not slanderous. I think we'd do best to let it pass."

I scarcely noticed the "we" crossing my lips. "In any case, Mrs. Belzner," I continued, "I don't think a letter of protest would be quite in order. I'm not sure what would be, but let me think further about it."

"You'll call me back?" she asked.

"Yes, of course," I said.

Before the week was out, my wife's water broke, at two in the morning. In good sitcom fashion, I woke our daughter and brought her over to our neighbors, the Hoffmans, with whom we had become good friends. And then, forgetting my wife's already packed small suitcase, I called a cab. We were waiting downstairs when I realized my error. Back in the apartment, I remembered that I might be spending hours in the maternity waiting room and scuttled about for something to read. I came up with *Yeshiva Bokher*, the novel in Yiddish that I had taken from Gerda Belzner on the day of our lunch.

Naomi was twenty hours in labor, during which time I finished more than 400 pages of Zalman Belzner's 626-page novel about life at one of the great rabbinical schools in Lithuania in the late nineteenth century. It was brilliant stuff, entrancing, absolutely dazzling. As I read its confidently cadenced Yiddish, all I could think about was proper English equivalents. A fair amount of the material in the novel had to do with complex Jewish texts, mostly legal, about which I knew next to nothing. Any translator would have to be versed in them and in the historical life of the time. Nearly twice the length of *Beyond the Pale*, *Yeshiva Bokher* was in every way a much denser and more difficult work, requiring at least two years, maybe more, to render into English. A job not likely to be undertaken again soon, if ever, it had to be done supremely well.

To be a translator was to be at best a secondary figure. To be a translator from Yiddish, a language now plundered for its idioms mainly by comedians and spoken by nobody under fifty not wearing a black hat — this was hopeless, to condemn oneself to the periphery of a periphery. Why was I so drawn to it? Even now I can't say. All I can provide by way of explanation, to myself if to no one else, is a line from Keats that I must have picked up at Yale, probably in Cleanth Brooks's class on the Romantics: "so I may do the deed / That my own soul has to itself decreed."

My newborn son weighed seven pounds six ounces. Two days before the *bris* in our apartment, my wife yielded to my wish to name him Zechariah. Since neither of our families had any relatives with names beginning with the letter Z, it was a mystery to everyone in attendance. To everyone, that is, but a small woman with dyed red hair and too much makeup who, with the look of a fanatic in her eye, stood off in the corner, spoke to no one, and never smiled. She had arrived at the *bris* without a gift for our new baby but with a heavily laden bag from Klein's, and she departed empty-handed before the food was served.

My Brother Eli

NEVER LET IT be said that my kid brother Eli failed to give me anything: he gave me five ex-sisters-in-law and seven (I think I have the number right) nephews and nieces, three of whom I met for the first time at his funeral. (My wife, Gerry, and I are childless.) At a memorial service I attended a few months afterward, a number of professors and writers and, yes, even the mayor of Chicago talked about the struggles, sensitivity, and soulfulness of a man bearing Eli's name but whom, tell you the truth, I wasn't able to recognize in any of these tributes.

My brother Eli is, make that *was*, the famous novelist, winner of all the literary prizes, national and international, a guy who scooped up most of the world's rewards (by which I mean money, women eager to sleep with him, praise from every quarter, international celebrity) without ever seeming particularly happy about any of them.

Eli took his life at the age of seventy-nine. You read about it, I'm sure. The official word was that he killed himself because he was diagnosed with Alzheimer's, but I'm not so sure something else wasn't behind my brother's putting a Beretta in his mouth and pulling the trigger. All the obituaries mentioned the Beretta, a nice detail that my brother himself would have appreciated. Eli always wore Borsalino hats; I wonder if he bought the Beretta in the same neighborhood in Rome where he bought his expensive hats, which, befitting the rake he became, he always wore at a rakish angle.

There were three of us: I was the firstborn, our sister Arlene came two years later, and then Eli (whose real name was Eliezer Schwartz) four years after that. Our old man worked for some-one named Schinberg in the produce market on Fulton Street. An immigrant, unable to read English, he came to this country at sixteen from Bialystok and, contrary to the standard American success story, never really made it. I don't think he ever felt at home here. He was stubborn, argumentative, a difficult charac-ter in almost every way, the old man. I call him "the old man" because I can't remember him young. He left for work at three A.M., took two different streetcars to Fulton Street, returned at four P.M., ate, and went to bed early. None of his children was sorry not to have seen more of him. He died at work, our father, outdoors, unloading cases of Texas grapefruits from the back of a truck on a blustery February morning when he was forty-nine years old. Unlike the case with Eli, at the old man's funeral no one knew what to say on his behalf.

Our mother was the hero of the family. She was from Kiev. I don't ever remember her other than without makeup, gray hair pulled back in a bun. She worked a sixteen-hour day: cooking and washing and cleaning for her family, then after supper taking out her Singer sewing machine, which she set up on the kitchen table, doing piecework for Hart Schaffner & Marx, the men's clothier, then on Franklin Street. In the few minutes she had for herself, she read novels in Yiddish. She died, worn-out, at fifty-four. Eli once told me that he thought our mother never loved him. I told him I didn't know when she would have found time, which wasn't the answer he wanted to hear.

The six-year difference in Eli's and my age was enough to keep us from ever establishing any real closeness. And then we led such different lives. I went to work in high school for Ben Belinsky, the used-auto-parts king, on Western Avenue near Augusta Boulevard, and never left. I worked for a few years out in the yard, with the Polacks and the colored guys, and then Mr. Belinsky, who was childless, took a shine to me. He was tough but straight, no crap about him, and he gave me a sense of what was honorable conduct, even in a competitive business like auto parts. If you worked hard for him — and I did — he took care of you.

He must have seen something in me. He had me to his home for dinner on Jewish holidays. When I was eighteen he brought me inside, into the office, and began to teach me the business. "Where you make your dough is in buying," he used to tell me. "Any shmegegge can move the goods if the price is right."

When I graduated from Marshall High School, I thought about going to college, maybe studying accounting. "What do you need to study accounting?" Mr. Belinsky said. "You don't *become* an accountant, Louis. You *hire* an accountant. Forget about accounting. Stick with me. You won't be sorry."

And I wasn't. At twenty I was making more money than my old man. In my middle twenties, Mr. Belinsky told me that, if I wanted it, really wanted it, someday his business would be mine. I wanted it, all right. None of this was ever put on paper, you understand. It didn't have to be. He was solid, Ben, though I never called him that. I always called him Mr. Belinsky, even when I was in my thirties and he was in his early eighties, still coming down five days a week, working half a day on Saturday. Not long before he died, I arrived one morning and saw a new neon sign across the front of the place reading BELINSKY & SON, AUTO PARTS. "That *Son* on the sign, Louis," he said, "that's you." I excused myself, went into the bathroom, and wept.

When Eli was in high school, I arranged for him to work in the yard at Belinsky Auto Parts. You could see right off his heart wasn't in it. Heavy lifting wasn't in my kid brother's line. He didn't like to get dirty. He was dreamy. He'd bring a book to work, which he read on breaks and which didn't at all please Mr. Belinsky.

What Eli didn't get in affection from our mother, he got from our sister Arlene. Eli was what you might call a sister's boy. Everything a person could do for another person without money, Arlene did for Eli: ironed his shirts, helped him buy his clothes, cooked special treats for him, slipped him an extra buck or two when she had it. Arlene and Eli looked a little alike. They both had our mother's fine features. I resembled more the old man. I have his large feet, thick wrists, big chest, black hair.

Arlene didn't have an easy life. Something in her eyes, in the way she carried herself, suggested vulnerability. She had two bad marriages, no children. Her second husband, a car salesman named Ralph Singer, used to beat her up. I didn't know about it until one day she turns up at our house for Passover with a black eye. I called Singer, asked him to come to my office the following Monday. When he showed up, I handed him an envelope with five grand in it, told him I wanted him to return home and get his things out of my sister's apartment, and that I never wanted him to bother my sister again. To show him I was sincere, right there in my office I broke his fuckin' nose.

Eli probably had no bigger fan than Arlene, who, later in life, used to keep scrapbooks filled with the reviews of his novels and the interviews he gave and everything else she found in the papers about him, which was quite a lot. I may not be the most careful reader of my brother's novels, but I did try my best to follow his career and his life, even if always from a distance. And I noticed a pattern over the decades, which was that Eli seemed to betray everyone who ever loved him. He never betrayed me, not really, but then maybe that was because I got off the love train for my brother fairly early.

What I sensed from the beginning was that Eli was in business for himself, and in a way that didn't make family love any easier. Maybe our father was unfeeling and our mother was certainly preoccupied. But in my mother's case at least we all knew that she would do everything she could for us, that, as best she was able, she was in our corner. Of course it wasn't like today, when if you don't tell your kid you love him every twenty minutes you could go to jail for child abuse. I always felt close to my sister, close to her and sorry for her both. But for Eli, as I say, I ran out of love fairly soon. I suppose I sensed that he didn't have much feeling for me, either.

When he graduated from Marshall, Eli came to tell me that he had a partial scholarship to Columbia University in New York, but he would need my help to pay his way. If I told you how little he needed, you'd laugh, because the sum today would sound trifling. Yet in those days, it wasn't; it seemed like a big ticket. Still, a brother is a brother, and I said sure, why not, and every month I sent him a check to cover part of his tuition and his living expenses. I never expected a regular thank-you note. But I did make a small mental note in later years, when Eli was making big money, that it never occurred to him to offer to pay me any of that money back, or to say thanks for helping him out when he needed it. Maybe I was supposed to feel privileged to have contributed to the education of the great novelist, though I note that none of Eli's three biographers ever mentioned how this poor kid from the West Side of Chicago found the money to go off to school in New York.

Because so much is known about my brother's life, I don't have to connect all the dots about how he fell in with a group of New

York writers when he lived there, how he met his first wife, his trips to Europe, things of that nature. But I first knew something was up when Eli published his second novel—I was still reading everything he wrote in those days—the book called *The Packard's Running Board*. I'm the so-called hero of that book, in which I'm called Eugene Siegel, and to Mr. Belinsky he gave the name Fred Armitage and made him a Gentile.

I don't read a lot of fiction. I tried, especially when my kid brother was gaining a reputation for turning the stuff out, but I never found the payoff was there, if you know what I mean. I like to read books about Franklin Delano Roosevelt and Harry Truman and about the periods in history I've lived through myself, like the Depression and World War II. Eli's first novel, about a young guy growing up in a neighborhood where no one understood his sensitivity, was tough for me to get through at all. I had to drag my eyes across every page, thinking who could possibly give a damn about all this. So the hero of the book is sensitive and the people he's forced to live among aren't. I didn't see the big deal.

In *The Packard's Running Board*, the character Eugene—me, that is—is on fire with ambition and wanting to impress his boss, who runs a large auto-parts store. (Eli, far as I can see, never did invent a hell of a lot.) So his boss, Mr. Armitage, who is an anti-Semite amused at his employee's eagerness to get ahead, assigns him the job of finding a running board, driver's side, for a 1942 Packard. Eugene goes scurrying all over, trying every scrap yard in the county, but no luck. Then one day he spots a '42 Packard parked on the street in Oak Park and waits outside to see who owns it. The owner turns out to be one of those old dames with blue-rinse white hair. Eugene follows her home to a mansion in River Forest. He hangs around the neighborhood. He finds out that the old broad's name is Emily Thornborough and that she's the widow of a successful architect. Although the car is old—the novel is set sometime in the late 1950s—the woman loves it, treats it like a baby, or so Eugene discovers by asking the mechanic at a nearby garage where she takes it in for servicing.

To make a long story short, Eugene realizes that he is going to have to steal the goddamn running board. And the rest of the book is about the complications of his doing that. A lot of comic hijinks follow: he nearly gets caught; he has the problem of how to get the unwieldy running board back into Chicago on public transportation. When he finally brings it to his boss, the man is unimpressed and says something like "You boys will do anything to get ahead"—"you boys," we are meant to understand, are Jews—and he fires Eugene on the spot, calling him a thief. End of story.

I took this book to represent Eli's opinion of me, his older brother, who was supposedly dedicated to the idea of getting ahead and willing to do anything to do so. Eugene is me, down to the gap between my front teeth, the hair covering the knuckles on my large hands, the way my face sweats when I'm under pressure. In the novel, I'm resourceful but also a major schmuck—and, when you get right down to it, a crook, too. For me the book wasn't exactly what you'd call easy reading.

I don't know why, but I never confronted Eli with his portrait of his older brother. I wonder if I wouldn't have done better to call him on it right then and there. I suppose I could have said, "Eli, where do you get off making me out to be such an obnoxious putz in your book? Is this what you really think of me? Explain this—and now." I was young enough in those days to put the hint—and maybe more than a hint—of menace in my voice. Maybe if I had done this, I might have saved a lot of grief to a number of other people Eli later put into his books.

Eli's first marriage was at City Hall in Jersey City, New Jersey. My sister and I heard of it after the fact. He married a girl named

Elise Lensky, whose family were big in the socialist movement. Jews went in for this left-wing stuff more in New York than in Chicago. Here we're happy just to make a living and get some kind of fix on reality. Our hands are full trying to cope with the world as it is. We don't waste a lot of time on the world as it ought to be.

Around this time, Eli himself turned socialist, with a big interest in Leon Trotsky. I learned this from his wife, who called me one day to tell me that she was pregnant, in her sixth month, and that Eli and a pal had gone off to tour all the Communist countries of Eastern Europe to view firsthand how Trotsky's teachings had been perverted under Stalin. She had medical and other expenses, and Eli had told her to get in touch with me if she ran out of the money he had left with her. The money was gone, and now she had nowhere else to turn. I sent her a grand by Western Union.

I have no idea why Eli needed to leave a pregnant wife the way he did, but when he returned two months later, he called to thank me for coming through with the money. He said that he had a new book in the works that his publisher thought might make some serious dough, and that he would repay me as soon as he could. I can't remember how I found out that he and his wife had had a son named David; probably through Arlene, who kept in better touch with Eli than I did. But less than a year later, he broke up his marriage to the Lensky girl.

Five or so years must have passed before I next saw my brother. The book his publisher had thought would make some money for him apparently did well, and it also evidently increased his reputation, putting him, as Arlene said, in the front rank of contemporary writers. He had a new wife, a painter of abstract art whose name was Serena, and he had taken to wearing expensive, somewhat gaudy clothes: suits with tight trousers, shirts with bold stripes, loud ties, pointy shoes. He was losing his hair, which may have explained why he was increasingly being photographed wearing a hat. He was in town to pick up a literary prize and give a talk at Roosevelt University.

I went with Arlene to hear the talk. The auditorium was filled. Eli was introduced as a writer who had changed the nature of modern writing. The talk was about an Irishman named James Joyce, who was evidently a great man for my brother. I couldn't make out a lot of it, but I did get that Eli admired this Joyce because he let nothing stand in the way of his writing, not the welfare of his family, nothing, even, I couldn't help note, continually borrowing from a brother, Stanislaus, I think the guy's name was, whom he never repaid.

Eli came up to Arlene and me at the reception after the talk. He embraced Arlene, put out his hand to me.

"How goes it, Lou?"

"Not too bad, Eli," I said, "but not so good as it seems to be going for you. This is a nice crowd you drew tonight."

"I provide artificial pearls for real swine," he said, looking around the room. He was wearing some sort of sharkskin suit, light gray, with high pockets in the trousers, a belt of matching material, and a silky green tie with a thick knot under a spread collar. I couldn't remember if he always had this drugstore wise-guy air about him. Or had it come with his success?

"How's auto parts?" he asked me.

"It's a living," I said, adding, "and a hell of a lot easier now that no one's asking for old running boards."

"Who'd have thought my big brother read my books?" he said with a smile. "Lou, you please me more than you can know. You astonish me, in fact."

I was about to tell him my opinion about that particular book but then thought better of it. He was my brother, after all, and I'm not good at telling people off. I tend to go too far, and I really didn't want to break things off with Eli, not yet anyhow.

The young woman who had introduced Eli, a Professor Shansky — Jewish, zaftig, in her mid-thirties — came up, excused herself for taking Eli away, but the president of the university and some of its larger donors were expecting him for a small dinner party. Eli smiled at her in a way that implied, if not possible past intimacies, certainly future ones. He was then married to his second wife.

"I better run," he said. He kissed Arlene on both cheeks and gripped my upper right arm.

"Stay well, both of you. I'll be in touch."

"You know, Lou," Arlene said to me on the way home, "he's not really our brother anymore. He belongs to the world now. He's a famous man, our little Eli."

"I suppose that's so," I said. "But I wish I liked him a little more."

"What's not to like?" Arlene said. "He's our brother."

"My guess is that he doesn't harbor many brotherly feelings about either of us, though probably more toward you than me. Eli's going to take what he wants and do what he wants, with very little obligation felt on his side. Eli's one of life's takers."

"I wonder, Lou, if you aren't being too hard on him. He's not like the rest of us, you know. Eli's an artist."

"I see where your brother's got his ass in a sling," My friend Al Hirsch said, smiling the kind of smile lawyers do when they discover fresh news of greed or other human depravity of the kind from which they make their living.

"What for?" I asked.

"As you probably know, he's going through his third divorce, and it seems that he left falsified tax documents around the marital apartment, to make it look as if he's been earning a lot less money than he's actually been earning. It's an old trick, and an extremely dumb one, if I may say so."

As a matter of fact, I didn't know that Eli was going through another divorce. I'd met his third wife twice. Her name was Sharon Lefkowitz, and she was a striking woman, good-looking, terrific figure, all-year-round suntan. Formidable, a tiger of a woman, is how I'd describe her. Unlike Eli's first two wives, she was no socialist or artist but the daughter of a Chicago dentist known for his cleverness at real estate deals. She didn't figure to be a girl who would take divorce lightly. She must have scared Eli good with her demands for him to hoke up fake tax documents. But now that he'd done it, my poor schmuck little brother had apparently really put his pecker in the wringer.

"Who's my brother's attorney?"

"A moron named Morty Silverman. He has an office on Washington, off LaSalle. A flamboyant guy who's known to bang his female clients and who's never really made his nut."

I remember Morty Silverman from the old neighborhood. His father had a dry cleaner's on Roosevelt Road. Morty was a little guy, dressed flashy, wore porkpie hats. Funny that Eli would use Morty Silverman when serious things were at stake. It showed a kind of loyalty, I guess.

"I thought your kid brother's supposed to be a genius," Al said.

"A limited genius," I said. "He's mostly a genius at telling other people what's wrong with the way they live. Not so smart, though, when it comes to his own life."

Eli had moved back to Chicago a few years before. In an interview he gave to the *New York Times*, which Arlene had sent to me, he said that he no longer needed to live in New York; its rhythms weren't his; he needed Chicago, where the grit of reality was in the air. Well, from what Al Hirsch said, Eli must by now have had a mouthful of this grit.

Arlene, always the family peacemaker, gave a dinner to which she invited me, my wife Gerry, Eli, and a new lady friend of his, a professor of some kind at the University of Chicago. She also invited another couple, named Wertheimer, who lived in her building. They were both shrinks, Arlene said, foreign-born, a little nutty, but nice. They were fans of Eli's novels and wanted to meet him.

Eli arrived after the rest of us. His lady friend, he explained, couldn't make it. "Illness in the family" is all he offered in the way of an excuse. We sat in Arlene's living room, the six of us. Eli seemed harried, tired; his face was pouchier than I remembered. He had dark circles under his eyes. He was wearing a tan suit with an emphatic glen plaid. He had a silk handkerchief in his jacket pocket, purple to match his wide necktie.

Before Eli had arrived, the Wertheimers asked me a number of questions about my brother. The Wertheimers were Jews who had escaped Germany and spoke with strong accents, Henrietta Wertheimer's stronger than her husband Karl's. Henrietta said that one of her special interests was in the childhood of artists, and she wanted to know what I could tell her about my brother's upbringing, particularly anything that might have contributed to his impressive career. The truth was, I couldn't think of a damn thing. A shame our father wasn't in the room, I thought; his gruff presence would have given the Wertheimers a lot to think about in connection with what Karl Wertheimer called "the developmental aspect of the artist's early years." I could have told them that Eli's father never gave him or any of his children the time of day, and he thought his mother didn't love him. Let them chew on that for a while. But I said very little except that my brother's talent had not shown up early, at least that I was aware of. He just seemed a very bright kid.

"You were an adherent of the doctrines of Wilhelm Reich, no?" Henrietta Wertheimer asked Eli. "Are you still?"

Eli laughed. "That was a long while ago," he said. "My brother Lou here, who is in used auto parts, probably never heard of an orgone box, but I had my very own such appliance. Kept it in a large closet in an apartment I lived in on West 106th Street in the late forties. Spent hours in it, brooding, in the hope of increasing my sexual energy, but mostly I sat there thinking of ways to advance the plots in my novels."

"Reich was of course a fascist," said Karl Wertheimer.

"I gather he was," Eli said, "but not so great a totalitarian as your man Sigmundo the Freud."

I didn't know what the hell Eli was talking about, but you had to be a dope not to recognize that he didn't like the Wertheimers.

"Well, totalitarian, I don't know," Karl Wertheimer said. "Freud was in possession of the most powerful ideas of the age, and I think it unfair to consider him more than judicious in guarding them from those who might dilute or otherwise corrupt them."

"Powerful ideas? You mean like the unrelenting desire of children to sleep with their parents? Lou," Eli said, turning to me, "funny, but I can't ever recall your mentioning your ardent desire to mount up on Ma. Or am I wrong about this?"

I didn't answer.

Things didn't get better at dinner, for which Arlene had obviously gone to a lot of trouble. Between the vegetable soup and the salad, Karl Wertheimer asked if anyone at the table had read Shakespeare in German. I felt like saying that I couldn't make him out so easy in English — except the play *Julius Caesar,* which they made us read in high school — but I clammed up. Dr. Wertheimer then went on to say that there is a school of thought that held that Shakespeare, in the Schiller or Schlegel or some other Kraut's translation, was even better in German. I was watching Eli, who up till now I thought was trying, if not very hard, not to wreck his sister's dinner party completely.

"You know," Eli said, "I think I've had just about enough of this German-Jewish bullshit."

You'd think that after making a remark like that he'd toss his napkin on the table, get out of his chair, and ask for his hat and coat. But Eli did nothing of the kind. He just sat there. Which meant that the Wertheimers had to get up and leave. They did so without much fuss, I'll give them that.

"Perhaps this meeting was a mistake, Arlene," Karl Wertheimer said. "I hope you will forgive us if we depart early." On the way out, Henrietta Wertheimer mumbled something about how nice it was to meet Gerry and me. I shook Karl Wertheimer's small soft hand.

Eli sat there, finishing his soup. When they left the room, Arlene followed them to the door, offering God knows what excuse for her brother's behavior.

"I've heard it said," Eli noted, "that if you dislike a person, it always helps to imagine that person as German. And if you really dislike him, it's best of all to imagine him as a German woman. I'll say this for Henrietta Wertheimer — under this arrangement she doesn't force the imagination into a lot of extra exercise."

"You were pretty tough on those people," I said.

"Lou," he said, "I've come to an age and stage in life where I no longer feel it incumbent upon me to listen to crap, and if there are greater purveyors of crap than intellectuals, then it is people with pretensions to knowledge of the soul, like Arlene's good German neighbors."

"A little hard on Arlene, though, wouldn't you say, Eli?" Gerry said. "I mean, these people were her guests."

"I don't worry about Arlene," he said. "Arlene'll understand."

When Arlene returned, I was a little surprised to discover that she didn't say a word to Eli about his treatment of the Wertheimers. She just served the rest of the meal as if nothing unusual had happened, and we talked about the old days on the West Side and, of course, about Eli.

"Is your new lady friend all right?" Arlene asked him.

"She's fine," Eli said. "We had an argument. She wants me to marry her. Her name's Karen Wilkinson, by the way. She's an astronomer at the University of Chicago. Not having had very good luck with wives in the humanities — and in the case of Sharon, my last wife, in the inhumanities — I thought I'd shop the sciences for a while."

"And you're not interested in remarrying?" Gerry asked him, with an unmistakable note of wonder in her voice.

"God, no. I'm already a three-time loser. And besides, it's 1974, and, as I'm sure you've noticed, it isn't such a hot time for marrying. Sex is hanging everywhere, like salamis in a delicatessen. The country's gone nuts. Everything's up for grabs. A man would have to be insane to marry today."

On the drive home, Gerry said that she didn't understand why any woman would want to marry her brother-in-law, since he was so obviously a bad risk, certain to bring unhappiness to any wife, not to mention his being a certifiably lousy father.

"And I would have killed your brother if he ever did anything like what he did to the Wertheimers to any guests of mine," Gerry said. "I don't get Arlene's being so calm about it."

"Arlene is devoted to Eli. She's sure he's a genius. She accepts his own idea of himself as a great man."

"And you, what do you think?"

"I think something's wrong with him. He may be talented, like everyone says, but I think he's got a screw loose. Something's missing in him."

"Maybe he's beginning to believe all the things that are written about him," Gerry said.

"Maybe, except I think Eli believed them even before they were written."

Three weeks later, we learned through Arlene, our usual source, that, despite all his talk about society and sex and salami and the rest of it, Eli had married his astronomer. I had another sister-in-law, my fourth.

As I said earlier, I didn't have much luck reading my brother's novels. I tried, but it was no-go. They weren't about a world I knew, nor did I find myself caring very much about how things worked out in them. Near as I could make out, they seemed to be mostly about Jewish intellectuals who thought that life had dealt them a bad hand and that reality was hard for them to locate. Gerry read them, and while she wasn't crazy about them either, she felt forcing her eyes across the pages to finish them was part of her duty as a sister-in-law. Occasionally she would call my attention to a passage where she thought I might know if Eli was writing about something or someone from the old neighborhood. She was usually right about this.

In the most recent book of my brother's, called *Leiderman's Kiss of Death,* Gerry pointed out some rough parts about a character he called Leo Leiderman, a failed lawyer, a little guy in a porkpie hat. He's unethical in every way possible. This Leiderman is also sex-crazed, not to be trusted around any skirt. He uses the same methods of seducing every woman he confronts. He quotes poetry to them and also a Russian named Berdyaev. When Leiderman at one point goes into the hospital, Eli has him flash himself in front of nurses. Leiderman is Morty Silverman, there can't be any doubt about it, and my brother has made his old pal out to be a real creep.

Why would Eli do this? Maybe he was paying Morty back for the stupid advice he gave him about faking his tax forms. This seemed a pretty stiff payback. I wondered if Morty himself would read it — I was fairly sure he would — and how he would react.

Gerry told me that Eli had done much worse with Elise, his first wife. In a novel with the title *Skolnik,* which I never got around to reading, he painted her as betraying him with another man and running off with him and their three-year-old son. This isn't the way I heard the story. I was told that Eli had left Elise because he said that an artist can't be tied down to a family, with a baby carriage in the hallway and the rest of it. I don't know the real story. What is true is that Eli made his first wife out to be a real *nafka*. What must she have thought of it? What would be the effect on their child in real life, who by now must be in his twenties? I recall being pissed off when my brother had written about me, and I felt all the more strongly that I should've kicked his ass and put a stop to this kind of thing right then and there.

What amazed me is that no one seemed to mind Eli's behavior much. His fame spread. Gerry was always calling my attention to some item about him in the Chicago papers. He gave a lot of interviews, Eli did, but he always seemed to do so reluctantly, almost as if he were being forced into it. I noticed, too, that whenever he won a prize, many of them involving fairly heavy cash, he would accept it with a slight grudgingness. "I am very pleased to have been awarded this prize, if only . . ." "I'm grateful to be the recipient of this prize, and though it pleases me greatly, it also makes me dubious of . . ." There was something phony about the whole deal, but it seemed to be working. I can't speak about the importance of my brother's writing, but he was a real public-relations genius.

Maybe Eli thought I was insufficiently impressed by him, or thought that, unlike the rest of the world, I didn't praise him enough, tell him how proud I was of him every other day, but then Gerry and I didn't see much of him, even though we were now living in the same city, we on Lake Shore Drive, Eli and his new wife in Hyde Park.

One day we get an invitation from the mayor's office for an event at which Eli was going to be presented with a medal from the City of Chicago. There was a dinner involved and an award

ceremony at Navy Pier. It was black tie. What the hell, I said to
Gerry, let's see how the other half lives.

"Which half is that?" she said.

This turned out to be not so dumb a question. At the reception before the dinner, every *tuchis lecher* in town was on display.
One of the first sights I saw after entering the hall was the gos-
sip columnist Irv Kupcinet hugging a small guy named Walter
Jacobson, used to be a batboy for the Cubs, who now does the local evening news. While they are hugging, I notice each of them
is looking over the shoulder of the other to see if there's someone
more important in the room. A strange little guy named Studs
Terkel, who has a radio interview show on the classical music station, is racing around pressing the flesh of everyone in the place.
I don't know much about him, but I remember Eli once calling
him "a cracker-barrel Stalinist" and his laughing at the pleasure
the phrase gave him. Gerry once asked me if I ever noticed that
Eli seemed to laugh a lot but rarely smiled.

Lots of women from the Gold Coast, the high-maintenance
kind, were there with their tired-looking husbands, who'd probably be happier if they'd stayed home to watch the Bulls-Lakers
game. I recognized a number of aldermen who, they don't steal
enough as it is, can always be counted on to show up for a free
meal. Mike Ditka, the former coach of the Bears with his thick
features, was talking to the mayor. Gerry spotted Jesse Jackson
leaning in close to talk to a striking black woman who does the
evening news on Channel 9.

Then Eli walked in with his wife, who, after four years of marriage to my brother, already looked exhausted. There was something dark and haunted in her eyes. She seemed thinner than I
remembered when I first met her. In her red gown and high heels,
she was a few inches taller than Eli. Eli was wearing a tux with a
wide sateen collar, a shirt with lots of big ruffles, and a red cum-

merbund and an enormous red bow tie of the kind which, if it flashed *Kiss Me* when you shook his hand, you wouldn't be in the least surprised. He looked like a Jewish trombone player in the old Xavier Cougat orchestra. His wispy, now completely white hair was combed over and patted down to cover his baldness. He got the family talent, wherever in the hell it came from originally, but I got our old man's thick hair, which maybe was the better deal.

The dinner was first class: large platters of seafood to start, choice of prime rib or salmon, lots of wine, cherries jubilee to end. When the dishes were cleared, the mayor, who wasn't known for fancy language, rose to say that culture has always been important to the city of Chicago, and then he reeled off the names of writers who had lived here, and he said that Eli was continuing in their line. In honoring Eli, he said, a man who had been born and grew up in Chicago and was now its greatest writer, the city was honoring one of its own, and he was proud to bestow the medal for literature on him, which he then did.

Eli stood at the podium, the heavy medal dangling from his neck on a red-white-and-blue ribbon, the large red bow tie just above it. He looked clownish. He waited for the applause to end. He grinned. I looked over at Karen, his wife, who was sitting across from me. She was staring down at the tablecloth.

"Well," Eli began, "this is quite an honor. I want to thank the mayor for his kind words. I want to thank Lois Weisberg and others in the city's Office of Culture. My big brother's here tonight, so I have to be careful what I say. He's a tough guy, and should I step out of line, he's sure to let me have it. Isn't that so, Lou?

"The relation of writers to power is a subject with a long and often squalid history," he continued. "I can't help wondering if, in accepting this handsome medal and eating this luscious food, I've not become part of that history. Literature is supposed to rep-

resent truth, and, as such, to tell truth to power, if only because
everyone else is frightened to do so." Here Eli looked over to the
mayor. "How're you doing, kiddo?" he said.

"Yes," he went on, "truth speaks to power, but the question is,
does power ever really listen? Or does it instead merely pretend to
listen and honor it with occasions such as this evening's gala? In
Communist countries they take writers very seriously — so seriously that they often kill them. Here in the United States, in the
city of Chicago specifically, they offer them a choice of roast beef
or salmon. Don't get me wrong, I'll take the salmon over a firing
squad any day. Still, it would be nice to be taken seriously, too."

And then Eli just stopped. That was it. Done. Finished. At first
people didn't know what to do. Everyone looked at the mayor,
who, after an interval of maybe ten seconds, began to applaud,
which allowed everyone else in the room to do so, though the
clapping was polite at best. I looked over at Eli's wife, who, returning my look, rolled her eyes back in her head, as if to say,
"He's your brother, you figure him out."

Eli, now back at our table, leaned over and said to me, "So,
how did I do?"

"I'd have to say that you didn't exactly knock 'em dead."

"That's OK," he said. "The main thing is that I knocked 'em."

Gerry took a cab home — she had an early-morning appointment the next day — and I stuck around a little longer. When I
was getting ready to leave, Eli asked me if I would mind taking
his wife home. He had some business to attend to after the party.
I said of course, why not?

I had been around my sister-in-law maybe four times, and never
alone. I wasn't sure what we'd have to talk about, but it turned out
that it didn't matter much because she did most of the talking.

"You know, Louis," she said as I pulled out of the garage at

Navy Pier, "Eli and I are splitting up. He's an impossible person, which you must already know."

"I've had some strong hints," I said.

"He needs to flirt with all kinds of women. His fame as a writer gives him some strange aphrodisiac quality for them, or so I suppose. They like to sleep with a famous writer. What I find hard to understand is that he doesn't seem to have all that much interest in what really, you know, goes on in bed. He's a very impatient lover, Eli. Forgive my not saying this more politely, but your brother doesn't know a clitoris from a kneecap."

I nearly drove over the median into onrushing Outer Drive traffic.

"It was a serious mistake on my part ever to start up with your brother. He humiliates me in public. He ignores me in private. I'm sure that someday he'll put me in one of his novels as a witch and whore and add a few bad hygienic habits at no extra charge. I don't care. I don't need money from him. To be free from him is gift enough. I'll be very happy no longer to be Mrs. Eli Black the Fourth. I'm sure there'll be a few more Mrs. Eli Blacks, all with numbers after their names, like ennobling suffixes."

When I pulled over to the curb in front of her and Eli's apartment at the Cloisters, before opening the door, she said, "Your brother thinks that because he's an artist he can do what he wants, hurt people whenever he likes. Everything is justified by his books. As an astronomer, I don't think Eli knows how small, how truly insignificant, he really is. Maybe someday he'll find out. Goodbye, Louis." She shook my hand as she left the car, and I never saw her again.

Maybe it was a year after this that Gerry and I went to a Jewish United Fund dinner and found ourselves seated at the same table with a young guy named Rick Feldrow. He was a lawyer who also wrote novels; all of them were made into movies, and damn good movies, too. He was bald, small, but looked firm, like he must've spent some time on treadmills. When we were introduced, he said he'd heard that I was Eli Black's brother. When I told him I was, he opened up to me in a way that took me a little by surprise.

"I can't tell you how much I admire your brother's writing," he said. "He's my personal hero — make that my household god."

"Why's that?" I asked.

"Because he writes like an angel. Because he understands what is really going on in the country. Because his novels will live forever."

"How's it you're so sure of all this?"

"Well," he said, "I can't of course be sure. But right now, of everyone who's scribbling away, he looks like the top contender to be read fifty or a hundred years from now."

"Have you met my brother?"

"Never," he said. "I'd still be daunted to meet him. When I was young, I used to imagine that Eli Black was my father, that I had inherited his talent, that he would guide me through the rocky places in life. My own father, who was a physician, never had much time for me, and when he did, he was hypercritical."

"Sorry to hear that," I said. "But I don't think you'd have had much luck with my brother Eli as a father, either."

"Really?" he said. "Why's that?"

I felt a light kick under the table from Gerry. "It's complicated," I said, and turned to the woman sitting on my left.

Eli and I were never in anything like regular touch. Six, eight months might go by without either of us calling the other. Sometimes we'd meet at the funeral of a cousin — Eli had a touch of family sentimentality. But one day he calls and says that he has to meet me on urgent business. How's tomorrow for lunch? he wants to know.

We met at the Standard Club. Eli was waiting in the foyer, dressed in one of his racy suits, this one black-and-white checks, a shirt with thick red stripes, white collar and cuffs, and a yellow necktie. As we walked to our table in the main dining room, I sensed people staring at us — at my brother, for Eli's picture was fairly often in the papers and he qualified around town as a celebrity.

After the waiter took our order, Eli, looking around the room, smiled and said, "Wouldn't the old man be amused to see us having lunch in this joint? We've both come a long way from Roosevelt Road and Kedzie."

"You a lot way farther than me," I said. "But what's on your mind?"

"I need a loan of a quarter of a million dollars," he said.

"That's a pretty serious number. For what, may I ask?"

"I'm in deep water with a man named Sid Gusio on a bad deal I made in an investment in nursing homes."

"Where do you come to know a thug like Gusio?" I asked.

"I met him at the Riviera Club, where I play racquetball," Eli said. "A very amiable fellow, or so he at first seems."

Sid Gusio was the Chicago Syndicate's man in charge of gambling and prostitution, and, as that job description implies, not a man to fool with. Eli had no more business with a man like Gusio than a mouse walking into the den of a lion.

"He's a dangerous character, Eli."

"Tell me about it," Eli said. "He was, he said, putting me onto a good thing. For a hundred-grand investment in a nursing home complex being built in Oak Lawn, I'd get triple my investment back within two years, or so he claimed. Only now he tells me that they vastly underestimated costs. I need to come up with another two hundred and fifty grand to protect my original investment. Except that Gusio made it evident that I didn't have much choice in the matter. It wasn't, he made it plain, an entirely voluntary matter. I couldn't just walk away and lose my original investment of a hundred thousand, though at this point I wouldn't mind doing that. But walking away, I strongly suspect, isn't really an option."

I couldn't help thinking: Eli, my schmuck brother, gets his ass in a sling every time he ventures away from his desk. Eli, who wouldn't know reality if it hit him in the face, the man who writes books telling everyone else they're living badly. Eli going up against Sid Gusio was no contest.

"What makes you so sure he won't come back to you for still more money?"

"Nothing," Eli said. I could sense his fear. Also his embarrassment. Always so goddamn knowing about everything, Eli was reduced to coming to his big brother for help.

"You don't have any of this money yourself?" I asked.

"I have a high nut, Lou, lots of ex-wives, kids, school bills, you don't know the half of it."

"Christ, Eli, every time I open the paper someone's giving you a new prize. You must get ten or twenty grand a shot for talks. And what about the dough your books bring in? How broke can you be?"

"Look, Lou, without going into details, all I can tell you is that I don't have the money and no prospects of getting it except from you."

I had already made up my mind to lend Eli the money, but for some reason I didn't want to make it easy for him. I hate to admit it, but I found myself enjoying this.

"Suppose I loan you the money," I said. "What're you offering in collateral? The Pulitzer Prize?"

"How about I give you the continuing royalties for my first three novels?" he said, quite serious.

"An IOU will do, with a schedule of repayment," I said. "But Eli, maybe you'll take a little free literary advice. Don't ever put Sid Gusio into one of your novels. Unless you want a couple of knee-replacement operations."

One day at the office, my secretary tells me that David Black is on the phone. I don't recall knowing any David Black, but I pick up the phone anyway.

"Hello, Uncle Lou," a voice says. "I'm your brother Eli's son, and I'm in Chicago for a couple of days and I wonder if we could maybe meet."

Then it clicked in. David was Eli's son by his first marriage. I remember him only as a child. He must be in his thirties by now. He lived in northern California — Santa Rosa, if I remembered correctly.

"Where are you?" I asked. "Staying with your dad?"

"No," he said, "it turns out that my father's out of town. I'm here on business, staying at the Continental Hotel on Michigan Avenue. I don't know Chicago at all. But is it possible we could meet for lunch or a drink?"

"Sure, kid," I said. "It'd be fine."

We arranged to meet the next day at a bar in the Drake Hotel called the Coq d'Or, which served good sandwiches and which, if you arrived after the lunch rush, provided a certain amount of privacy, though I wasn't sure what this boy and I had to talk about.

The first thing I discovered was that my nephew was no kid. He was balding, slightly paunchy, with his father's nose and slightly flared nostrils. He was taller than Eli and darker. Something a little soft about him, vulnerable, but something, too, that made my heart go out to him. It was probably his having grown up without a father.

"Thanks for meeting me," he said, putting out his hand.

We took a table against the far wall and ordered beers and hamburgers. I asked him what brought him to Chicago.

"I'm here for a conference," he said. "I'm a civil engineer and work for the California highway system. The conference is about state highway funding. Dull stuff to most people, I suppose, but important in my line of work."

"Have you seen your father recently?"

"I called him before coming to town, but he told me that he was going to be in London."

"Are you in regular touch with him?"

"Irregular touch would be closer to it. Sometimes a year or two will go by without any contact. Usually I call him on his birthday."

Eli had divorced David's mother when he was three years old. She took him to California and remarried there a few years later. Eli hadn't much money in those days and saw his son no more than once a year, if that. When he remarried and had other children, he saw him even less.

"I learned to get on without my father," David said. "When I was a teenager, I sort of followed his career in the newspapers. At school nobody knew that my father was the famous writer, which was fine by me. My stepfather, who died two years ago, was a decent man. My mother had two other children with him, but he always treated me fairly. I have no complaints."

David told me that he had three children of his own. Eli had not yet seen the youngest, a boy who was four years old. I thought how much my own wife missed having grandchildren.

"I suppose the one grudge I hold against my father is the way he portrayed my mother in one of his novels, where he makes her out to be so vengeful and little more than an obstacle to his own career. I've always wanted to say something to him about the meanness of that, but I've never had the guts. When it comes to his writing, he can be very touchy, my father."

"I haven't had much luck reading your dad's novels," I said.

"Maybe it's because they don't have plots. I'm just an engineer, what do I know, but my father's books seem to be mostly about men like him, Jewish intellectuals who feel the world has screwed them in some vague, deep way. His main point, near as I can make out, is that nobody understands the modern artist and just about everyone is an anti-Semite. But his books seem to charm lots of people. I don't think there's a prize left he hasn't won. And he's been translated into all kinds of languages."

David went on to talk about his wife, who is a graphic artist, and his children and how he came to study engineering. When he asked me about my own family and business, he listened carefully as I told him about my life. He seemed a solid kid, my nephew, and I wished I could do something for him, something to make up for all the things that my brother didn't do. Eli's and Arlene's and my father wasn't much, but at least he was on the premises, and he sure as hell didn't attack our mother in public. Thank God for small blessings.

Out on the street in front of the Drake, David and I exchanged business cards, and he said he hoped I would visit him and my grandnephews and grandniece if I should ever find myself in Santa Rosa. "It's the wine country, you know, Sonoma Valley," he said. I told him I'd try to stay in touch, but life being what it is, I sensed that we wouldn't meet again.

A few weeks later, I called my brother to tell him about my meeting with his son and what a fine young man I thought he is. "You're lucky to have such a kid," I said. "It's none of my business, but you probably ought to see him more than you do."

"You're right, Lou," Eli said. "It isn't any of your business. Look, I don't expect you to understand this, but all the energy I have goes into my books—all of it. There isn't anything left for anything else."

"Whaddaya writing, the Bible?" I said. "They're only novels, Eli. We're talking about human beings here, a son and grandchildren."

"What the hell do you know about the life of an artist?" he said, and hung up on me.

Arlene had had a bout with breast cancer, and now, four years later, she called one night in tears to tell us that the cancer had returned, metastasized to the brain. It was inoperable. Arlene's two marriages, like my own marriage, produced no children. She hadn't gone to college, and she'd worked for many years as the bookkeeper at Zimmerman's Liquors in the Loop. I helped her out a bit financially when her building went condo and she wanted to buy her apartment; I also gave her some investment advice that worked out well. But she had no one in the world except Gerry and me, who loved her, and Eli.

She was given between six and eight months to live.

Arlene was the most generous-spirited person I ever knew. She had no meanness, no anger, no envy — at least none that I ever saw. When I went with her to see Al Hirsch to discuss her will, she decided to divide everything she had among Eli's grandchildren. I learned then that she had a list of their birthdays and every year sent each one of them a card with a fifty-dollar bill in it. She made me promise not to tell Eli about the return of her cancer. "He hates death," she said. "He can't stand hearing about it. I'll tell him when the time gets nearer."

Arlene had also arranged another dinner with her neighbors the Wertheimers. She had a bad conscience about the way the previous one had turned out, and she hoped that we would come again. Of course we said yes. She told us, too, that she hadn't told the Wertheimers about the return of her cancer, and we were instructed not to mention it.

The going was much easier without Eli there. We talked about the Wertheimers' and Arlene's neighbors, about the American infatuation with sports, and about how foreigners like the Wertheimers viewed American politics. "Too much virtue in American politics," Karl Wertheimer said. "I prefer a straighter kind of political engagement. I mean one in which one votes one's interests and beliefs and doesn't think people who vote otherwise are monsters or idiots."

Arlene is a good cook, and the dinner was excellent. It was only at dessert — a pineapple upside-down cake — and coffee that Henrietta Wertheimer asked if we minded talking about Eli. No one seemed to object.

"Your brother, you know, is a peculiar but not entirely unknown type," she said. "Nothing, it seems, makes him happy. Not his successes, not his wives and children, not all the world's lavish praise of his work. Psychotherapy doesn't really have a label for such a condition. He isn't a depressive, nothing so simple as that. Yet one could tell from a single meeting with him, and from the many seemingly grudging interviews he has given to the press, that the world — how to say this? — the world disappoints him. It isn't, somehow, good enough for him."

"I note from a recent interview," Karl Wertheimer joined in, "that your brother has begun a dalliance with the doctrines of Rudolf Steiner. Perhaps you know of this man Steiner?"

None of us did.

"A quack not even of the first order," he continued. "In his doctrine, spirits are aloft, souls join in the empyrean, all sorts of other fun and games. But what I find interesting in all this is your brother's need for a higher doctrine, for a system of ideas, no matter how foolish. He was a Trotskyist, I understand, as a young man, and then there was the Wilhelm Reich period, which we talked about earlier, and now there is Rudolf Steiner. Perhaps, who knows, in the end he will die, your brother, as a Catholic."

I didn't know how to respond. The Wertheimers knew a lot more about the intellectual side of Eli than I did. But what I took from their account of my brother's adventures among the quacks was his basic unreality. He grew up on the same streets I did. We had the same parents. How could two people be so different?

"What do you make of all my brother-in-law's marriages?" Gerry asked.

"A number of possible ways of viewing this," Henrietta Wertheimer said. "Perhaps they express a yearning for the settled life that he thinks he wants but does not really want. Perhaps he operates, your brother-in-law, under a theory of muses, like the painter Picasso or the choreographer Balanchine, who had different wives and mistresses for different phases of their respective careers. This, too, is possible."

"What seems clear to me," Karl Wertheimer joined in, "is that Eli Black believes in the myth of the artist. This is a myth that holds that everything must be sacrificed for art. It may not be a foolish myth if one is, say, Michelangelo or Beethoven. But if one is less than that, then the myth of the artist is very destructive, sadly so for the people who become too closely involved with him."

When it was finally time to tell Eli about the return of Arlene's cancer, he did come to visit. He had by then moved to Washington, planning, he said, to write a political novel, though he never did. (Instead, Gerry tells me, he wrote a novel attacking his fourth wife for not understanding the condition of the artist and for her unconscious anti-Semitism.) He stayed at Arlene's apartment over a long weekend. I never found out what they spent their time talking about, but I'd bet it wasn't about death. When I tried to talk to Eli about hospice and other arrangements for Arlene, he seemed very uncomfortable. Nobody likes death, but Eli seemed to take death personally. He didn't see why death should one day have to happen to him, too. He seemed to feel there was something unfair about it, at least in his case.

Now that he was near seventy, he did what he could to fight it. When he came over for dinner at our apartment, he told Gerry beforehand that he no longer ate meat. He spent a lot of time in gyms. He took up yoga. He became thin, which only made him look older. A picture of him published in the *Chicago Tribune* Sunday magazine shows his skin sagging, his hooded eyes looking wrinkled like a lizard's, his nose larger. He's wearing one of his crazy suits (blue-gray with red stripes outlined faintly in yellow), a pink shirt, a bandanna around what appeared to be his goiterish neck. He looked, Gerry said, like an ancient Jewish parrot.

I also noted a strong strain of sentimentality in my brother. Although Eli didn't go to Arlene's funeral — he said it would have been too much for him — once she was dead he spoke of her as if she were a saint. "She was the only person who ever truly loved me," he told me, "who took me exactly as I am, no questions asked." He even had kind words for our father. He was super-critical of other writers, but if one of them died, he spoke more kindly about him. To earn Eli's respect, apparently you have to die first. That seemed to me a very steep price to have to pay.

Eli had repaid my quarter-million-dollar loan, right on schedule. His life seemed, at least as far as I could tell, on a firmer basis. He was married to the same woman, the dean of a university in Washington, where he now lived, for eight or so years. He published a new novel. As a writer, he was respected more than ever, or so Gerry reported from reading the reviews of this latest book. I was headed toward eighty; my brother was seventy-three.

And then I hear that Eli had left his wife to marry a graduate student at Georgetown University, a woman not yet thirty. Which means she was more than forty years younger than he was. Something in my brother evidently can't stand peace and quiet. I knew nothing about the girl, but I could imagine what her parents must have felt when she told them she was going to marry a man older than they were. I wouldn't be surprised if Eli, in his vanity, felt his sexual attraction was still there, that he was still in the game, still a player. Gerry jokingly wondered if her brother-in-law and his new bride were registered at Marshall Field's. I felt sorry for the girl.

I felt even sorrier when, a year or so later, Eli's son David called to tell me that his father and his young wife had had a Down syndrome child, a boy they named Frederick. What the hell was Eli thinking! No doubt jacked up on Viagra, was he going to show the world he was still virile? Hadn't he already proved he was a misery as a father? Why prove it again? Gerry thought that a child probably wasn't Eli's idea but his young wife's. She said that it sounded like the notion of a young woman to want the child of the much older husband, something to have after he had gone. A part of me felt sorry for Eli. I found it hard to imagine the life he led with a young wife, with whom he couldn't have all that much in common, and now a retarded son.

Eli never called to tell me that he had remarried or that he had had a child, and this time the lapse in our relations ran four or so years. I sold my business. Gerry and I now lived half the year in a condo we purchased in Boca Raton. Our health had held up fairly well, though I had begun to have arthritis in my elbows and ankles, about which there isn't much to be done but grin and bear it. I try to find pleasure in each day. The truth is that I feel myself damn lucky: I'd always made a good living, I wasn't dependent on anyone my whole life, and I still enjoy my wife's company.

I'd pretty much lost touch with Eli's son David — his other kids I can't say I ever knew to begin with — when one day I decided to call him to see how things were going.

"Things aren't too bad, Uncle Lou," David said. "I've had a

promotion. My kids are in good shape. We bought a larger house. Can't complain."

"How's your father?"

David told me that his father was suffering from dementia.

"How bad?" I asked.

"I guess it tends to be day to day — that is, some days he's better than others. I went to visit him in Washington. He sleeps a lot. He knows who everyone is, but his sense of time is way out of whack. He sometimes thinks people who died years ago are still alive. Maybe you ought to try to see him before things get a lot worse."

The next day I called Eli's young wife and asked when it might be convenient to see my brother. Anytime I wished, she said. When I asked how he was, she said, "Some days he's pretty good. Today happens to be one of his bad days."

I took a cab from Reagan Airport to Eli's house, on Hoban Road. His wife greeted me at the door, saying that her husband was sleeping. She was not a beautiful woman, my new sister-in-law, but she had an intelligent face. When I addressed her as Mrs. Black, she said, "Call me Sandy, please."

She made coffee, which we drank sitting in the large kitchen. Her son, she said, was off at something called Playschool. She asked if I knew anything about Down syndrome kids.

"They have their own charms, you know," she said. "Frederick is very dear."

"How is my brother with him?"

"Before his illness, he was marvelous with him, though at first he was shocked, and blamed himself, his being so old, for the child's not being normal."

Eli now entered the kitchen. He was in slippers, pajama bottoms, an undershirt with a V-neck. He looked tired; his skin sagged badly; his left eye was almost closed. If you hadn't known him and someone told you he was ninety, you'd have believed it.

"Lou," he said. "What a nice surprise! Did Arlene come along? Arlene always loved me, you know. She was my first and best friend."

I thought to tell him that Arlene had died more than a decade ago, but then figured that it would only agitate him, and so I said nothing.

"No, Eli," I said. "Arlene couldn't make it this trip. Why don't you join us for some coffee?"

"A good idea, Louie, sure, why not?" He never called me Louie before; nobody ever called me Louie.

"We have a son, Louie. Frederick the Great, I call him. Cute kid. You'll like him. So tell me, Louie, how's the old man? Still working for Schinberg on Fulton Street?"

"He's fine, Eli. He still doesn't say much. What do you suppose he's thinking? You're the novelist. You probably know."

"He's thinking what am I doing in this damn country? He's thinking who needs this goddamn English language? He's thinking life is full of dirty tricks. It really is full of dirty tricks, Louie, an endless variety of them, I'm here to tell you. But then you probably noticed on your own."

"Hard not to notice, Eli."

"Take me," he said. "Take me, Louie. Somewhere along the way I slipped off the track. Could never get back on. Not good. Wrote the books, though. That must stand for something with someone or other. Only one life to live, I'm afraid, and it's getting obvious that I'm not going to be allowed to live mine as a blond." He put a hand to the few fluffy white hairs that remained on his head.

"Think I'll take a pass on that coffee," he said. "Wake me when Frederick gets home, Sandy. There's lots of things I have to tell him. Next time bring Arlene, Louie. She's my true friend, always was, always will be." And then he shuffled out of the room, my kid brother, and I never saw him again.

I don't know how Eli got the gun, the Beretta, he killed himself with. And of course I don't know what the exact motives for his suicide were. It may be that he was terrified of slipping any farther down the dark hole of his dementia. Maybe he found he lived his life so badly that he wanted to end it. When I remember how much he feared death, I shudder at the picture of him getting up the courage to put the gun in his mouth and then pulling the trigger. He slipped off the track and couldn't get back on, he told me that morning in his house on Hoban Road. What in the hell did he mean? I'll never understand him, my kid brother Eli.

Bartlestein's First Fling

L ARRY BARTLESTEIN HAS PLAYED it safe all his life, and playing it safe has paid off. At sixty-four he is a wealthy man, his two daughters are married, he has two grandchildren and another on the way, and he and Myrna will soon celebrate their fortieth wedding anniversary. In his set of friends, this last fact is nearly worthy of *Ripley's Believe It or Not*. There were lots of early divorces, and a number more when couples reached their mid-forties. Some had still not settled in. Bartlestein read in *Chicago* magazine last month that his high school classmate Joel Meizels, the real estate developer, had just forked over $40 million to his third wife. The figure made him whistle. The two earlier wives probably hadn't done much worse.

To Bartlestein, playing it safe came naturally. He had been a passably good student in high school, majored in business at the University of Illinois, taken and passed the CPA exam, and married Myrna Perelman, his high school girlfriend, soon after graduation. Myrna, who had gone to the National College of Education in Evanston, taught grade school for the two years that it took Bartlestein to get his MBA at the University of Chicago. A job offer from Merrill Lynch followed, but it involved moving to

Dallas. It was around then that his father-in-law made Bartlestein one of those offers not many people could refuse.

Perelman Plumbing is a major manufacturer of sinks, tubs, and faucets in the Midwest, one of the four or five largest in North America. Irv Perelman, the first Jewish licensed master plumber in Chicago, built the business out of a small warehouse on Western Avenue, near Diversey, after returning home from World War II. A genuinely modest man, he retained the thick, callused hands of a plumber, grime permanently encrusted under his fingernails.

"Larry," Irv Perelman said when his daughter told him about their prospective move to Dallas, "what's it going to take to keep you two here? I'd like the business to stay in the family, and Myrna's mother and I like having our daughters close by." Myrna's older sister, Susan, was married to a dentist in Highland Park.

"What do you have in mind?" Bartlestein asked.

"I was thinking about making you a vice president in charge of the administrative side of the company and eventually let you run the whole business if you turn out to be good at it. Starting salary of fifty thousand a year."

In 1966, $50,000 was serious money, more than twice what Merrill Lynch was offering to move Bartlestein to Dallas. Besides, Myrna wasn't eager to leave Chicago. Why not, Bartlestein figured. He told his father-in-law he was grateful for the offer and ready to give it his best effort.

Irv Perelman was of the my-word-is-my-bond school. He had no craving for power or status or glory, and he felt no need to bully or lord things over his son-in-law or anyone else. He just wanted to turn out a good product at a reasonable profit. His employees, who after five years became automatically vested in the company's profit-sharing plan, tended to stay put, many for their entire working lives. "No need to be a pig," he once said to

Bartlestein. "Run this business right and everyone will do OK."

Bartlestein spent long hours mastering the details of the plumbing business. When Irv Perelman turned seventy-five and stopped driving, Bartlestein began picking him up on the way in from Northbrook. Most mornings, Irv read the *Trib* and then, after he put down the paper, the two generally talked business: investing profits, enlarging the plant, designing a new line, patching up troubles. After much careful effort, Bartlestein had gotten the firm's less expensive sinks and faucets into Home Depot, which turned out to be a shrewd move. His father-in-law treated him without condescension, as if he were a full partner, which is what Irv made him on Bartlestein's fiftieth birthday.

One morning, on the drive down, Bartlestein mentioned that he was thinking of getting a new car, a Mercedes. His father-in-law came alive. "Do me a favor," he said, "and buy another kind of car." Bartlestein asked why. Irv, who never talked about his wartime experiences, answered that even today he didn't like to think about it, but his battalion had been among the first to liberate the Jews at Treblinka. "I don't consider myself a prejudiced man," he said, "but the least I can do to keep the sights of those days out of my mind is not to have to drive to work with my son-in-law in a German car."

Bartlestein bought a Lexus, and from then on he purchased a new one every three years. He found the Lexus to be the perfect car for him: dependable, not too showy, efficient, quietly luxurious. He has himself become a kind of human Lexus.

After the death of Irv Perelman — at eighty-one, of a heart attack, early one morning at his desk — Perelman Plumbing has continued as a family business, with Lawrence R. Bartlestein as chairman and chief executive officer. Bartlestein has invested both the company's and his own personal profits well. He has twice been president of Temple Jeremiah. He is among the major contributors in metropolitan Chicago to the Jewish United Fund, manufacturing division. He golfs at Bryn Mawr Country Club. Myrna, a better golfer than he, regularly wins the over-fifty women's title at Bryn Mawr. His daughter Debbie is married to a cardiologist and has two children of her own. Jennifer, his younger girl, married a documentary filmmaker and is now, after two traumatic miscarriages, in her eighth month. Her husband, Charlie, isn't making his nut, so Bartlestein helps out with a couple of grand a month.

At his annual physical less than two months ago, Bartlestein was assured by his internist that he is in excellent health. He does the treadmill and rowing machines at the East Bank Club, his weight is about what it should be, and all his numbers—cholesterol, blood pressure, PSA, and the rest—are good. Financially, medically, domestically, he is in the black, in the clear, sailing in calm waters.

So the question is, what is Lawrence R. Bartlestein doing in his office at 6:45 on a Wednesday night, slipping his hand under the blouse of a young woman named Elaine Leslie, a designer at Perelman Plumbing? Elaine at this moment has her hand on Bartlestein's belt buckle, loosening it with what seem like very deft hands.

Only minutes before, Elaine Leslie was standing behind Bartlestein's chair as he studied the designs and production costs for a new midpriced line of faucets, a project she had brought in for his comments. He felt her hand touch his shoulder, then go upward, massaging gently, her fingers raveling the hair on the back of his neck. He pushed his chair away from his desk, and before he had time to say anything, she slid smoothly onto his lap, and his arms were around her. Presently she will descend to do unbidden what Bartlestein, head of a company whose estimated worth is well over $100 million, has never found the nerve to ask his wife to do.

Bartlestein feels himself trembling slightly as Elaine, moving quickly, removes her blouse and slips out of her skirt. Now they are on the floor, Ms. Leslie (as he persists in thinking of her) directing the show. Bartlestein feels oddly detached, hugely excited yet curiously outside himself, looking in. He recalls that he is a grandfather. He has had back trouble of late, and hopes he will not throw something out of whack before this session on his office floor is over. Until now, he has never in his life slept with anyone but Myrna.

Earlier this year, Bartlestein had lunch with Eddie Jacobs, who handles his brokerage account at Bear Stearns. Eddie's third wife is in her early thirties, and, Eddie confided, he is sexually very active. That was the bragging phrase he used, "sexually very active." Bartlestein's own sex with Myrna is and always was decidedly less so. He enjoyed it, and tried to be a patient and in no way brutish lover; Myrna was without expressed complaint. But after the first year or so of their marriage, sex had never been at the center of their life. When their daughters arrived, and his responsibilities at the office increased, most of Myrna's complaints were about the hours he worked at Perelman Plumbing. Bartlestein's adult life has been lived through a very sexy age, and he has tried his best not to be swept up in the craziness.

Bartlestein and Elaine Leslie are now lying on the Oriental rug in front of his desk, she on her stomach, he still on his back. He looks at his watch: 7:18. The Polish cleaning women, he knows, come on at 9. Clothes are scattered across the floor. He is still wearing his T-shirt and black socks — "executive length," as the saleswoman at Marshall Field's described them to him. Now they remind him of those ridiculous movies shown at the stag parties he used to attend for friends on the night before their weddings.

"What exactly are we doing here?" he hears himself ask.

"I believe there are several names for it," Ms. Leslie answers.

"I guess I mean, why are we here?"

"For pleasure," she says. "It pleased me. I hope it didn't displease you."

Bartlestein feels complimented. "I'm still not putting it right," he says. "How did we get into this position?"

"I got us into it, Larry," she said. "It's OK to call you Larry, isn't it? I thought you could use a little relief."

Relief, Bartlestein thinks: interesting word.

They dress, and Bartlestein asks if she would like dinner; he can tell Myrna he has to entertain a customer at the last minute. She says no, thank you, but since her car is in the shop, she would appreciate a ride home.

On the way, Bartlestein finds conversation awkward. He asks if she grew up in Chicago, and she answers New York, but she has lived here for almost twelve years. "I still think of myself as a New Yorker," she adds. "Can't help it. Being a New Yorker is like being a member of an ethnic group." This makes Bartlestein wonder. Is she Jewish? Her name doesn't give much of a clue.

He drops her in front of her large apartment building on Armitage, off Lincoln Park. No talk about his coming up; no mention of their getting together again. Looking back as she closes the car door, she says, "Thanks for the ride, Mr. Bartlestein," forgetting to call him by his first name.

Driving home, Bartlestein attempts to decipher Elaine Leslie's motives. He rules out simple sexual attraction, at least on her part. Although, like all men, he still checks out every woman in sight, and figures he will probably do so on his deathbed, there is nothing of the flirt in him. He is careful to send no signals to his female employees, and has certainly never sent any to Elaine Leslie, who was hired not by him but by his father-in-law. He is without illusions about his own attractiveness; women, he knows, find him easily resistible.

Perhaps, Bartlestein thinks, still searching for motives, she views sex with him as a way of getting ahead in the office. Blackmail is always a possibility. A wealthy man with a settled home life, Bartlestein has put himself in a position where Elaine Leslie could do him real damage. His mind racing, he conceives the possibility of an office pool, with the prize going to the first female employee to bang the boss. Who knows?

He thinks back to the day when, near high school graduation, he and Myrna first made love — "going all the way" was the name for it then, a phrase, it occurs to him now, that assumed there was no way back. Having taken her virginity and in the same moment given up his own, he felt, rightly or wrongly, beholden to her. In those days, the sex act was not only exciting but a matter of the deepest intimacy, implying trust on every level. There was nothing trivial about it. Now, for Elaine Leslie, it was a means of relief. Which was the better arrangement? Bartlestein hasn't a clue.

He is not disappointed to discover that Myrna isn't home. A note in the foyer tells him she has gone to her book discussion group at Sue Levin's. There's lasagna in the fridge, with instructions for warming it in the microwave. She may not be home until after 11, and will try not to wake him. Bartlestein, who gets up at 5 A.M., is usually asleep by 10:30. The note, as always, is signed "Love, Myrna."

Eating the lasagna quickly, Bartlestein moves to the bedroom, where he checks his shirt for lipstick and his clothes for perfume, and — always the safe player — showers before getting into bed. He is sure sleep won't come quickly, but it does, and without any of the anxiety dreams that have plagued him since he turned sixty.

In the morning, Bartlestein looks over at his wife, her face, even in sleep, shining with kindness. He and Myrna don't confide in each other regularly; there are many things, chiefly business worries, that Bartlestein keeps to himself. But their marriage is built on being able to count on each other, on never being a cause of embarrassment, let alone humiliation. What happened last night, if it were to come out, could only cause Myrna both.

Usually they have coffee and toast together, but this morning he decides not to wake her. After he has shaved and dressed, he kisses Myrna gently on the forehead and tells her he is leaving a bit early. "Love you," she says, pulling the covers up and falling back to sleep.

In the office, checking Elaine Leslie's file, Bartlestein learns that she is twenty-three years younger than he, is a graduate of Pratt Institute, earns just under $70,000 a year, and is divorced with no children. She has been with Perelman Plumbing for eight years. According to the reports of the people she has worked for, she is excellent at her job. She is also, Bartlestein reflects, good-looking, petite, and vibrant. Not to mention fine in bed, or on the floor.

The question is how to erase what happened last night. These days you have to be very careful about letting someone go, even someone who royally deserves to be fired, which Ms. Leslie clearly does not. Screwing the boss hardly qualifies as a reason, especially when the boss has put up no resistance whatsoever; more likely it qualifies as grounds for a high-publicity sexual harassment suit.

Earlier, driving to work, Bartlestein wondered whether he might arrange to have her lured away by another firm, perhaps even fix things so as to pay part of her salary. He is on friendly terms with Teddy Mohlner, head of a rival and larger plumbing firm. What if he confessed to Teddy his "indiscretion"—that is the word he decides he will use—and asked him to take Elaine off his hands by hiring her for $20,000 more than she is now making. He would come up with the additional money out of his own pocket. Once the deal was in place, he could tell Elaine he had heard Mohlner was looking for designers and was willing to pay up to $90,000. Was she interested?

But now Bartlestein thinks, What am I, nuts? Imagine confessing his problem to Teddy Mohlner. Imagine signing up to pay twenty grand or more a year for the foreseeable future, all for a quick roll on the floor. Talk about dumb schemes!

"Hi. Larry Bartlestein," he says to Elaine Leslie on the office phone. "I think we should probably have a talk. Are you free for dinner any night this week?"

"Tonight I can't," she says. "But tomorrow night's OK."

"Great," he says. "You know Erwin's, on Halsted? How about we meet at seven."

"See you there," she says.

Bartlestein's heart is racing. How the hell did he get himself into this? He sees scandal, lawsuits, a divorce, his careful life going down the tubes. The problem facing him is how to disengage smoothly, without bad feelings and worse consequences, but his mind floats off when he seeks a solution.

At the bar at Erwin's, it occurs to the waiting Bartlestein for the first time that maybe he doesn't really want to disengage from Elaine Leslie. Doesn't he deserve a little time off for an entire life of good behavior? He can afford a lady friend, and what with his long working hours and frequent business travel he feels reasonably sure he could arrange to bring the affair off. Maybe it makes sense to let this business unfold, wind down of its own accord.

Erwin's is a restaurant with good food and a fairly low level of pretension. Hoping that he won't be seen, at least not by friends or business associates, Bartlestein has scanned the room with care. Elaine Leslie is only a few years older than his daughter Debbie. Seeing them together, would people take him for her father? Better that, he thinks, than for some old guy chasing young broads, a sugar daddy. As he ponders whether people use words like "broads" and "sugar daddy" anymore, Elaine walks up to him at the bar.

She is wearing jeans, close-fitting, and a red cashmere cardigan over a white T-shirt. Her dark hair, cut short and brushed back, accentuates her delicate ears. On them she wears simple silver ball-shaped earrings; on her feet, moderately high heels. Her lipstick is darker than what she uses in the office. Noting these things, Bartlestein thinks that Myrna, who jokes about his obliviousness to her clothes and jewelry, would be amazed at his powers of observation. He also thinks he would have a hard time convincing anyone that this young woman, dressed for the attack, is a niece from out of town or a business associate.

"I don't know this restaurant," she says. "Looks like a good place for a tryst. Or are trysts only in the afternoon?"

"Good place for dinner, actually," Bartlestein says, "and for talk. What're you drinking?"

She orders an apple martini, something Bartlestein has never heard of. From a small bag she takes out a white box of long, slender cigarettes. Lighting one for her, Bartlestein feels he is in a movie from the late 1940s, which, he reminds himself, is well before Elaine Leslie was born. In fact, everyone in the restaurant seems young to him: the fellow who asked for his reservation, the bartender, the woman who has shown them to their table, the waitress who recites the list of the evening's specials. After the first two specials, Bartlestein can never keep track. Elaine orders a veal chop, he the swordfish.

"So," Bartlestein begins as the waitress goes off. "What do you see happening here?"

"Between us?" she says. "I kinda think that's your call."

"I'm a lot older than you, I'm your employer, I'm married, I'm even a grandfather."

"Really," she says. "I don't think I've ever slept with a grandfather before. I certainly never slept with my own."

Her jokiness puts him off, but he persists. "Why would you want to waste your time with me?" he asks.

"Think of me as Florence Nightingale," she says, lifting her martini glass — tall, with a blue stem — in a toast to herself. "I like the idea of bringing comfort to the wounded troops."

"Wounded?"

"Maybe not wounded. Maybe stifled. I don't know, but when I was standing behind you at your desk, I felt an overpowering sadness, as if you were a little boy who always did what he was told and didn't have all that much fun doing it."

"I don't think of myself that way at all," Bartlestein says. "I think of myself as a lucky man, in lots of ways."

"I'm only reporting what I felt," she says. "Funny: you say 'think,' I say 'feel.' Difference between men and women, I suppose."

When their food comes, Elaine's veal chop is enormous.

"They don't spare the horses here," Bartlestein says.

"Let's hope they do," she replies with her quick smile.

Bartlestein is impressed by the way she tucks into her food. Myrna, who worries about her weight, nowadays rarely eats anything but salads and fish, and never much of either.

"How do you eat like this and stay so slender?" Bartlestein asks after she has polished off the chop, the potato, the broccoli, and a large salad, and ordered a dessert of chocolate mousse and raspberries and a double espresso.

"The torture of exercise," she says. "The choice for me is simple: jog five times a week or buy my clothes at maternity thrift shops."

"Which reminds me to ask, if it's not too personal, how come you've never had children?"

"Pretty personal," she says. "My ex-husband turned out to be a child himself, and since he didn't show any signs of growing up, I didn't see much point in raising another one. There's another reason. I had an alcoholic mother. I'll spare you the details except to say that my dad took off and left my brother and me in her very shaky care. When your own childhood has been a misery, you think hard before bringing more children into the world. At least I did. Still do, actually."

Bartlestein finds himself touched by this young woman. He learns that her younger brother died in a car accident. She went to college on Long Island, to a school called Adelphi that he had never heard of. To help pay her way, she had waited tables. She wanted to be an actress, but auditioning made her too nervous. She had always been good at visual art, had an instinctive sense of design, and was able to get together a portfolio that won her a scholarship to Pratt. Her marriage, she tells Bartlestein, lasted four hellish years.

What Elaine described was a life lived pretty much on her own. How different from the case of Bartlestein's own daughters. Mostly thanks to Myrna, the girls had been carefully guarded and ushered through a gentle girlhood ending in safe marriages to Jewish boys of roughly their own background. They had been backed up all the way. Elaine Leslie flew solo, and was still doing so. Bartlestein admired that.

"You know," he says, driving her back to her apartment on Armitage, "we really haven't talked about the purpose of this dinner."

"You mean the purpose wasn't strictly nutritional?" she says.

"I mean where we're going."

"I think I'll let you decide that," she says. "I understand your situation is much more complicated than mine. If you want to put a stop to things now, we can do that, too."

"You're an amazing kid," Bartlestein says, pulling up in front of her apartment. "But maybe you already know that."

"I do," she says. "But it's nice to get reinforcement." She steps out of the car before he can come around to open the door for her. "Have to be up early," she says, looking in. "I work for a real tyrant. Thanks for dinner."

On the drive home, Bartlestein feels exhilarated, youthful, high, and happy as he hasn't been for years — decades, really. He knows men whom he thinks of as terrific chaos managers. At the East Bank Club, he occasionally runs into Jack Meltzer, a friend from high school days. On his fourth marriage, all of them to much younger women, Jack has twice declared bankruptcy, is in serious hock to the IRS, and at one point had Mafia goons after him for too-slow payment of juice loans. Yet he shows no obvious traces of stress. At the club he still takes more than his share of shots at half-court basketball, flirts with women, tells jokes at which he himself laughs the loudest.

Bartlestein is not like that. If a shipment is delayed or profits are down by a half point from last year, he can't sleep. How he has avoided ulcers is a mystery. "Know your limitations" was one of his father-in-law's great mottos, and Bartlestein, taking it seriously, had discovered his early. He needs his risks to be closely calculated, his days to be orderly, his life to be routinized. Take care of the details, he believes, and the larger matters will take care of themselves.

Are we talking about a midlife crisis here, Bartlestein wonders. He had never put much stock in the notion. Men of a certain age become interested in younger women and want to drive around for a while in red convertibles. Not much crisis there, it seemed to him, just random desire conquering good sense. So isn't he entitled, too? At sixty-four he is already well past midlife. Hasn't he earned a last — make that a first — fling?

Details, it is all a matter of details, and details are Bartlestein's specialty. If he could master the details of the sink-and-bathtub business, surely he can master the details of a relatively simple love affair without stirring up trouble. True, the stakes are high. If he is caught at it, Myrna will never again regard him in the same trusting way; she might even want a divorce. He will lose the respect of his daughters and their husbands.

Before he turns off the freeway at the exit for Dundee West, he has decided not to break things off with Elaine Leslie.

"Larry," Myrna says as soon as he enters the house, her voice shaking, "I've been trying to reach you for hours."

Bartlestein takes out his cell phone. He'd turned it off before going into the restaurant.

"What's the matter?"

"It's Jen. The baby was stillborn, strangled on its umbilical cord. She went to the hospital by ambulance, but it was too late. Larry, it's horrible. Almost full term, and now this nightmare." Tears are in his wife's eyes. She embraces him. She sobs, clutching at him. Bartlestein holds her, rubbing her back slowly in a circular motion. He tries to block out everything he has been thinking on his ride home. The thought crosses his mind that his own behavior may have had something to do with his daughter's misfortune.

Bartlestein does not think of himself as religious, but he leads his life as if cosmic justice prevailed. A man does good, and good is likely to be his reward. The reverse is also true — not always, not inevitably, but mostly. He knows there are thousands of exceptions, but somewhere firmly lodged in his mind is the certainty of cause and effect, of acts having roughly predictable consequences, of people getting what they deserve. Somewhere, an accountant keeps a careful record.

"Dr. Oberman says that Jen isn't going to be able to have children, ever," Myrna says. "She's heartbroken. The hospital put in a cot, and Debbie is going to spend the night. Thank God Jen won't be alone."

Bartlestein's mind, usually so concentrated at moments of business crisis, is scattered. Despite himself, he can't help comparing his wife, her makeup ruined by tears, body slumped in grief, eyes red, exhausted by her daughter's suffering, with Elaine

Leslie's youthfulness. He feels a perfect son of a bitch. And he feels his own age.

Early the next morning at Highland Park Hospital, Bartlestein finds his daughter sitting in a chair near the window. Her older sister has gone home. Her mother is coming in later. Jennifer is his perennially troubled child. True, until now her troubles, though real enough to her, have been minor. She needed glasses, then braces. Her skin wasn't as good as Debbie's. She turned out to have a bit of a learning disability, and needed remedial teachers in grammar school and special tutoring later on. She sulked through adolescence, her sadness strong enough to send her to a therapist. She was unhappy with her nose — the Bartlestein nose, high-bridged, nostrils flared. Bartlestein didn't protest when Myrna said it should be fixed.

Nothing has seemed to go easily for Jen. Maybe because of this, Bartlestein loves her even more than her sister, though he tries never to show it. He loves her more because she needs him more.

"You OK, baby?"

"I'm OK, Daddy," Jen says, and her eyes begin to tear up.

"How's Charlie taking it?"

"He's been great. He's talking about adopting. I wanted my own children so much." All her efforts at bravery collapse, her head drops to her chest, and she begins crying. "Why me, Daddy? Why always me?"

Bartlestein holds her, kisses the top of her head, rubs her back as he did her mother's last night, murmurs over and over that everything's going to be all right. He feels her thinness through the robe. He stays for twenty minutes, holding his daughter's hand, neither of them saying much. He leaves after hugging her at great length, feeling inadequate.

Will this inability to have a child become the story of his daughter's life? Maybe he has raised both his girls too protectively. He has done everything he could to make them safe, has been the net over which they safely flew. Except they never quite flew, not even Debbie; they never quite got off the ground. They are conventional girls — decent enough, not mean or selfish, but in no way out of the ordinary.

But then, Bartlestein thinks, neither is he. Through cautiousness he has ventured little while gaining much. He has concentrated all his energies on his business: making and selling sinks and tubs and faucets. But what has he given up in return? Passion is what Bartlestein feels is missing from his life. If he lived more by his instincts, he would already have begun to let his affair with Elaine Leslie play itself out, to see where it led. But he doesn't live by his instincts; he lives by rules, by repression and self-sacrifice, by fear of shame and worry about guilt, by what he has always taken to be moral principle. At the moment, he doesn't feel particularly moral.

On the floor of his Lexus, Bartlestein notices a small suede bag. Opening it, he discovers lipstick, tweezers, a small mirror, a compact. It must belong to Elaine: lucky thing he didn't take his wife to the hospital. It's only a little past 7:30, so he decides to drop the bag off before Elaine leaves for work.

On the freeway, his cell phone rings. Myrna.

"What do you think?" she asks anxiously. "Is she going to be all right?"

"She's obviously very depressed. It's understandable enough."

"What terrible luck!" his wife says. "She wanted this baby so much."

"Rotten luck," Bartlestein agrees. "Crappy, crappy luck."

"We have to stand by her, Larry. Jen's going to need a lot of help."

"Right," Bartlestein says. "Look, babe, I'm just getting off the freeway. Call you later."

Bartlestein finds a parking spot half a block from Elaine's building. Ringing her up from the lobby, he's answered by a man's voice. Bartlestein says he has Elaine's cosmetics bag. The owner of the voice says she's out jogging but he'll come down to get it. A minute or so later, a young guy, tall, in shorts and a tank top, a baseball hat worn backward on his head, greets Bartlestein.

A relative of Elaine's? Bartlestein asks.

"No, a friend. Scott," the young man says with a smile, putting out a hand for Bartlestein to shake. He has large good teeth, very white. Bartlestein, a grinder in his sleep, has lost four teeth on the lower left-hand side and now wears a bridge.

"Thanks," the young man says. "I'm sure Ellie will be glad to have this." As he walks away, Bartlestein notes his long suntanned legs and athletic calves.

Bartlestein goes through his day, takes meetings, deals with suppliers over the phone, answers correspondence. Part of his plan is eventually to leave the business. He has thought he'd probably sell it to one of his larger competitors. What he will do with the time available, he doesn't know. He'll find something.

Actually, until meeting Scott, he had been thinking that one of the things he might do was to show Elaine a few bits of the world in an expansive, expensive way. Now he is thinking about his foolishness in imagining this could ever have happened. At a little past four, his secretary buzzes that Myrna is on the phone.

"Larry," she says, speaking quickly. "Bad news, but everything's OK."

"Myrna, be clear, please."

"Jennifer stuffed a fistful of pills down her throat. Thank God they got to her in time." Myrna is sobbing.

"My God!" Bartlestein says. "What do we do now?"

"I don't know," she says. "Please come home right away. I need you. We all do."

Bartlestein drives in a dark rain along the Kennedy Expressway. Myrna's last words on the phone had been "You're so good in emergencies, darling." Vaguely he wonders if he will ever create an emergency or two of his own before he leaves the earth. But that is not his role. He tries, without much success, to imagine his daughter's despair as she grabbed and gobbled down those pills.

A list is forming in his mind as he turns off the freeway. He will press ten grand on his son-in-law to take Jennifer on a vacation once she has her health back. He'll find the best shrink in the city for handling this sort of postpartum problem, if postpartum depression is what Jen is going through. He'll call Marty Cohn, his lawyer, to see what he knows about adoptions in China, in Korea, in Guatemala, here at home. He'll look into the business of surrogate mothers; another lawyer he knows, Henry Waller, has made a minor legal specialty of this. Naturally, Bartlestein thinks, I'll pay the expenses.

Tomorrow he'll call in Elaine Leslie. In his office he'll tell her that, pleasing as the prospect is, his life is too complicated just now for them to continue seeing each other. He'll mention serious family troubles, not going into any details. He will always be grateful to her, he'll say, leaving unspoken what, exactly, he is grateful for. What he is truly grateful for, he realizes almost with relief as he pulls into the driveway, is that she showed him a kind of life he is now certain he could never lead. He pauses for a second or two as the engine of the Lexus dies away, breathes deeply three times through his mouth, and heads for the house. It's a little past five. Marty Cohn never leaves his office before six-thirty. Might as well call him now, Bartlestein reasons, his spirits picking up.

Kuperman Awaits Ecstasy

D RIVING TO THE LOOP to take his tax stuff to Schapiro, his accountant for nearly forty years, Milton Kuperman, at the lengthy stoplight at Thorndale and Sheridan, had the appalling thought that his death, which couldn't be all that far off, would matter to no one, not a soul. A widower, Kuperman would be eighty in August. His only child, his daughter Rivian, lived in Los Angeles and saw him once a year; and that, when you got right down to it, was generally less than a visit and more like someone checking in dutifully to pay her respects.

Kuperman was also without grandchildren. Married to a successful patent attorney and unable to have children of their own, Rivian and her husband many years ago adopted a child from Chile, a boy they named Eric — Eric Cohen — who hadn't, as his daughter used to say, "worked out." By this she meant that, from his adolescence until now, a man in his late twenties, Eric was a drug addict, in and out of one clinic, sanatorium, hospital, and halfway house after another.

Richard Cohen, Kuperman's son-in-law, was a powerful moneymaker, so the inheritance that Kuperman planned to leave his daughter — somewhere in the range of $3 million — didn't figure to change the couple's life much; it would probably present nothing more than a complicated tax problem. At odd, perverse moments, Kuperman thought of leaving his money to his adopted grandson, whom he barely knew. Let him smoke it or shoot it up, inhale it or stuff it up his nose, who knew what. At least someone would get some pleasure out of the rewards of Kuperman's lifetime of work.

Kuperman had spent the better part of his life in the auction business. He had found a niche, as his son-in-law had put it. He bought up the inventories of failed businesses — known as closeouts in the trade — and sold them, along with other items he had acquired, at auction. A good part of his success he owed to his always keeping very liquid; an even larger part had to do with his talent for knowing what goods he could move. "You make your money in buying," he used to tell his nephew Stuart Siegel, his wife's sister Florence's son, who worked for him. "Buy right and the rest will take care of itself." Whether it be throw pillows, costume jewelry, outdated neckties, or whoopee cushions, if Kuperman could get it for the right price, and he usually could, he could turn a profit.

"What's the point, Milt?" said Schapiro. "What're you still knocking yourself out for? You've got more money than you can possibly use. What do you need the aggravation for?"

"I've come to like aggravation," Kuperman replied. "Within reason. It's part of life, part of the game."

"What do you need the game for? Enjoy life. Watch the sunset. Gaze at the stars. Do you want them to drag you out of your business feet-first?"

"Someone's going to drag me out of someplace feet-first, so it might as well be from my place of business. Besides, if I retire, what do you suggest I do, chase golf balls with the rest of the morons? Maybe I should take courses in Chinese stamp collecting or the history of Peru at *Loch in Kop* University downtown?"

"Milton, my friend, there's got to be more to life than close-outs."

Kuperman knew Schapiro had his best interests in mind. He liked Lou Schapiro — little Louie Schapiro, as he first knew him at Humboldt Grammar School and later at Roosevelt High, the shortest kid in class, who went on to win the gold medal in the state CPA exam at the age of twenty. But Schapiro didn't — couldn't possibly — know what was in his, Kuperman's, heart.

"Of course there is, Lou, but what's left of me if you take my work away? I'm not sure there's anything left."

"Whaddya mean? You read. You're a thoughtful guy. So quit working and just think, at your own pace, with no pressure on you at all. Maybe travel a little. Does that sound so bad?"

Kuperman could have turned the tables and asked Schapiro why he didn't retire. But then Lou had a son in the business, and he himself went into the office only three days a week, mostly to take care of old clients like Kuperman, who would have felt strange with their business in the hands of anyone else.

As for Kuperman's capacity for leisure, true, he was a reader, mostly of biography, especially of the lives of scientists. Had he gone to college, he would have liked to have studied engineering. Growing up when he did, engineers and inventors — Ford, Edison, even Charles Lindbergh held a few patents — were the great heroes of the age. But that wasn't any longer a possibility. One of the saddest things about growing older, Kuperman long ago concluded, was the closing off of one possibility after another.

Kuperman's only concession to retirement was to begin going into the office later in the morning: at ten o'clock instead of his usual eight-thirty. He continued to wake at five-thirty, as always. Although he said he didn't believe in the current exercise fad — "I'm a fatalist," he liked to say. "When your number's up, it's up" — Kuperman did use the early part of the morning for walks around the neighborhood. In bad weather he walked in the mall off McCormick Boulevard near his apartment on Touhy Avenue, off Kedzie, at Winston Towers.

On his third lap around the mall, in front of Foot Locker on a gray Tuesday morning, he met Faye Schwartz, the furrier's wife, who used to play cards with Miriam, Kuperman's wife. She was with another woman, petite, with red hair, whom she introduced as Judith Neeley.

Faye asked Kuperman how things were with him, said that her and her husband's health was good, they had a lot to be thankful for, and mentioned that Judith, who lost her husband last year, lived on the same floor as the Schwartzes, two buildings down from Kuperman's own building at Winston Towers.

"Judy taught high school," Faye said. "She was a music teacher at New Trier."

"That's nice," said Kuperman, not listening very intently.

"Interested in music, are you, Mr. Kuperman?" Mrs. Neeley said, showing a bright and winning smile.

"Well, not all that much, maybe," he answered, and even here he was lying, for Kuperman went to no concerts, kept no phonograph, and listened to the news exclusively on his car radio. He had vaguely heard of something called CDs, but had not actually seen one. When Miriam was alive, she dragged him to musical comedies; and though he went along, he didn't see the point of sitting uncomfortably in a seat at the Shubert Theatre, on Monroe, while young men and women, with great expenditures of false energy, belted out the lyrics to *The Pajama Game* and other such nonsense. He recalled the line "Seven and a half cents doesn't buy a heck of a lot . . ." Pure *narrishkeit*, nonsense.

"Without music," she said, "life for me wouldn't have much point."

"Really?" Kuperman asked.

"Absolutely," she said.

Kuperman looked at his watch. Faye Schwartz remarked that they had better keep moving. Judith Neeley put out her hand, which Kuperman shook before heading off in the other direction.

Driving down to his warehouse, on Ashland Avenue near Belmont, Kuperman thought about Mrs. Neeley. Not a Jewish name, Neeley. Irish, he thought. Of course, Neeley was her married name. Handsome woman, though, looked to be in her late sixties. He liked her manner; there was a note of seriousness about her he found appealing.

Kuperman had been a widower for a little more than four years. His wife had had liver cancer, and lived three years before it finally swept her away. As a husband, he was a good provider, but the fact was that his life was never concentrated in his marriage. He was most alive at his business. He loved his wife, or thought he did. But did he miss Miriam? At first, yes, a lot, but by now days, whole weeks, went by when he didn't think about her. His best guess was that, had he died first, he would not have been constantly in her thoughts, either. We forget the dead, and the living forget us when we die. That was all right, that was the deal, that was the way the world worked.

After hesitating for more than a week, Kuperman decided to call Judith Neeley. He wasn't sure why. At his age, the blood didn't run as fast as once it did. He was no lady killer. He didn't think of himself as lonely. During the day he made his business calls, worked with his nephew Stuart at the warehouse, made his own dinner or brought home Chinese, read the *Trib*, watched new shows on television, and was usually in bed before ten o'clock.

His health had held up. He figured he had nothing to complain about.

Still, here Kuperman was dialing the number of Judith Neeley. "Yes," she said, "of course I remember you. Faye introduced us at the mall."

Feeling like a high school boy, Kuperman heard the hesitation in his own voice as he asked her if she would like to meet one evening for dinner or maybe a movie.

"I don't go to the movies much anymore," she said. "But I have two tickets to a chamber music concert at DePaul this Sunday. Would that interest you?"

"Yes," Kuperman heard himself say, "it would, a lot."

That Sunday, before picking up Mrs. Neeley, Kuperman wasn't sure what to wear. He wasn't sure what a chamber music concert was, and his nephew Stuart, who had gone to the University of Wisconsin for three years, was no help. He decided on a business suit and one of his quieter neckties. He wasn't clear about why he was putting himself through this. At least, he told himself, he didn't have to travel far to pick up this broad.

On the way to the concert, Mrs. Neeley — she asked that he call her Judy — told him that her husband had been a lawyer working in a small firm with three Jewish partners. Neeley was Irish, but he had gone to Sullivan High School, where the kids were mostly Jewish, and he had become, as he liked to say, an honorary Jew. Over the years he had acquired more Yiddish words and expressions than she. Her parents, who had departed Austria in the early 1930s, weren't happy when she married Ned Neeley; her mother warned that someday, in anger, he would throw her being Jewish in her face. But her mother was wrong; it never happened. Her late husband hadn't any interest in music — he used to say that his musical education ended with "Mairzy Doats and Dozy Doats" — and he didn't mind her going off to the Chicago

Symphony and the Lyric Opera (she was a season subscriber to both) with lady friends.

Kuperman didn't say much about his own wife. Miriam had in fact been a bookkeeper in a firm he did business with, a thorough and well-mannered woman, pretty, five years younger than he. After marrying Kuperman, she stopped working, raised their daughter, cooked, kept house, had her special charities—the Jewish Home for the Blind, Hadassah, a cancer foundation named after her friend Edie Weitzman—played cards. She left Kuperman alone; never gave him a hard time when he needed to work extra hours or go down to the place on weekends. Kuperman never cheated on her; the thought that she might have cheated on him was not possible. Before she died, she thanked Kuperman for giving her a good life. Did she have her own unspoken yearnings? Would she have preferred another kind of life? While she was alive, Kuperman neglected to ask.

Kuperman parked his Cadillac on Belden, off Halsted. The hall for the concert also served as a chapel. There were no crucifixes on any of the walls, but the seats were pews with red cushions added. Bright light flooded in through the tall side windows on this cool afternoon. The audience made Kuperman, at seventy-nine, feel positively young. Much osteoporosis; a number of people on walkers; most of the women had white hair and several of them seemed bulky; the majority of the men were bald, bent, haggard. Hard to imagine that many in the audience were ever desirable, even when young, Kuperman thought. He had overdressed. Only one other man, a doddering guy who looked to be in his nineties, wore a tie.

When Kuperman, seated, looked at the program he had been handed at the door, he saw that he was about to hear something called the Vermeer String Quartet. When Judith Neeley mentioned the name on the drive down, he thought she said the

Vay Iz Meer Quartet. They were going to play works by Mozart, Hindemith, and Schubert. Kuperman had heard of Mozart and Schubert, but not this guy Hindemith.

Four men came out, all oddly different. When Kuperman was a kid, they used to call this kind of music "longhair," but all of these musicians were fairly kempt, at least in the hair department. His attention was attracted to the man who sat up front on the left and who played the violin. His name, according to the program, was Shmuel Ashkenasi. Heavyset, with curly hair, florid, the fiddle under his double chin, he looked, Kuperman thought, Jewish to the highest power. Kuperman remembered that in the Chicago public schools of his day they offered music lessons for twenty-five cents, and you could rent the instrument. He thought that he might like to try the trumpet; his mother, though, was interested only in his playing the violin. Even at age eight he could not imagine himself carrying a violin case around Albany Park. The violin was, he thought, looking at Mr. Ashkenasi, the Jewish instrument par excellence.

During the Mozart, Kuperman noted people around him beginning to drop off to sleep. He tried to find some attractive women or vigorous men in the audience, but was unable to do so. Why had they come here, he wondered, all these people, at some inconvenience and expense, on a sunny Sunday afternoon? What was the attraction? Did the music offer them consolation of some sort for the things that their lives didn't offer?

The Hindemith, the second selection, was just noise to Kuperman. He fidgeted while the four men onstage seemed to saw away at the music. The Schubert, which came after a break, was more like it. Under its melodiousness, his mind wandered, but wandered pleasantly. He remembered his army unit marching into Paris near the end of World War II. He was young, without plans; all his days were in front of him. The time that it took to play the Schubert seemed to pass much more quickly than that of the other two pieces of music, but in checking his watch, he noted that it was in fact longer.

Several times during the concert Kuperman glanced over at Mrs. Neeley. Her face, in profile, radiated intelligence, thoughtfulness, something blissful about it. She seemed quite beautiful when concentrating on the music. Kuperman sensed that she was hearing things he didn't. What might they have been? Whatever they were, for her they were obviously enchanting, entrancing, filled with a significance unavailable to him, though he thought he would like to be in on it.

After the concert, Kuperman asked Mrs. Neeley if she'd like to have dinner. She said she was sorry but she couldn't, because she was expected at her daughter's in Highland Park that evening. Perhaps another time. Before dropping her off, he suggested they go to another concert sometime, his treat, so he could repay her for this afternoon. She said that she would try to find something interesting upcoming at Orchestra Hall and get back to him.

What she came up with was a Saturday evening performance of a man named Alfred Brendel playing Beethoven sonatas. Kuperman looked up the word "sonata" in the dictionary, but didn't find it very helpful. He also bought a little blue book containing musical terms. He quickly saw that any command of the subject of music was not going to be possible, at least not at his age. Mainly he wanted to avoid embarrassing himself by saying or doing something stupid.

The audience at Orchestra Hall was peppered with more younger people than the one at DePaul. Lots of old GJs — German Jews — as Kuperman always referred to them. People seemed rather better dressed, though still less than glittering. Does musical culture, Kuperman wondered, make its followers a trifle shabby in appearance? This world that Judith Neeley was taking him into was mysterious to Kuperman, who didn't much care for mysteries.

The greatest mystery of all, of course, was the music. Alfred Brendel — born in Moravia, Kuperman learned in the program notes — sat upright at his piano and played with an air of the greatest seriousness. He assumed that Brendel was Jewish. Kuperman felt that he had previously heard some of the melodies that came booming out of Brendel's piano, or at least wisps of them. He stole glances at Judith Neeley, who had on her normally pleasant face an expression quite as serious as Brendel's. Kuperman was not bored by the music — not at all — but if you asked him what he had heard, he couldn't have told you, couldn't have hummed a note. Judith Neeley seemed in a state resembling ecstasy. In the program notes he read that one of the sonatas had an "incomprehensible sublimity." Kuperman got only the incomprehensible part.

Judith Neeley — Kuperman for some reason found it difficult to call her or even think of her as Judy — continued to invite him along to concerts and even twice to the opera. He cared less, cared really not at all, for opera; the improbability of the proceedings — heavyset men madly in love with vastly overweight women, whose response to being stabbed was usually to sing louder than ever — didn't seem to work for him. Studying the audience, Kuperman concluded that opera was chiefly for homosexual men and for women whose dreams and fantasies obviously were not going to be realized. He didn't of course mention this to Judith.

But the concerts fascinated him. He came to like chamber music more than symphonies. The blend of so many instruments when played by a full orchestra tended to confuse him, whereas in listening to a chamber group of from three to eight players he could tell which instruments were contributing what sounds.

He sensed an order here that pleased him, though he could not say exactly why it did so. He began to tune his kitchen radio at home to WFMT, the local classical music station, to the accompaniment of which he ate his breakfast. But when he would hear something played that he thought he had heard before, he could never call up what it was. Along with his other inadequacies, he had, it seemed, almost no memory for this music. Hopeless, the whole damn thing seemed hopeless.

Kuperman sensed that a lot of music was about setting up anticipations and then satisfying them, but often in unpredictable ways. Sometimes his mind seemed to him fairly sharp in the concert hall, but sometimes it wandered all over the place and, strain as he might, he couldn't keep it in the room and on the music. Once, presumably listening to a Handel oratorio in a church in Oak Park, all he could think of was the hundred gross of long-out-of-fashion neckties he had bought that afternoon at eight cents apiece. Could he move them? At eight cents a shot, how could he go wrong? Still, a hundred gross?

He also noticed that time itself operated very differently with and without music. While listening to some music, time sped by much more quickly than usual; other pieces seemed to slow time down painfully, making twenty minutes seem longer than a poor fiscal quarter. Why? What caused this? Another mystery Kuperman couldn't pierce.

The larger meaning of music escaped him. Where, he wondered, was the payoff? What was the bottom line? Was there a meaning to it all that evaded him? One night, on the ride home after an all-Russian evening at Orchestra Hall — Tchaikovsky, Mussorgsky, Prokofiev — he put the question to Judith.

"I shouldn't worry overmuch about it, Milton," she said. "Music is directed to the emotions. If you like, you can try to put into thought what the great composers wanted to suggest emotionally. I suppose that's what the good music critics try to do, though not all that many succeed. But I gave up on that project long ago. I love music because it allows me to get out of myself into something larger, which I find it not easy to specify. I am content to listen as carefully as I can and let the music come to me, if you know what I mean."

Kuperman, in fact, didn't know what she meant — hadn't, really, a clue. But he decided not to press the point, lest he look as boorish as he felt.

Kuperman and Judith Neeley had been going to concerts together for roughly four months. All this while his own movements with this woman were, you might say, strictly *adagio*. He did not call her every day; some days he wanted to, just to check in, but decided doing so would be pushing things. Sex wasn't anywhere near up for negotiation, though Kuperman, obviously no longer a boy, wouldn't have minded if it were.

Judith had invited him to a Passover Seder at the home of her daughter, the one who lived in Highland Park. Judith's other daughter and her son and their families — seven grandchildren in all — were there. Kuperman sensed he was on display, being considered for his worthiness as a companion for their mother and grandmother. He also sensed that he was failing the test. The conversation wasn't on any of his topics. Judith's family talked about recent plays, and books, and colleges, lots about colleges, since one of her grandchildren, a boy with bad skin and braces named Dylan Kaplan, was applying to colleges in the fall. (Kuperman could have gone to college on the GI Bill after the war but was too eager to get back into the stream of life, to start making some money, once he was discharged in '45.) Kuperman decided to say little among Judith's family and hope that his silence would pass itself off as the wisdom of the aged. More likely, he felt, they found him a schlepper.

One evening in May, she took him to St. Paul's, an Episcopal church in Evanston, to hear something called the St. Matthew Passion. By now Kuperman had heard a fair amount of music by its composer, J. S. Bach, some of whose things he liked — the liveliness of the Brandenburg Concertos, which he'd heard more than once, always pleased him — and others of which seemed like so much sawing away. He wasn't sure what to expect.

What he didn't expect was the sight of tears dribbling down Judith's face. As the chorus boomed away, Kuperman took her hand in his. She did not remove it. He did not know quite how to describe, for himself, the look on her face. He could only think of an old-fashioned word — transported. This woman wasn't really here with him; the music had sent her — transported her — elsewhere. As the tears continued to flow, her face took on a radiance that made her, even in her late sixties, more beautiful than any woman he had ever seen.

That evening, after the concert, Judith invited Kuperman to come up for tea. When he had settled in one of the two chairs alongside the glass coffee table in the living room, she brought in, on a tray, two cups of tea with a dish of plain sugar cookies.

"I need to tell you something, Milton," she said after she settled into the other chair, stirring the sugar into her tea. "Four years ago I had breast cancer, and now it has returned, but metastasized to my bones, including my spine."

Kuperman had no notion of her earlier bout with cancer. They were not in the habit of retelling their medical histories, or much else of an intimate kind, to each other. He didn't know how to respond. "I'm sorry," he said, which sounded, as he said it, as if the returning cancer were his fault.

"I've decided not to put myself through another round of chemotherapy. The last time nearly did me in. The insidious thing about cancer, as you may or may not know, is the hope — there's

always that slight wisp of hope on which patients bet and too often lose their last days on earth. I'm not taking the bet. Anyhow,
I'm told that I'll probably have no more than three or four months
before the end."

"Is there anything I can do?" Kuperman said. "Is there any
place you want to see, in Europe maybe? Monuments? Great music halls? Name it, I'll take you."

"No," she said, "I want to be near my family. I want to hear lots
of music. And I would like it if you would stay close by."

Kuperman was shocked and touched by this last item. He had
little notion that he meant anything to her much beyond being an
escort and driver to her musical entertainments.

"If that's what you want, it also happens to be what I want," he
said. "I mean the last part."

"You are solid, you know," she said. "There's something very
solid and real about you that's comforting to me."

"I'll do anything you want," Kuperman said. "Anything. Just
ask."

"Stay near," she said.

Kuperman did not move into Judith's apartment. But he began taking his breakfasts and dinners with her. He kept a robe
and pajamas, a toothbrush and razor, at her place. Some nights
he slept over, holding her. They fell asleep listening to Schubert
Impromptus, played by a French pianist named Marcelle Meyer,
on a small CD player Judith kept in the bedroom. He still went
to work every day, still bought his closeouts, ran his auctions. He
even unloaded those eight-cent neckties for a decent profit.

Fortunately, Chicago had enough musical life for them to go to
one or another kind of concert almost every night. The summer
festival at Ravinia was beginning. He made a $5,000 contribution
so that he could get good seats to everything Judith wanted to
hear. They would drive out along Sheridan Road, stopping some
nights in Hubbard Woods for Chinese food; other nights Judith

would make a light cold dinner that they ate on the lawn. After the night she told him about its return to her body, she never again mentioned the word "cancer," and he didn't, either.

They sat in the little Martin Theatre at Ravinia and watched and listened to a vast quantity of Bach, Mozart, Beethoven, Brahms, and endless French composers whose names Kuperman couldn't keep straight. Judith listened to the music with a concentrated serenity that filled Kuperman with admiration. They had taken to holding hands through these Ravinia concerts. Kuperman tried to take Judith's advice and let the music come to him. He paid the strictest attention; his mind wandered less. He heard patterns, felt themes emerge and reemerge, detected what he thought were subtle turns and twists in the music. But the mystery of it was never revealed; ecstasy, the deeper meaning of it all, escaped him.

By early August Judith's appetite had all but disappeared. She grew thin. Her energy dwindled. They stayed home most nights, sat on the couch in her living room, and listened to CDs, holding hands. Kuperman made and served her tea; she might take a single bite of a cookie. What a lottery life was, Kuperman thought, the lousy luck of the draw! A pathetic bit of wisdom to arrive at after eight decades of living, but he had no other.

Kuperman received the call from Angela, one of the practical nurses looking after Judith round the clock, that she had died on a sunny Tuesday morning. He was at work. Her children were with her at the end. Nothing he could do. He finished the day at his place of business, locking up, as usual, at five-thirty.

"Jews bury quickly," he remembered his father saying to him long ago, "they don't drag it out." The service for Judith, at Piser Chapel on Church and Skokie Boulevard, was on Thursday. Richard Blumberg, Judith's son-in-law, called Kuperman to inform him of the time and place of the service and asked him if he would like to join a few members of the family and say a word or two about his mother-in-law at the service. Kuperman thanked him and said he would like to say something.

The chapel for the Neeley funeral was filled, with perhaps three hundred people present. Some among them must have been Judith's former students at New Trier. Kuperman was glad that he had written out the little he planned to say. All three of Judith's children spoke, and two of her grandchildren, also a former student who had become a friend. They talked about what a good mother and, later, friend she had been. The former student, herself a teacher of music at Roosevelt University, recalled what a personal inspiration Judith Neeley had been when she was in high school. Except for the rabbi, Kuperman was the last to speak.

He walked to the lectern with some nervousness and took out of the inside pocket of his suit jacket the two index cards on which he had written out what he intended to say.

"My name is Milton Kuperman," he began, "and I was lucky, make that privileged, to be Judith Neeley's friend during the last year or so of her life. She was a woman of real refinement, culture, and genuine courage." Kuperman felt his eyes fog up, his throat catch, and he heard himself saying something he had not planned on saying.

"Tomorrow I am going to call the Steans Institute at Ravinia and donate a million dollars for Judith Neeley scholarships to help train young musicians, in the hope that Judith and her love of music will not be forgotten."

Leaving the lectern, he felt his face flush, his ears grow hot. There was a buzz of talk around him as he took his seat, but he couldn't hear any of it. Instead, in his mind he heard a beautiful joining of a flute and a harp. Mozart? he wondered. Yes, Mozart, definitely Mozart. Whole passages of the flute and harp concerto came back to him. The music filled him with pleasure of a kind he had never known before. Although Kuperman may not have been fully aware of it, he had just achieved ecstasy.